MOST DEADLY HATE

Sara Woods

MOST DEADLY HATE

'Sweet love, I see, changing his property,
Turns to the sourest and most deadly hate.'

King Richard II, Act III, Sc ii

St. Martin's Press
New York

MOST DEADLY HATE. Copyright © 1986 by Probandi Books Limited. All
rights reserved. Printed in the United States of America. No part of this
book may be used or reproduced in any manner whatsoever without
written permission except in the case of brief quotations embodied in
critical articles or reviews. For information, address St. Martin's Press,
175 Fifth Avenue, New York, N.Y. 10010.

Library of Congress Cataloging in Publication Data

Woods, Sara, pseud.
  Most deadly hate.

  I. Title.
PR6073.063M59   1986   823'.914   85-26052
ISBN 0-312-54914-8

First published in Great Britain by Macmillan London Limited.

First U.S. Edition

10 9 8 7 6 5 4 3 2 1

MOST DEADLY HATE

HILARY TERM, 1976

MONDAY, 15th March

They had had lunch together and lingered over the meal. Afterwards Geoffrey Horton accompanied his friend, Antony Maitland, back to the Inner Temple, and followed him up the rather dim-lit staircase to Sir Nicholas Harding's chambers. Maitland spent a moment in the clerks' office, reassuring old Mr Mallory of his safe return from the wilds of Yorkshire, but he lingered only a moment before leading the way down the narrow corridor to his own room.

'I don't know why you can't do something to cheer this dismal place up,' Geoffrey grumbled, as Antony crossed the room to turn on the desk lamp, which was needed even on the sunniest day.

'Tradition, my dear Geoffrey, tradition,' said Maitland, walking round the desk to his own chair as he spoke. 'Jenny did offer, when I first took this room over, to re-decorate it in a lighter shade – primrose yellow I think was mentioned – but Mallory wouldn't have liked it and you know Uncle Nick, he can't bear disturbances unless he makes them himself.'

'I suppose that applies to the chairs too,' said Geoffrey, seating himself in the one that he knew from long experience to be the least uncomfortable of the three provided for visitors.

'I'm sure it does, but they have the added advantage of keeping my clients awake during the dullest conference,' Maitland assured him. Several new sets of papers had arrived on his desk while he was away, and he glanced at them briefly before pushing them to one side and giving pride of place instead to a foolscap-sized yellow pad of lined paper. Someone – Willett of course, no one else would have been so optimistic – had sharpened his pencils during his absence, and

9

he possessed himself of one now and looked enquiringly at his companion. 'Now then, Geoffrey, what's all this urgent desire for my company?' he asked.

Geoffrey Horton was a solicitor, with a strong sense of propriety where his clients' affairs were concerned that often masked the fact that he was in private life a very cheerful companion. He was a few years younger and a few inches shorter than Maitland, and had built up over the years a very successful criminal practice, in the course of which he had briefed his friend perhaps more frequently than any other advocate. Now, however, he seemed strangely unwilling to come to the point.

'The case itself isn't exactly in your line, Antony,' he said after a moment's hesitation, 'but I'd be glad if you'd refrain from pointing that out until I've explained why I want your advice.'

'All right, I won't say a word,' Antony promised obligingly.

'It's a custody suit,' Geoffrey explained, and sat back awaiting the protest that he knew, whatever good intentions Maitland had expressed, was inevitable.

Sure enough, it came. 'No really, Geoffrey. You must know by now that I don't like getting mixed up in other people's domestic dirty linen.'

'Don't worry, I'm not asking you to see them through the divorce court,' said Geoffrey soothingly. 'I know you wouldn't, anyway. That was all taken care of three years ago.'

'But surely—' Antony broke off and started again. 'It isn't your kind of thing either, Geoffrey,' he said. 'Surely Bernard deals with all that kind of thing.' (Bernard Stanley was Geoffrey's partner, and, whether by accident or design Antony didn't know, the work of their practice had come to be divided between them on those lines.)

'There are certain aspects of the matter,' said Horton carefully, 'that made it seem more appropriate that I should deal with it.'

The sight of Geoffrey picking his words instead of speaking with his usual bluntness was too much for Antony's sense of humour. He said, smiling, 'I can see that you rehearsed that carefully, Geoffrey, but I still can't see why you want to bring *me* into the affair. It's practically routine to give custody to the mother, and I should have thought that would all have been taken care of when the divorce went through. What's her name anyway?'

'Mrs Phillipa Osmond. But she isn't our client.'

'If you're quite determined—'

'I am,' said Geoffrey stubbornly.

'Then you'd better tell me the worst.'

'Our client's the father.'

'Tell him to forget it.'

'If you'd just listen. His wife left him and the child five years ago.'

'In that case it ought to be duck soup,' said Maitland. 'I don't see why you want to wish it off on me at all.'

'Hardly a professional way of expressing yourself, my dear boy,' said Geoffrey, in a poor imitation of Sir Nicholas Harding, who was Antony's uncle as well as the head of the chambers to which he belonged. 'As for it being straight-forward, I shouldn't jump to conclusions if I were you.'

'What is the position then?'

'The child – a girl – has been with her father all these years, but now Mrs Osmond wants her back. Her name's Jennifer, and she's eight years old.'

'I still don't see—'

'I know it sounds as if it ought to be quite simple, but Osmond's story is a queer one and I don't quite know what to make of it. I'd like your opinion as to whether he's telling me the truth.'

'Come now, Geoffrey! It isn't like you not to be able to make up your own mind about a thing like that. What exactly is his story anyway? And why should he need one, when he already has custody? As it was the mother who did the deserting she doesn't seem to have much of a case now for reversing the arrangement.'

'It's a little more complicated than that. As for his story, I'd like you to hear it from him; that will give you more chance to make up your mind about him.'

'But—'

'The thing is,' said Geoffrey in a burst of candour, 'I'm

11

inclined to like the chap and my instinct tells me he's truthful. But what Mrs Osmond alleges is so extraordinary . . . I really should like your opinion, Antony.'

'Then of course you shall have it, for what it's worth. But I think – don't you? – on an informal basis at first.'

'You mean a meeting at my office, rather than a full-blown conference here?'

'That's it exactly.'

'Could you manage tomorrow?'

'Just a minute till I see what's come in while I was away.' The new sets of papers were subjected to another cursory inspection. 'Nothing that won't wait,' said Maitland, looking up and smiling at his companion. 'Make it first thing, if that'll suit you and Mr Osmond. Then I can put in the rest of the day in getting the hang of these.'

'It will suit me, and I'm pretty sure Osmond will agree to anything I suggest.'

'Nine o'clock then, unless I hear anything from you to the contrary,' said Maitland briskly. But he spent some time staring vacantly at the pad in front of him – on which was written the one word, Osmond, though even that had snapped the point of his newly sharpened pencil – before pushing it aside again and reaching for the topmost of the papers that had just come in. If he knew anything of Willett these would be arranged in strict order of precedence, and if he was to waste time on this wild goose of Geoffrey's the sooner he got a start on them the better. There had been from the beginning, as he knew well enough, no likelihood that he would refuse Horton's request. Over the years too many common causes had bound them together; and though his friend would certainly not regard the matter in that light his own sense of obligation made it inevitable that he would have agreed to an even more outrageous request.

TUESDAY, 16th March

I

If Maitland had chosen to retort the previous day that Horton's own office gave him little right to criticise other people's he would have been well within his rights. He arrived there a few minutes before nine o'clock to find that Geoffrey's client had been even earlier. Horton performed the introductions and left the two men a moment or two to take stock of each other.

Robert Osmond was a large, craggy man, impeccably dressed and probably impressive under any normal circumstances. But, it took Antony no more than a moment to realise that the veneer of self-confidence was very thin indeed, and that under the surface the other man was far from being calm. He himself sustained a hard look with tolerable equanimity before Geoffrey interrupted this mutual inspection, inviting them both to sit down, and explaining Maitland's position – or lack of it – in the matter in a few tactful words. How successful he was in this remained doubtful in Antony's mind when Osmond turned to him and remarked, 'It was good of you to see me on such short notice. Or, perhaps in the circumstances,' he added dryly, 'I should say it was good of you to see me at all.'

Maitland only smiled at that, having had in his own opinion very little to say in the matter. However, he replied gravely, 'I understand it's a matter of some importance.'

'Of vital importance, to me and to Jennifer. Do either of you mind if I smoke?' Osmond added abruptly.

'No, not at all,' said Geoffrey. Antony contented himself

with nodding, and was silent while he watched Osmond fumble for matches and a moment later draw deeply on his cigarette. He noted with detached interest that the other man's hand was shaking.

'I forgot to ask Mr Horton yesterday,' he said, breaking the silence when he felt it had lasted long enough, 'whether he or Mr Stanley handled your divorce.'

'No, they didn't. I've never had much need for a solicitor and picked Mr Horton's firm out of the blue, as I couldn't stick the fellow who dealt with the other business for me. He obviously didn't believe a word I said.'

'The child has been in your care ever since?'

'Yes, that's true.'

'Her name's Jennifer, Mr Horton told me. That's my wife's name too' – no harm in digressing a little if it would help to set the chap at ease – 'but we always call her Jenny. I gather the court must have had good reason for awarding you custody.'

'The best of reasons; Phillipa left us both.'

(And what lay behind that, I wonder?) 'You must remember,' said Maitland, 'that I'm coming into the case with no previous knowledge of any of the circumstances. Mr Horton seems to want me to hear them from you, and I admit so far I find the affair a little bewildering. Perhaps it would be best if you started at the beginning and told me the whole story.'

Osmond tapped the ash from his cigarette and leaned back in his chair. 'That's what I came here for, at Mr Horton's bidding,' he affirmed. 'But you know, even with hindsight it isn't easy to say exactly what went wrong.'

'Perhaps we could begin with some personal details,' Maitland suggested. 'About you, and about your wife.'

'Very well, though you'll find them rather dull, I should think. I'm a photographer . . . portraits. Which is something, I think,' he added reflectively, 'like being an artist; to get a good likeness you have to look beyond the face your subject presents to the world. Now you, Mr Maitland, if you'll forgive me for being personal, are a more complicated person than you look.' He took a moment to study Antony with unconcealed interest: a tall man with dark, unruly hair, and an

14

amused look lurking in his eyes though his expression was just now carefully schooled to seriousness. 'You haven't always found life easy, but your experiences have left you, I should say, with a penetrating eye for other people's idiosyncrasies. At the moment you're thinking, I wonder why she left him' – this was so near the truth that Antony felt a momentary discomfort – 'but I'm hoping to be able to convince you that the faults weren't entirely one-sided. Not that I'm holding myself up as a model husband.'

'I know who you are now,' said Maitland. 'I ought to have realised it before. You do a lot of those society photographs, and I think Meg has sat for you several times . . . Margaret Hamilton, the actress.'

'Yes, but they aren't necessarily the most interesting ones, even if they are where I get most of my bread and butter. Though I must admit,' he added reminiscently, 'that Miss Hamilton was an interesting subject. However, that's enough about that. My parents are still alive, living in the North of England. Jennifer and I go up for Christmas and for our summer holidays. I've no other family.'

'And Mrs Osmond?'

'Phillipa? I met her about eleven years ago and married her a year later when I was thirty. Nobody could have been more surprised than I was when she agreed. She's two or three years younger than I am, and always seemed completely wrapped up in her profession.'

'Which is?'

'She's an architect.' He smiled suddenly and glanced around the room. 'She wouldn't approve of your surroundings if I may say so, Mr Horton. Given half a chance and she'd have you installed in something plushy and modern and probably not nearly so appropriate. I mean, there's a sort of tradition about lawyers' offices, isn't there?'

'So you knew your wife for a year before you were married?' said Antony, not giving Geoffrey a chance to reply, though he was pretty sure, from his friend's amused look, that he was remembering their conversation the day before.

'Yes, we . . . she's a tremendously attractive woman, you know, perhaps when she left me even more so than she was then. Certainly I'd tried to pin her down to some permanent

15

relationship long before the year was up, but she said she wasn't ready.'

'Had she many friends?'

'Oh yes, a great many. She . . . well, we slept together sometimes – before we married, I mean – but I was under no illusion that I was the only one. Not that I'm saying there was anything wrong with her way of life by today's standards, but I wanted marriage and I think that with me in the long run it was all or nothing. Nobody could have been more surprised than I was when she suddenly changed her mind and said she'd marry me as soon as I liked, next week if that would please me.'

'This was ten years ago?'

'Yes, and Jennifer is eight, so there's no question of her not being my daughter,' said Osmond quickly. 'And if you're thinking, Mr Maitland, that perhaps Phillipa thought she was pregnant and wanted to regularise the position, I'm sure you're wrong about that. People do make mistakes, but the point is she wouldn't have cared. The single parent idea is so well accepted nowadays, but even if that weren't the case she's a very modern person. I believe liberated is the right word.'

'You must have thought about this, Mr Osmond. Have you come to any conclusion as to why Mrs Osmond suddenly decided to get married?'

'Not at the time. I was just happy that she said yes, I never thought about the reason. It was only later, after she'd left me, that I began to wonder about it, and to tell you the truth I never did reach any conclusion.'

'How did things go between you in those early days?'

'Pretty well. She had her job and I had mine and we were happy enough to be together in our spare moments.'

'No disillusionment?'

'Not on my part at least. Nor on hers I think. She's a woman who needs a man's company sometimes – I needn't be more explicit, need I? – but I had the impression that the way she played the field before we were married was more to keep me in my place than anything else. Once we were together that satisfied her. And then Jennifer was born.'

'Do I gather that made a difference?' The change in

16

Osmond's tone had been unmistakable.

'It certainly did. All through her pregnancy I was conscious of a dissatisfaction about Phillipa, in fact she'd have had an abortion if I hadn't put my foot down pretty firmly. I felt I had some rights in the matter. And, of course, the time came when she couldn't go to the office; that didn't please her either. And when we tried to get a nurse for Jennifer as soon as it was reasonable to do so we couldn't find one for more than a couple of days a week. That left nights and weekends, besides the three days one of us had to stay at home. We rigged up a space where Phillipa could work, though I can quite see it was difficult while she had sole charge of Jennifer, while as for me there was no possibility of moving all my stuff from the studio. I also did my best to do my share when we were both at home, but you know what babies are.'

That didn't seem to call for any direct reply. 'Do you think that's what caused Mrs Osmond to leave you eventually?' Maitland asked.

'Yes, I'm afraid I do. For one thing, she blamed me for her pregnancy in the first place, which I suppose was fair enough. And then – here is where I must blame myself, Mr Maitland – I admit to having been a little preoccupied with the baby, perhaps not taking so much notice of Phillipa's whims as I'd done before. But, frankly, parenthood bored her, and one Friday evening when I got back from the office she was waiting for me with her bags packed. "I'm leaving," she said abruptly, and of course I asked her for an explanation but I never really got one. And that was the last I saw of her for two years, when I heard from her solicitor that she was suing for divorce.'

'She never tried to see Jennifer?'

'No, never.'

'About the divorce . . . you made the remark, Mr Osmond, that you thought your solicitor didn't believe a word you said. Have I got that right? As you were the aggrieved party I don't see how it arose.'

'That's because you don't know Phillipa. She'd waited the mandatory two years and hoped for an uncontested divorce. Irretrievable breakdown of the marriage, isn't that the phrase?'

17

'Are you telling me you didn't agree?'

'I wasn't quite sure what she was up to. You see I'm so . . . perhaps I'm too fond of Jennifer, so I did wonder if Phillipa was having some belated maternal feelings and wanted her back.'

'Jennifer was how old by that time?'

'Five. No, I think she had just turned six. She doesn't really remember her mother at all, incidentally, as far as I can tell. But what I thought, you see, was that perhaps Phillipa might regard a child of that age rather differently from a baby. More fun and fewer problems . . . something like that.'

'So you told your solicitor to contest the divorce?'

'That's right.'

'But I understood—'

'Two things changed my mind. We had a meeting with our respective solicitors present. And she was all ready to quote causes for her desertion. It isn't important now; I knew she was lying but there's no way *they* could have known.'

'The two solicitors, you mean?'

'Yes, of course. Someone told me—'

'I think I see. Correct me if I'm wrong, Geoffrey. Before this breakdown of the marriage business became the only cause for divorce there was a thing called constructive desertion. In other words she was saying that your conduct had been the cause of her leaving you?'

'Yes, and if the court had believed her they might have thought I wasn't a fit person to bring Jennifer up. But the clinching reason – for my not contesting the divorce, I mean – was that she said quite plainly she'd leave the child with me. Even so, the decree absolute was delayed while the court satisfied itself that Jennifer was well cared for. And after a while things settled down again.'

'Are you paying Mrs Osmond alimony?'

'No.'

'And now out of the blue she's decided she wants custody. That raises two questions, Mr Osmond. First, why does she want the child after all these years? And secondly, what cause does she think she can show that custody should be awarded to her?'

'As far as the first question is concerned I don't know the

answer but I suppose it doesn't really matter . . . she wants Jennifer and that's that.' Osmond, whose cigarette had run out long since, ran his fingers through his hair, so that he presented all at once a dishevelled appearance quite at variance with the neatness of his dress. 'But as for the second point, she's pulled the same sort of stunt as she did over the divorce' – he smiled suddenly and leaned forward – 'and when you hear about that I don't want to have you two looking at me askance and believing every word she says.'

'She can't divorce you twice,' Antony pointed out.

'No, but there's the question of being a fit parent.' He wasn't smiling now. 'She says she has witnesses – four of them to be exact – who can prove conclusively that living with me is of harm to Jennifer. Moral harm I mean, not physical, which could be disproved easily enough.'

'And you've no idea, no idea at all, of what these witnesses have to say?'

'Not the remotest idea in the world. Except that it's probably the same kind of thing she brought up when the divorce was in question. Moral turpitude,' he added, obviously dredging the phrase up from some forgotten corner of his mind.

'I see. You say Jennifer doesn't remember her mother, and she hasn't seen her for . . . how long? Five years?'

'Nearly five years, and she's got it into her head that Phillipa is dead. I swear I never told her that outright, but when Phillipa left us I may have said something like "Mummy's gone away", the sort of thing you say to a child, and then later she jumped to the conclusion that was what I meant and I have to admit I've never disillusioned her, it seemed easier than explaining.'

'She'll have to be told,' said Maitland thoughtfully.

'Yes, and can you imagine what kind of a shock that's going to be for her? I shall put it off for as long as I can. Mr Horton says his firm will accept service of the papers on my behalf—'

Geoffrey interrupted at that point. 'All in good time,' he said. 'First there's our meeting with Mrs Osmond's solicitor. I hope you haven't forgotten about that because I arranged it for ten-thirty.'

'I hadn't forgotten but is it absolutely necessary?'

'It's essential,' said Geoffrey firmly. 'If we went into court without a preliminary attempt to resolve the matter the judge would take a very dim view.'

'I'm not prepared to accept any arrangement that will give Phillipa access to the child.'

'Talk first, decisions later,' said Maitland decisively. 'I suppose you mean,' he added, turning to Horton, 'that Mrs Osmond will be present at this meeting.'

'Yes, of course.' Geoffrey looked rather closely at his friend for a moment. 'Does that mean you propose to attend?'

'I think so. With Mr Osmond's permission, of course. You can introduce me as a colleague if you think it's rather early in the proceedings to be bringing counsel into the affair. I want to know a little more about these witnesses and what they're going to say.'

'That's all very well and I know your weakness for getting everything at first hand. But Mr – Mr Begg,' said Geoffrey, consulting the note pad by his telephone, 'will certainly know your name.'

'Mumble it,' said Antony cheerfully. 'I'll keep a very low profile,' he promised, 'and not give you any chance to be ashamed of me.'

Osmond was looking from one to the other of them in a rather bewildered way, which perhaps wasn't surprising. 'I ought to warn you,' he said, 'whatever Phillipa has up her sleeve won't sound good. And even now I don't know whether you believe me when I say I wasn't responsible for her leaving me.'

'Is it any good my reassuring you that I'll do my best for you,' Geoffrey asked, from which Antony deduced that the solicitor was still not absolutely sure about his client's good faith. 'And if it's any consolation to you,' Horton went on, 'if the matter does get into court Jennifer's welfare will be the first consideration.'

'That might console me if I thought the court would know what was best for her,' Osmond grumbled.

'No use borrowing trouble, let's think about that after the meeting,' Geoffrey told him. He glanced at his watch and added, 'We needn't leave for a little while yet so I'll get some coffee sent in.'

II

Messrs Wilkins and Begg, who were acting for Mrs Phillipa Osmond, had a suite of glossy new offices in a glossy new building which for some reason – probably pure contrariness – put Maitland out of all charity with them before he even reached Mr Begg's office. His client they found, on being shown in, was already with him.

In saying that his former wife was an attractive woman Robert Osmond hadn't exaggerated in the least. She was seated in a chair by Mr Begg's desk – the décor of the office struck Antony as being vaguely Scandinavian – and didn't attempt to get up to greet them. Perhaps, even if she had done so, being tall himself he wouldn't have noticed particularly that she was above average in height. What he did observe immediately was her exquisite fairness, features that were almost classically beautiful, and the sheer elegance of her brown dress. That, and the accessories she wore with it, must have set her back a pretty penny, not to mention the fact that there was also a mink coat draped casually over a chair near the door. Obviously her career was a well-paying one, and one thing seemed certain: on material considerations alone the court would have no difficulty in regarding her as quite capable of looking after Jennifer's welfare.

'So here you are, Robert,' she said. Her voice was low and husky and very faintly insolent. 'You've forsaken Mr Matthews, I see. Who are your new solicitors?'

'Mr Geoffrey Horton, of Horton, Stanley and Company,' said Mr Begg fussily. He was a small man, vaguely pear-shaped, with heavy eyebrows and almost completely bald. 'And – er—?'

'An associate of mine,' said Geoffrey smoothly, and as the other man made no comment didn't put himself to the trouble of the mumbling Antony had recommended. 'As there seemed to be some suggestion that the matter was not completely straightforward I took the liberty of bringing him along.'

21

'Certainly, certainly, there can be no objection. This is Mrs Phillipa Osmond, Mr Horton. I'm glad to see you again, Mr Osmond,' he added with obvious insincerity.

'I'm sorry I can't return the compliment,' said Osmond rather abruptly. His eyes were on his wife's face. 'You're looking well, Phillipa,' he said.

'Why, I am, darling, very well,' said Phillipa. 'Never better, in fact. Come and sit down all of you,' she went on, rather as though she were in her own drawing-room. 'We can't talk comfortably with all of you looming over me like this.'

'Certainly, certainly.' Mr Begg moved chairs a fraction of an inch, saw his visitors seated – Maitland was keeping well in the background – and went round behind the desk. A huge expanse of polished mahogany, almost free from papers, now separated him from the others. He took a pad from one of the drawers and laid a ball-point pen across it to show that he was ready for anything. 'This is a very distressing situation,' he said sententiously, 'and Mr Horton and I agreed, after some consultation, that the best thing was for the parties to meet to talk things over quietly. Perhaps then—'

'Come off it, Wilf,' said Phillipa, who obviously didn't hold her man of law in much respect. 'It may be distressing for Robert, in fact I think it will be, but you and Mr Horton and his companion aren't interested parties, and as for me I'm going to get exactly what I want.'

'Don't be too sure of that,' said Robert gruffly.

'Oh, but I am sure,' she said lightly.

A cough from Wilfred Begg called the meeting to order. 'Mr Horton feels, as I do, that we should discuss first the possibility of some compromise between the two of you,' he said. 'Surely some amicable arrangement can be reached that is satisfactory to both parties.'

'No!' said Robert and Phillipa together.

'You mean you wouldn't even grant me – what are they called – visitation rights?' said Phillipa reproachfully. 'Shame on you, Robert! How can you be so unkind?'

'It was your choice to leave us,' Robert retorted. 'After that I don't think rights come into it at all.'

'That's where you're mistaken. My own daughter! I can't wait to see her,' said Phillipa soulfully.

'Well, you're not going to and that's that,' Robert told her.

Geoffrey intervened at that point. 'Mrs Osmond, I think you'll agree that your husband – your ex-husband – has a certain amount of right on his side. If you yourself would adopt a more reasonable attitude, however—'

'Why should I be reasonable? I hold all the cards,' she said.

'We'll come to that in a moment.' Her confidence was disconcerting, but one thing at a time. 'First of all, Mrs Osmond, may I ask you to consider the effect of what you're asking on your daughter? She believes you to be dead.'

'Did you tell her that, darling?' said Phillipa, swinging round to face Robert. 'How naughty of you.'

'I didn't,' said Robert. 'It must have been something I said to her before she was old enough to understand. She persuaded herself that that's what had happened.'

'It's a good story, of course,' said Phillipa. 'However, in the circumstances I don't think I can afford to take Jennifer's short-term feelings into consideration. Her best interests—'

'In all what circumstances?' snapped Robert.

'We'll come to that in a moment, darling. Just now we're interrupting Mr Horton, I feel sure he has some perfectly marvellous suggestion to make.'

'It's not exactly a suggestion, Mrs Osmond. I should like to know how you'd feel if Mr Osmond, on mature consideration, decided that some scheme for you to see Jennifer regularly could be worked out.'

'That's what you'd like too, isn't it, Wilf?' asked Phillipa, turning to Mr Begg.

'It's a possibility that must be given consideration before we can proceed any further,' he said non-committally.

'Very well then, I have considered it and I won't agree to it . . . not at any price. I want custody and full rights over the child's upbringing, then I might think about allowing Robert to see her . . . sometimes.'

'That won't do for me,' said Osmond bluntly.

'I'm afraid it may have to, my dear.' Her tone was silkier than ever.

'I don't see it,' said Robert, shaking his head. 'First you deserted us – any judge would agree that meant you didn't care at all about Jennifer's welfare – and now suddenly you want her back. Do you suppose that anybody will believe that's more than a moment's whim?'

'Of course they'll believe it. No, Wilf, let me speak' – as Mr Begg started to say something – 'I want to convince Robert that his case is quite hopeless.'

'I'll take a good deal of convincing,' said Osmond.

'Yes, you always were of a stubborn disposition,' said Phillipa thoughtfully. 'But don't you see that it's just because I care so much for Jennifer that I didn't insist on having custody of her from the first. What they refer to nowadays as single-parent families are bad enough, even when the father is the only one concerned. But a man is at a great advantage in these things, he can always get help from a doting house-keeper who will look after both him and the child. Aren't I right, darling?'

'I did succeed in finding a housekeeper,' said Robert grudgingly, 'who is also willing to undertake the care of Jennifer when I can't be with her, though I should hardly refer to her as doting. But I don't see—'

'A woman is much worse off in those circumstances,' said Phillipa. 'She hasn't a hope of getting that kind of support. So, dearly as I love Jennifer, I left her with you for her own sake.' If she was acting, Maitland thought, she was very good. Her whole soul seemed to be poured into that statement. But at the same time he was aware of revulsion, and a rising tide of sympathy for Jennifer's father.

Robert Osmond, however, didn't seem impressed. 'In that case you won't try to disturb the *status quo*,' he said. 'Jennifer is perfectly happy as she is.'

'Ah, but things have changed. I can't reconcile it with my conscience any longer—'

'What has changed?' demanded Osmond, interrupting without ceremony.

'I'm going to retire, darling. I shall be able to devote my full time to Jennifer.'

'If you think I'm going to maintain you—' began Robert hotly.

'I think that might be managed too.' Phillipa was thought-ful. 'However, you needn't worry, darling, I've no intention of asking you for a penny. I'm going to be married.'

The two parties most concerned had taken over the discussion completely. From Maitland's point of view as an observer this was all to the good; if Phillipa was in a mood to talk it was certainly instructive to listen. Geoffrey, he thought, was also content with a passive role, but he wasn't too sure how Wilfred Begg viewed the situation. But Phillipa had made it only too clear that she intended to conduct things her own way and her lawyer had no choice but to acquiesce. There'd be time enough later for Geoffrey to put any questions that Osmond left unasked, but Antony had a feeling there wouldn't be many of those.

'Who's the lucky man?' asked Robert, with an undeniable sneer in his tone.

'You wouldn't know him, darling, though I think most people who take a moderate interest in what is going on around them would at least have heard of him . . . Matthew Leighton.'

'Never heard of the fellow.' He turned quickly towards Maitland, and then recollected himself and let his eyes travel on to fix on Geoffrey's face. 'Have you, Mr Horton?'

'Yes, I think I have. He's the sort of person the papers usually refer to as a wealthy industrialist, but I must say my knowledge stops short of having any idea what industry he's connected with.'

'The aerospace industry,' said Phillipa rather grandly, without leaving any of her hearers much the wiser. 'And I assure you he's the soul of respectability and quite capable of taking care of both Jennifer and me. And I can't help feeling, Robert dear, that the court might conclude that a family atmosphere would be better for the child.'

'And what does this paragon of yours think of having a ready-made daughter wished upon him?'

'Oh, he's delighted with the idea. In fact . . . but that's beside the point. Do you really want to deny Jennifer this opportunity, Robert?'

'I can give Jennifer anything she wants.'

'Any material thing perhaps, but not a mother's love,' said Phillipa sentimentally.

'As a matter of fact I can,' Robert retorted. 'I'm about to get married too.'

25

'Are you though? Do you think Jennifer will like having a stepmother?'

'I'm quite sure she will. She knows Amanda well and can't wait for us all to be together. There's no difficulty there.'

'You're not living together then?'

'No,' said Robert shortly. 'And when we consider what you're proposing – a new stepfather, a mother she hasn't seen for five years and doesn't even remember, and a complete removal from everything familiar to her – I don't think the court will consider your request for a moment.'

Phillipa seemed unimpressed and Maitland was beginning to be even more bewildered by her attitude, an emotion that he saw, on glancing at Geoffrey, was shared by his friend. 'In that case,' she said lightly, 'I can quite see I shall have to call up my big guns.'

'My dear Mrs Osmond!' Wilfred Begg expostulated.

'What is it, Wilf?' His regard for the proprieties concerning the client–solicitor relationship obviously meant nothing to her.

'There's no need at this stage—'

'Nonsense. You explained it all to me. Sooner or later I'll have to tell him the basis of my claim in detail, and it may as well be sooner.'

Mr Begg sat back and held his peace, but he didn't look happy.

'Everything I've told you is perfectly true, but I've another reason for asking – no, for demanding – the custody of Jennifer,' Phillipa went on, turning to her former husband. 'It has come to my notice that you aren't at all a proper person to have the care of a child of her years.'

'What on earth are you talking about?'

'Do you really want me to spell it out for you?'

'If you've anything to say, say it!'

'To begin with let me ask you a question. You live in a flat—'

'You know perfectly well that I do. I wasn't the one who left when we separated.'

'Let me finish, Robert. I'm not quite sure where your housekeeper sleeps—'

'She doesn't live in. I keep my working hours pretty

regular now – I've no choice about that – so she leaves when I come home in the evening and doesn't come at all at weekends.'

'I see. It's quite a comfortable flat, I grant you that . . . two bedrooms and a good-sized living-room. But do you really think, Robert, that it's quite *comme il faut* to conduct your amours there?'

'You must have gone mad,' said Robert with conviction.

'Far from it, my dear. I don't pretend to know how many women you've entertained in this way, but I do know about three of them. And, as I believe you've been told already, they're quite willing to testify at the hearing if we ever get that far.'

For a moment Robert Osmond just stared at her. 'I haven't the faintest idea what you're talking about,' he said at last. 'I knew you were up to your old tricks, but who are these imaginary women anyway?'

'I don't think I'll tell you that, my dear. I needn't, need I, Wilf?'

'Not at this stage,' said Mr Begg rather faintly.

Geoffrey obviously thought it was time he took a hand. 'You must realise, Mrs Osmond, that this is a very serious accusation,' he said. 'When we reach the stage of exchanging pleadings – I'm sure Mr Begg has explained this to you – you will cite this alleged circumstance as a reason why custody of your daughter should be given to you, and we shall be in a position to ask for proof of your statements. Whereas if you tell us now—'

'I meant to anyway.' She flashed him a sudden and quite devastating smile, apparently quite unconscious of any inconsistency in her attitude. 'Their names are Norma Martin, Ella Boyd and Laurie Kinsman, and if you want their addresses Wilf will give them to you.'

'My dear Mrs Osmond,' Begg protested again, 'no action has been started yet—'

'And if Mr Horton can convince Robert of the hopelessness of it all perhaps none ever need be,' said Phillipa, with devastating logic. 'I don't want a day in court any more than you do, Robert,' she added, whirling round to face him. 'Don't you think it would be better to give in gracefully?'

27

'I'll see you in hell first,' growled Osmond rather unoriginally. But all of a sudden an idea seemed to strike him. 'Stew Brodie!' he said. 'That's who you've got doing your dirty work for you.'

'Well, I needed help,' said Phillipa with rather pathetic dignity. 'Naturally I went to an old friend.'

'Naturally!' Robert laughed. 'And he dug up these so-called witnesses of yours. I wonder you stopped at three,' he added bitterly.

'I'm sure we could have taken it further, but there seemed no reason to do so,' said Phillipa sweetly. 'You'd better face it, Robert, Stew is well known in his profession.'

'If you call it a profession.' He turned to Horton. 'Stewart Brodie calls himself a private enquiry agent,' he said.

There didn't seem to be any comment that could usefully be made on that. Geoffrey looked instead at Phillipa Osmond. 'I wonder what his main line is,' he said, 'now that divorce is so often by consent.'

'I'm sure I don't know.' Phillipa was being the helpless little woman again. 'But he's worked for some quite big companies. Matthew knows of him,' she added, as though that clinched the matter.

'Your future husband?'

'Yes, and as I told you he's intensely respectable. I'm sure he'd impress the judge,' she added, with a sidelong glance at her former husband. 'And he wouldn't – Matthew, I mean – ever allow me to have dealings with anyone who wasn't perfectly respectable too.'

'Thank you.' Geoffrey was getting to his feet and Antony lost no time in following his example. 'I think that's as far as we can take things today,' Horton went on. 'Did I understand correctly, Mrs Osmond, that you would postpone any action until my client has had time to consider the matter?'

'I feel sure that if anybody can make him see reason it's you, Mr Horton,' she told him demurely.

'And that you, Mr Begg – on behalf of your client – would have no objection to my having enquiries made about these three women?'

'If it would help to convince you that the matter is hopeless—'

'The decision as to whether to contest the action will be Mr Osmond's, not mine.'

'Quite so.' Wilfred Begg pushed back his chair and came to his feet in his turn and Robert Osmond followed suit more slowly. 'I have the addresses here, Mr Horton.'

'Thank you. There only remains to ask how long Mrs Osmond will be willing to wait for our decision.'

'Until the weekend perhaps,' said Phillipa negligently.

'And what exactly are the alternatives you're offering us?'

'Some kind of legal action will be necessary, I suppose. Wilf will advise me about that. If Robert doesn't contest my suit I imagine a statement from him that he now felt Jennifer would be better with her mother would suffice.'

'You seem to have an excellent grasp of essentials, Mrs Osmond,' said Geoffrey rather dryly, and turned just in time to grip his client's arm as Robert Osmond lurched forward.

'It's all right,' Osmond assured him, 'I'm not going to do anything violent. But she'll never get the statement from me, never, and she may as well understand that now.'

'Very well, but I think we should talk more about this . . . not here,' Geoffrey insisted. 'Good morning, Mrs Osmond. I'll be in touch with you again, Mr Begg,' he concluded, and managed to steer his unwilling client and his silent associate in the direction of the door.

III

'You don't believe me,' said Robert Osmond accusingly as soon as they got out into the street. He stopped dead as he spoke and Geoffrey, very conscious that they were blocking the pavement and anxious to avoid a scene, glanced around anxiously.

'We need to talk,' he said. 'Will you come back to the office?'

'My studio is nearer. Or . . . I need a drink.' He glanced at his watch. 'Not quite twelve o'clock; is that too early for you for lunch?'

'Not really, and in any case we needn't order immediately.'
He turned to look at Maitland. 'What about you, Antony?
Will you come with us?'

'I've never been the sort of person who leaves a book half
read,' said Antony lightly. 'I want to hear the end of the
story. If this is your area, Mr Osmond, I expect you know
where we should go.'

'This way.' Robert looked very much as though he would
like to propel his two companions by force in the direction
that he wished them to take. 'Of all the damned unreliable
women,' he said as they went. 'I might have known she'd pull
a trick like this, and that you'd fall for it.'

'You're going too fast for me, Mr Osmond,' said Geoffrey,
and he wasn't referring to the rate at which they were
covering the ground. 'At this stage it isn't a matter of whether
I believe you or not, and I haven't said—'

'You needn't try to be tactful. If you believe me why do
you want to make enquiries about these damned women?'

'I only want to know how convincing they'll be as
witnesses.'

'I can tell you that without any further trouble. Their
stories will be rehearsed down to the last detail, so as to
squeeze the last drop of emotion out of what they're going to
say.' Antony happened to be nearer to him and he grabbed his
arm as he spoke, fortunately the left one. 'In here!' he said.
'It's new and not many people know about it yet. We can
talk.'

Maitland went with him willy-nilly, not that he had any
inclination to refuse. The interview with Phillipa Osmond
and her solicitor, who appeared to be so very much under her
thumb, had obviously left Geoffrey even more a prey to
doubts, but it was only fair – as well as being reasonable – to
hear her husband's side of the story as well. He waited,
however, until Robert had led the way to a table at the far end
of the long room, where no one else seemed to have
penetrated, and waited again until drinks had been ordered
and the waitress had disappeared in the direction of the bar.
Then he said quietly, 'Do you think they'll all confirm what
Mrs Osmond said?'

'Of course they will!'

30

'And they weren't friends of yours . . . clients perhaps?'

'I tell you I've never heard any of the names before.'

'That doesn't make it terribly easy for them. If you decide to contest Mrs Osmond's suit Mr Horton will engage counsel—'

'When you agreed to come to the meeting at Mr Begg's office with us I hoped that you'd decided to take it on.'

'There's a good deal to talk over first. You may have made up your mind to go to trial, but we don't know yet what Mr Horton's advice will be. However, let me tell you what's in my mind. If you go into court your counsel – whoever he may be – will want to know a good deal of detail from these witnesses Mrs Osmond has promised to produce . . . where you met, exactly what dealings you had together, and a description of the flat, of course.'

'I'm a creature of habit,' said Robert. 'Phillipa knows that perfectly well. She also knows the flat, let me remind you.'

'So you're telling me that whatever these three women say will be a complete fabrication from beginning to end?'

'I hoped I'd made that clear already.'

The waitress arrived with their drinks at that point, but it was quite obvious that Maitland intended to continue the interview in his own fashion. Geoffrey sat back and prepared to listen, amused at this reversion to Antony's usual form, the more so because he couldn't imagine how his friend had managed to maintain silence all through the recent confrontation. Maitland took time to taste his drink before putting his next question. 'Mr Osmond, supposing you wished to indulge in an affair such as your wife described, how would you set about it, the circumstances being what they are?'

'I wouldn't take the woman to the flat where Jennifer would be bound to see her,' Robert retorted vehemently. 'I tell you that child means everything to me. I wouldn't—' He broke off and looked at his interrogator helplessly. 'Can you think of any way of putting it that doesn't sound like a romantic novel? I can't, so I'll say it right out. I wouldn't do anything to sully her innocence. Does that satisfy you?'

'It doesn't quite answer my question,' said Antony, sidestepping that one neatly. 'I asked you—'

'You asked me how I'd set about it. I couldn't use the

studio . . . too many people about. There's my receptionist and there's my assistant . . . no privacy. But I suppose I should tell you there were a few occasions just after Phillipa left me, very casual encounters . . . we went to an hotel. I don't pretend to be any better than the next man, but the whole atmosphere revolted me. Sordid,' he explained. 'So the question didn't arise again until I met Amanda. We've known each other for two months and we're going to be married and I'm content to wait.'

'Would you mind describing your flat to me, Mr Osmond?'

'Of course not. It's a fairly conventional design: a narrow hall with a big cupboard, a large living-room off to the right with a dining area at the far end and a door leading into the kitchen. It's one of the not-much-bigger-than-a-cupboard variety, though fitted up with every imaginable gadget. On the other side of the hall there are two bedrooms and a bathroom. Phillipa didn't like that . . ., having only one bathroom, I mean. We were thinking of moving when she left me. As it was the rent was quite high enough so Jennifer and I just stayed on.' For the first time something of his anger seemed to have left him and he looked from one to the other of his companions almost quizzically. 'Does that help at all with our problem?' he asked.

Again it was Maitland who answered. 'I think it may do.'

'How?'

'It doesn't sound as though you and Jennifer would have had many opportunities for keeping secrets from each other.'

'None at all I should say. It's awkward at Christmas and birthdays when I want to hide her presents but—' He broke off there, stared at Maitland for a moment, and then crashed his fist down on the table. 'Understand me, I won't have Jennifer mixed up in all this.'

'You may have no choice if you want to keep her with you.'

'But even if I would agree . . . a child's evidence?'

'She's eight years old, hardly a baby. The court would be very gentle with her and—'

'Suggest that I'd coached her in what to say,' said Robert bitterly. 'No, Mr Maitland, it won't do.' He sat back and sipped his drink. 'You're beginning to puzzle me,' he observed.

'Am I? Why?'

'You're beginning to sound as though you believe me.'

'Do I?' Antony wondered. Then he smiled. 'I believe at least that you wouldn't do anything to hurt your daughter in any way, and that's the essence of the matter, Mr Osmond. Without these allegations the hearing might go one way or it might go the other. I have to tell you this – and I'm sure Mr Horton will agree with me – because I don't want to get your hopes up unduly. Mrs Osmond may be sincere, though I'm inclined to the view that she's a clever actress. She certainly made no secret of the fact that she was only too glad to find some way of tormenting you, but in court I'm sure she could put over the impression of a loving mother wanting only what's best for her child. If she played her cards right Matthew Leighton's name might be something like the ace of trumps. On the other hand, it must be obvious that it would be less upsetting for Jennifer to stay with you. So, as I say, the decision might go either way.'

'But with an unpleasant touch of scandal introduced by this story of Phillipa's . . . I see what you're getting at. But I still won't let you call Jennifer to give evidence.' He paused there and then said, as though the thought had just occurred to him. '*They* couldn't call her, could they?'

'They could, but they won't,' said Maitland confidently. 'If you're telling the truth she'd be bound to come down heavily on your side. But at least, Mr Osmond, will you let us see her?'

'Is it necessary?'

'To confirm my wavering belief,' said Antony, and this time when he smiled at the other man, Robert Osmond smiled back. 'But don't you see, if we have her evidence in your favour up our sleeve it will go a long way to counter Mrs Osmond's case? Mr Begg won't know that you've refused to let us use it, he may be able to persuade Mrs Osmond that it would be better to let the matter drop.'

'You don't know Phillipa if you think she'll give in so easily,' Robert told him. 'But if you can trust me, at least partially, I suppose the least I can do is to trust you in return.

33

Mrs Arbuthnot will be fetching her from school about four o'clock. If it's convenient for you I suggest that we're at home when they arrive.'

'That sounds like a good idea.'

'Can you manage it?' Robert insisted.

'Oh yes, certainly.' If he was thinking of all the things he had intended to do that day no one would have known it. 'What about you, Geoffrey?'

'I can make it all right,' said Horton, 'unless you prefer to see her alone, Antony. I know you always say people are more willing to talk to one person than to two. Though in this case I'm sure Mr Osmond would want to be present, so perhaps I should say to one stranger.'

'That's quite true in the ordinary way, but it won't do in this case. If we're to have any hope of persuading Mr Begg we must both be there to hear what she has to say.'

'Then of course I'll come along.' It was Geoffrey's turn to smile at his client. 'I think I can promise you that Mr Maitland won't frighten her,' he said, 'and I'll do my best not to look too much like an ogre.'

'Thank you,' said Robert, apparently taking this with perfect seriousness. 'I suggest we have another drink before we order, then you can tell me why Phillipa was so frank with us.'

'She'd have had to be eventually,' said Geoffrey. 'Do you want me to go into the matter of the pleadings again?'

'No, I understand that all right. I meant, why was she so frank at this stage?'

'I suppose it was as she said, she doesn't want to go into court if it can be avoided.'

'I don't see that, not if her case is as good as you say it is. And there's another thing, five years ago – even three years ago – she didn't care what happened to Jennifer. Why has that all changed now?'

Geoffrey's look at Antony was an obvious invitation to reply to that. 'Something to do with her forthcoming marriage,' Maitland hazarded. 'Perhaps Leighton is fond of children.'

'If that's the case Phillipa has quite a number of years left for child-bearing,' Robert pointed out.

'Then we'll have to leave it as a mystery for the moment. But I think you must accept the fact that she's genuine in her desire to get custody.'

'Yes, I realise that. You realise too – don't you? – it's about the only thing that is genuine about her.'

'What I should like to know, Mr Osmond,' said Horton, sensing that his friend would prefer to ignore the question, 'is, who's this Stew Brodie you spoke of?'

'An old acquaintance,' said Robert shortly. And then, as though relenting, 'To say he's a private detective is to dignify his calling, I think. And you heard what Phillipa said of his present activities.'

'I did. I got the impression perhaps . . . some sort of industrial espionage? And it crossed my mind that there might be some connection between him and her new fiancé.'

'That's something I couldn't tell you about.'

'But you know Brodie?'

'Yes, I . . . well, I can't say we were ever particularly friendly.'

'Does that mean he was more Mrs Osmond's friend than yours?'

'I suppose so. She used to ask him to dinner parties, a spare bachelor is always useful – that's what she told me. Afterwards I wondered if there'd been anything between them, but perhaps I shouldn't even suggest that because I don't know.'

'How would you rate his honesty?'

'That's not a thing you consider about people you know,' said Robert, and saw his companions exchange a smile. 'Well, perhaps I should say not unless you're a lawyer,' he added, smiling himself. 'I didn't like him, but I'd never any reason to question his integrity. However, if he's behind these three women who Phillipa says will give evidence of having had relations with me it's obvious that he's as crooked as hell.' He paused there, and then went on not quite so calmly. 'It makes me furious every time I think about it. I'd never do anything to hurt Jennifer or start her in life with the wrong set of values.'

'Well, the next thing is for us to talk to her,' said Geoffrey, 'and I'll set Cobbold's – who are in the same line of business as your Mr Brodie, though I doubt if they include industrial espionage in their list of activities – on to finding out something about the women in the case. Meanwhile,' – he produced a notebook – 'what's your home address, and what time shall we get there this afternoon?'

IV

In the event, by the time they had finished their luncheon there wasn't too much time to put in before they had to set out. Osmond went straight home, and Antony – not knowing what complications might be lying in wait for him if he went back to chambers – accompanied Geoffrey to his office. 'I take it your advice to me is to treat my client's word as gospel,' said Horton rather sourly, almost before Antony had time to seat himself.

'I'm certainly inclined to believe him,' said Maitland slowly, 'but mainly because of his obvious devotion to his daughter.'

'I grant you that. What worries me is that he was very ready to accept the fact that his wife's witnesses would come up to proof,' said Geoffrey.

'Yes, but that's a clever woman, Geoffrey, and expert in getting her own way, I should imagine.'

'Now there I *can* agree with you. But in my line of country, Antony, I see more of domestic squabbles than you do, and when we heard exactly what her witnesses were going to say I must say it shook my belief in Osmond's integrity rather.'

'If you ever had any. Wasn't that why you asked me to look him over?'

'You're right, of course. And you think—'

'I think we should make a push to help him if only for Jennifer's sake,' Antony interrupted firmly.

'But if he's the sort of man—'

It seemed that afternoon that Horton was never destined to be able to finish a sentence. 'You forget he's going to be married. That should put a stop to that sort of thing, and at

36

least if it continues Jennifer will know nothing about it. Think of it from her point of view, Geoffrey, we've got to help him if we can.'

'We?'

'That's what I said. I seem to remember your asking me to take a hand.'

'Well, of course I'd be glad if you decide to, but I must admit the most I thought I'd get was your opinion of Osmond,' Horton confessed.

'Does that mean that you want to see the witnesses yourself?'

'No, I don't think so. I don't see what good it would do.' He grinned suddenly. 'And if we get into court I'd prefer on the whole not to be greeted as a familiar friend by three ladies of the town.'

'Don't let that worry you,' said Geoffrey, amused. He pulled out his notebook and turned the pages until he found the one he wanted. 'One's a model, which might mean anything I suppose, but the other two are an assistant in a flower shop and a schoolteacher. And don't tell me you're going to have an easy time upsetting their stories.'

They left in what seemed to them to be good time for their appointment, but it took a little while to find a taxi and when they arrived at their destination they were by no means too early. Antony stood for a moment looking up at the block of flats until Geoffrey had paid off the cab and joined him. 'Almost palatial,' he murmured then, admiringly. He had always looked upon photography as a rather expensive hobby, but crossing the lobby almost ankle deep in a shag carpet of a lustrous red, and going up in a rather ornate lift to the second floor he revised that opinion a little. Obviously if one went about it the right way there was a good living to be made, though he thought it most likely, as Osmond had said, that an artist's eye was also a necessity. He was thinking as the lift bore them aloft that Osmond was almost the exact antithesis of everything he expected from the artistic community; his physique would have been well enough suited to a rugger player, and no doubt the way he dressed was dictated by the impression he wanted to make on his clientele.

Robert opened the door to them himself and ushered them

into a big living-room which was expensively furnished but had a pleasantly lived-in atmosphere. 'Mrs Arbuthnot has just gone to fetch Jennifer,' he said. 'They should be back in a few minutes.'

'Good,' said Maitland. Horton seemed to have decided to let him conduct matters in his own way, which was too familiar an attitude to surprise him.

'Sit down and make yourselves comfortable.' Osmond seemed unaccountably nervous for a man entertaining in his own home, but his next words explained it. 'I've been thinking things over since we parted; Phillipa really has a good case, hasn't she?'

'On the face of it, yes. But we've only just begun, Mr Osmond, it's far too early to despair.'

'You see, I don't know what I'd do without Jennifer,' said Osmond, dividing what was obviously a confidence between the two visitors. 'We've been so close for so long. And I'm lucky there, Amanda understands perfectly. She's quite happy to take on a ready-made daughter, in fact everything seemed perfect until all this blew up.'

'Perhaps we should talk to Amanda as well. Is she Miss or Mrs?' asked Maitland, anxious to get it right.

'Miss – Miss Amanda Herschell. She's never been married. I don't know how she's managed to avoid it,' Robert added thoughtfully, 'though I'm pretty sure what my mother would say: she's been waiting for Mr Right.'

'It sounds as though congratulations are in order,' said Antony.

'If it weren't for this other business, Mr Maitland. I've been thinking about that too. What do you want of Jennifer? I know what you say, but I don't want her upset.'

Antony took his time to reply to that, wondering how well honesty would repay him. 'I suppose I'd like to see how she'd answer the kind of questions I might ask her in court,' he replied rather cautiously.

'To check up on me?' asked Robert quickly.

'As a matter of fact, no. I seem to be taking you pretty well on trust,' Antony admitted. 'I think I explained to you what was in my mind; when Mr Horton talks to Mr Begg again we want all the ammunition possible at our disposal.'

'I told you I won't let her give evidence.'

'Yes, but you may not be the best judge of that. You see I think that's just what Mrs Osmond is counting on . . . that you'd do anything rather than let Jennifer testify. Until I've seen her I can't form an opinion, but I might feel it my duty to advise you that we should call her after all.'

'And let her in for the sort of cross-examination Phillipa's counsel would subject her to? Oh no, Mr Maitland, not that.'

'Think about it,' Antony urged him. 'A child in court, particularly in a case like this, would be treated with kid gloves. Any attempt at the sort of thing you seem to have in mind would be so unpopular as to bias the court in your favour immediately. No, I think you can take it she'd be dealt with very gently, even by the other side.'

'That opens up a new train of thought,' said Robert, 'but I can't say I like it even now. Are you going to tell her Phillipa is alive?'

'I don't intend to but I think you should, Mr Osmond.'

'And tell her also that there's a possibility she may be taken from me?'

'I think she's going to find out about the case some time, and if the worst happens – which I hope it won't – it would be a terrible thing for it to come as a complete shock to her.'

'You're right, I suppose. I'll think about it.' He broke off as they heard a sound in the hall. 'Oh, there they are now,' he said.

The remark was prompted by the sound of a key being turned and of the front door opening and closing quietly. Then came a woman's voice. 'This won't do, Jennifer. Do you want your father to see you like that? You know he phoned me and said he'd be home early today, probably before we arrived.'

There was no reply to that unless you could count the sound of a sob. 'Give me your coat, my dear.' That was the woman's voice again. 'Then you can go and wash your face and we won't say another word about it.'

'If daddy's here I want to see him. Thank you, Mrs Arbuthnot,' the child's voice went on; obviously she was remembering her manners. There was a very brief pause, presumably while her overcoat was being removed, and then she burst into the living-room. So far as she was concerned neither Geoffrey nor Antony might have been there at all. 'Daddy!' she said, and rushed across the room. Robert's arms went around her, she buried her face against his jacket and clung to him tightly.

'Here, hold on, sweetheart,' said Robert, smoothing back her hair. 'What's all this about?'

Jennifer Osmond was tall for an eight year old, as fair as her mother but otherwise not much like her; the brief glance Antony had of her showed a rather serious-looking child with a distinctly snub nose. Now a woman appeared in the doorway behind her, presumably Mrs Arbuthnot who had fetched her from school, a short woman who affected a style of dress that was subtly out of date, and who managed to look all the more respectable by doing so.

'She's been like that all the way home, Mr Osmond,' she said in a worried way. 'I can't think what's come over her.'

'She'll be all right now,' said Robert, and Antony thought immediately that he was voicing a confidence he did not feel.

'Come along, old lady,' he went on, and now he took Jennifer's shoulder and shook her very gently. 'Did something happen at school to upset you?'

There was no reply to that except another sob and a violent shaking of the fair head. 'Did you see anything that might explain this, Mrs Arbuthnot?' Robert asked.

'No, indeed I didn't, Mr Osmond. I waited on the corner as I always do, and most of the other children had come out by the time Jennifer appeared. But when she did she just ran towards me without seeming to realise I was there at all. I had to grab her arm to stop her, and it was very difficult getting her to walk home quietly and not run all the way.'

'I see.' This time Robert Osmond's eyes met Antony's. 'Well, I'm grateful to you, Mrs Arbuthnot, but I'm sure I can handle things now. As I'm at home there's no need for you to stay any longer, and I'll see you in the morning at the usual time I expect.'

'Very well, Mr Osmond.' If she was curious enough to resent her dismissal she gave no sign. 'Good night, Jennifer,' she added.

Jennifer, her face still hidden, muttered a stifled 'Good night'.

'She's not usually like this,' said Mrs Arbuthnot to the room at large and went out, closing the door behind her. A moment later they heard her leave the flat.

'Now!' said Robert, and put Jennifer away from him gently. 'You've got some explaining to do, young lady. What's all this about?' And suddenly Jennifer came to life. Her hands became fists, battering against her father's chest as though she were afraid he might pull her to him again.

'You lied to me, daddy,' she said tragically. The tears were running down her cheeks. 'All these years you've lied to me.'

'I never lied to you, sweetheart.' He took her wrists and held her away from him. 'Let's sit down and talk about it quietly, shall we? And you haven't said good afternoon to these gentlemen, Mr Horton and Mr Maitland.'

Jennifer gave a great gulp, which seemed to be her method of turning off her tears, and turned to look at the two lawyers. 'Good afternoon, Mr Horton; good afternoon, Mr Maitland,' she said obediently, but to Antony's surprise neither then nor later did she question their presence.

'Sit down, Jennifer,' said Robert again. 'You know we have to stay standing as long as you do and you don't want to tire us out, do you?' He waited until she had followed his suggestion, and then gestured to the other men to return to their chairs. His own he pulled close to his daughter's. 'Now then, sweetheart, what's all this about my telling you lies?' he asked.

'You said mother was dead,' she told him simply.

Robert glanced rather quickly at the other two men, his expression bewildered. 'You're wrong about that,' he said, giving his attention again to his daughter. 'I know you assumed it, and I admit I never contradicted you. Do you think that's quite as bad?'

Jennifer heaved an enormous sigh. 'Quite as bad,' she said.

'Now, think about it for a little.' A sudden thought distracted Robert from what he was going to say. 'How did you know that Phillipa – that your mother isn't dead?' he demanded.

'There was a man—'

41

'What man?' asked Robert sharply.

'I don't know, I don't know. In the playground when we came out of school. He said that mother didn't die at all and that now I have to go and live with her.'

'What else did he say?' Robert was suddenly very still, but his voice had a note of urgency.

'All sorts of things. I can't tell you—' She broke off, staring at him, and two small tears began to trickle down her cheeks.

'Well, let's get back to this question of my lying to you,' said Robert very quietly. 'You're old enough to understand what happened now. Your mother left us. I told you she'd gone away, and later on I told you she wouldn't be coming back. You were three years old—'

'Nearly four!'

'—and I found it difficult to explain to you that she didn't want to be married to me any more.'

'But that's what people say when other people have died,' Jennifer protested.

'Yes, I understand that. I understood it when I heard you talking about her as being dead, but I didn't want to hurt you any more, sweetheart, and I thought explaining would do that. What would you have done?'

'I don't know,' she said miserably, not looking at him now.

'Well, if you think about it a little you'll see it was quite reasonable on both our parts. But now, about this man who spoke to you. What was he like?'

'I didn't like him,' said Jennifer positively.

'No, but . . . we're going to have to talk this out, Jennifer, however much you dislike the subject. Was he tall . . . short . . . stout . . . thin . . . dark . . . fair?'

'As tall as you, daddy. I don't know about grown-ups' ages, and he had a beard which made it harder than ever to tell, but he was dark and good-looking and his eyes were very, very blue.'

'And what did he say to you besides what you've told us?'

'Lots of things.' She was becoming agitated again and Robert, hearing the rising note of hysteria, changed course immediately.

'Don't worry now, Jennifer. We'll talk about it later when you feel like it. And I'm sorry you had to learn this way, but

42

after all these years your mother has changed her mind. As this man told you, she wants you to go and live with her. There may even be a case in court about it, that's what Mr Horton and Mr Maitland are doing here. Mr Horton is my solicitor, and Mr Maitland is a barrister. Do you know what that means?'

'A sort of lawyer.'

This time Robert's glance at Antony was enquiring and Maitland shook his head slightly. He thought the other man was doing pretty well with his questioning and that the child would respond more readily to her father. 'Well, Jennifer,' said Robert turning back to his daughter, 'there's one question they'd like an answer to before they decide what is best to do on my behalf. Now that you know your mother is still alive would you rather go and live with her or stay here with me?'

Jennifer looked at him for a long, long moment. Maitland found himself holding his breath, as though unwilling to disturb the silence even in that small way. Then suddenly the child was on her feet. 'Don't ask me that, daddy, don't ask me that,' she said. A burst of noisy sobbing followed, and then she was at the door struggling with the knob and a moment later was out in the hall with the door closed behind her. The three men were left looking at one another.

'Should I go after her?' asked Osmond uncertainly.

'You're the best judge of that,' Antony told him, 'but I'd say she'd be better left alone for a little while at any rate.'

'Yes, I suppose so.' He smiled suddenly, though rather ruefully. 'In any event I don't think I'd do much good. Jennifer isn't given much to tears, still less to letting anyone see her crying. Though when anything upsets her badly – the death of a kitten for instance – she'll lock herself in the lavatory and not come out until the worst of her grief has expended itself. I don't think it would help at the moment if I shouted at her through the door.'

'I don't think so either. I got the feeling you knew the man she described, Mr Osmond.'

'It was Stewart Brodie, there can be no doubt at all about that. The question is, what was he trying to do?'

Maitland hesitated, but if his conclusion was correct the

43

other man had the right to hear it. 'I think he was trying to turn her against you,' he said. 'That's the part she wouldn't tell you . . . remember? The first move in the game.'

'Of course I remember. She wouldn't tell me either what she herself would like to do in the circumstances. Do you think that's out of consideration for my feelings too?'

'There's no way of knowing. I only hope that she'll confide in you when she's calmer, and I'm afraid you ought to prepare yourself for what may be the worst aspect of this encounter with Mr Brodie. I said to you before that there was no chance of the other side wanting to call Jennifer. Now I'm not so sure I was right.'

Osmond thought about that for a moment. 'That's the last thing I want,' he said. 'Do you think I ought to throw in my hand straight away?'

'No!' Antony's tone was vehement and both Robert and Geoffrey eyed him curiously. 'If they want a fight we'll give them one,' he said with determination. 'I'll leave Jennifer to you.'

'And trust me to tell you what she has to say about all this, however unpleasant it is?' asked Robert wryly.

'She'll obviously confide more readily in you. I think I have to trust you,' said Antony smiling. 'Meanwhile Mr Horton will put in hand the enquiries he spoke of, and then we'll compare notes and see where that gets us.'

They left it there and Maitland and Horton took their leave a few minutes later. There was no sound as they went through the hall, which Antony hoped meant that Jennifer's fit of crying had finished, but Robert indicated a closed door at the other side from the living-room and said in a depressed way, 'I told you that's where she'd be.'

Maitland was thoughtful as they made their way to the main road where they had some chance of picking up a taxi, and after one glance at his face Geoffrey felt that it was no time to start another discussion. He asked only, 'Do you really mean to see Miss Herschell?'

And Antony replied rather vaguely, 'Perhaps. We'll see,' and then added, 'There's nothing more to be said, is there, until you've heard from Cobbold's? Give me a ring when you do.'

V

As well as Maitland's professional connection with his uncle he and his wife Jenny occupied an anything-but-self-contained flat which comprised the two top floors of Sir Nicholas Harding's house in Kempenfeldt Square. Sir Nicholas's marriage to Miss Vera Langhorne, barrister-at-law, was still not five years old but it had changed none of the pleasant traditions that had grown up between the two households over the years. One of these was that Sir Nicholas – originally as a refuge from the cold collation his housekeeper insisted on leaving him on Tuesday nights, when it was her invariable custom to attend the cinema, but now because they all enjoyed the arrangement too much to give it up – dined with the Maitlands every Tuesday evening. And now, of course, Vera accompanied him.

Naturally she would have been quite capable of taking over the kitchen quarters and doing everything that was necessary, but though Sir Nicholas's small staff, who had done exactly as they liked for years, had taken his marriage very well, this, they all felt, would have been carrying matters a little too far. Antony had been known to voice his regrets that his new aunt's arrival had made it quite certain that Gibbs, Sir Nicholas's aged retainer, would now never consent to retire, a consummation which they all felt was devoutly to be wished. As it was – though he had given up one at least of his more annoying habits in her honour – he still did exactly as he pleased, one of the ways in which he played the martyr being to hover at the back of the hall at the time when he expected his employer or his employer's nephew to be coming home from chambers. Gibbs was an old man of saintly aspect and disagreeable temper, and he'd disapproved of Maitland ever since Antony had joined his uncle's previously bachelor establishment. Since this event had taken place when Antony was thirteen years old he should have had time to get used to it by now, but his disapproval continued and that night when

45

Antony let himself into the hall he remarked austerely, 'Sir Nicholas and Lady Harding joined Mrs Maitland quite some time ago.' But the note of reproof was too familiar to cause Antony any qualms; he said, 'Thank you,' rather vaguely and set off up the stairs.

He heard the murmur of voices as soon as he let himself into his own hall, so Gibbs's warning had been unnecessary. Antony dropped his coat untidily on a chair and went into the living-room, standing quietly for a moment before he closed the door behind him to savour the moment of homecoming as he so often did.

It was a big room, a little shabby but undeniably comfortable, and with a tranquil atmosphere for which he certainly could take no credit. There was Jenny turning her head to smile at him, the lamplight gilding her brown curls. She had what he always called to himself her serene look, and he took a moment to thank heaven that this unpleasant case of Geoffrey's in which he seemed to have become entangled was unlikely to involve anything that might disturb her. Vera, beside her on the sofa at the end nearest to where her husband was sitting, said in her gruff way, 'Not been in chambers all day, Antony. Nicholas was getting quite worried.' Which, if Sir Nicholas's attitude was anything to go by, was a downright lie; he was stretched out in his usual chair, completely relaxed, and raised one hand in languid salute to his nephew.

'I expect, my dear Vera,' he said in rather a bored tone, 'that Antony is about to explain his – his truancy to us . . . probably at some length.'

Maitland crossed the room, greeted Vera punctiliously, as was still his habit – though his rather exaggerated air of politeness didn't often last much beyond the moment of meeting – said casually, 'If you really want me to, Uncle Nick,' and bent to kiss his wife before adding firmly, 'but I want a drink first. No, don't get up, love,' he added as Jenny started to scramble to her feet. 'I'll help myself and do the honours if anyone wants a refill.'

When this had been accomplished he came back to the group near the fire, placed his glass on the mantelpiece, and stood looking down at them in a satisfied way. 'As a matter of

46

fact I'd be glad to tell you what's kept me all day,' he said. 'It's a disagreeable matter, and getting more disagreeable by the moment, and I am not quite sure whether I've made the right decision.'

'I'd be only too happy to give you my advice, my dear boy,' said Sir Nicholas cordially, 'if I thought for a moment that you'd take it. Unless, of course, it happened to coincide with what was your intention all along.'

This was too true to admit of argument, so Antony ignored it. 'As Geoffrey said, it isn't at all my line of country,' he began. 'Bernard had passed it on to him because it seemed that some enquiries might be necessary, and he lured me into it by saying he wanted my opinion of his client. You see, Robert Osmond's wife left him and their child five years ago, and since then Jennifer – your namesake, love – has been living with her father, but now her mother, whose name is Phillipa, has changed her mind and wants her back.' He went on to tell them exactly what had happened so far, finishing up with Jennifer's arrival home from school and the scene that had followed, which was still extremely vivid in his mind.

'Do you think this man Osmond had really lied to her?' Vera asked when he had finished.

Antony took a moment to consider that it was very unlike Vera to direct her attention first to a quite unimportant point. 'I think it was just as he said, that she assumed her mother was dead and he'd taken the easiest way out by not contradicting her. I don't think you can blame him for that.'

'The point we should first consider is your part in this, Antony,' said Sir Nicholas, putting down his glass. He was a man as tall as his nephew, though very unlike him in feature and even less so in manner, being authoritative where Maitland preferred a casual approach whenever possible. 'Since you went so far as to accompany Geoffrey and his client on their visit to Mr Begg's office, and subsequently had lunch with them to talk matters over – not to mention your later visit to Osmond's flat – I must presume that you came to the conclusion that the allegations his wife was making against him were false.'

'Until we met Mrs Osmond and her solicitor I didn't know exactly what her allegations were,' Maitland pointed out.

47

'The only thing I was sure of, the only thing I'm really sure of now, was his genuine concern for his daughter, and I felt – rightly or wrongly – that if any efforts of mine could contribute to his retaining custody I ought to make them. I thought it was obvious that it would be very upsetting for a child of that age to have to go to live with a mother whom she hadn't seen in five years and whom she had believed was dead. I felt that even more strongly after I'd heard what Mrs Osmond had to say.'

'Didn't believe her?' asked Vera.

'I didn't like her,' said Antony, 'but she seemed quite confident that the evidence to back up her story would be forthcoming. At the same time I like Osmond and should prefer to believe his version of things, though I realise that these days, when even the nicest people are so confused about right and wrong, he might not have seen anything very dreadful in conducting his affairs so that Jennifer couldn't help knowing about them. He's going to be married, so that won't be a problem in the future, but the question is: was I right, having these doubts, to commit myself to helping him?'

'It's a little late to be asking that,' said Sir Nicholas. 'Would you be in any doubt if it hadn't been for that last scene at Osmond's flat?'

'No, that's the real trouble, of course. Osmond asked her which of them she'd rather live with but she wouldn't answer him and ran out of the room. To lock herself in the lavatory,' he added, 'which is apparently her custom when she's particularly upset.'

'Well, I think you're doing the right thing,' said Jenny. 'A woman who would desert a child of three —'

'Nearly four,' said Antony, smiling when he remembered Jennifer's insistence on the point.

'That doesn't make any difference. A woman who would do that isn't fit to have charge of her now, however upset she may have been by what this mysterious man told her.'

'Think you're right,' said Vera nodding. 'What do you feel, Nicholas?'

'As I said before, it is rather too late to be giving an opinion but I'm inclined to agree with you, my dear. And if you're

48

right about Osmond's affection for his daughter, Antony, I don't think you need worry too much as to whether his denials of his wife's story are true. However confused he may be on moral matters he could hardly fail to realise the unsuitability of taking these women to a small flat where Jennifer couldn't possibly fail to know exactly what was going on.'

'That's what I think, but I took such a violent dislike to Mrs Osmond that I might easily be deceiving myself. For instance, I came away from the meeting quite convinced that whatever her motives are for wanting her daughter with her now, maternal affection isn't one of them.'

'If you're right that is a small mystery to which we may never know the answer,' Sir Nicholas told him. 'But the child's interests must come first, and I can't help but agree with you that her place is with her father. What do you propose to do now?'

'Try to find out what's upsetting Jennifer, and have a word with Osmond's intended, a lass called Amanda Herschell. Geoffrey is putting enquiries in hand about the three women concerned and this man Brodie who seems to have been instrumental in finding them.'

'And is also the man who spoke to the little girl tonight and upset her so much,' said Vera. 'We know he told her her mother was alive, but what else do you think he said?'

'I have my own ideas about that, of course, but they're pure guesswork and Uncle Nick wouldn't like them.'

'Don't let that deter you, my dear boy,' said his uncle, in a tone which only too obviously invited him to dig a pit for his own undoing.

'I can only suppose he spoke to her of her father, and whether what he told her was truth or lies I haven't the faintest idea. But I'm afraid it may mean that an attempt has been made to prejudice her, which will be followed by calling her to give evidence in court that she'd rather live with her mother.'

'I don't think Mrs Osmond sounds at all a nice woman,' said Jenny severely, a remark so un-Jennylike that all her companions turned to look at her. 'You agree with me, you know you do,' she added, dividing the remark indiscrimi-

49

nately between them. 'And I know it's not the sort of case Antony can possibly enjoy, but I think he's quite right to do what he can.'

'At least,' said Maitland, retrieving his glass and coming to sit in the chair opposite his uncle's, 'it will make me grateful – if I hadn't been before – for the advantage of a peaceful domestic circle.' He saw Sir Nicholas's smile and added outrageously, 'If any place within a hundred miles of you, Uncle Nick, can be called peaceful.'

WEDNESDAY, 17th March

I

The following day Maitland got down to the work he had been neglecting. He had first to endure old Mr Mallory's disapproval, his absence on Tuesday having been more protracted than he had expected, but that also was too familiar to cause him any surprise. Mallory was set in his ways and had suspected from the beginning that his employer's nephew would add nothing to the dignity of chambers; an opinion in which he had been confirmed many times during the years that followed, as Antony would have been the first to admit, though his relationship with his uncle – which might appear to an outsider to be a stormy one – precluded him from any feeling of guilt about the upheaval his arrival in Kempenfeldt Square had caused in Sir Nicholas's previously peaceful existence. Fortunately for his comfort in his professional life he had acquired an ally in John Willett, now second in command in the clerks' office, who had turned out to be somewhat of a psychologist and had his own methods of obtaining his own way when the question of the acceptance or otherwise of a brief arose.

Maitland had finished his afternoon tea when the telephone rang and when he picked up the receiver he found that Geoffrey had been put through to him without Hill's intervention, which wasn't surprising if he had spoken to the clerk as urgently as he now did to his friend. 'Robert Osmond has just been on the phone,' he said, without wasting time on a greeting. 'Jennifer hasn't come home from school and he

51

wants me to go round to see him right away. Would you like to come too?'

'I certainly should,' Maitland told him, with a look of mingled dislike and relief at the document he had been studying. 'We decided yesterday, didn't we, that a cab would be quickest? Will you get one and meet me at the usual place?'

Geoffrey agreed and was obviously fortunate in getting a taxi without too much delay. When they reached Robert Osmond's flat they found their client pacing up and down his living-room with a distracted air. Mrs Arbuthnot had let them in and now retreated to a chair in the furthest corner, where she probably hoped to remain unnoticed, her eyes following her employer's movements anxiously.

Robert stopped his pacing and turned towards the new-comers eagerly. 'I'm glad you could get here,' he said.

'Anything we can do,' said Geoffrey, a little at a loss in a situation which was so far outside his experience. 'What time is Jennifer due home from school?'

'They get out at four o'clock.'

It was now barely five. 'Isn't it rather soon—' Geoffrey ventured.

By way of an answer Osmond swung round on the unfortunate Mrs Arbuthnot. 'Tell him!' he commanded.

'Well you see, Mr Horton – I have got your name right, haven't I?' asked Mrs Arbuthnot, just as if it mattered. 'I got to the corner of the street just before four as I always do and waited for Jennifer to join me. But the school came out and she didn't come. I recognised some of her classmates so I knew she ought to be with them. And when I was sure no one else was coming I went along and enquired. They told me Jennifer hadn't been there at all this afternoon.'

'Weren't they worried about that?'

'No, the teacher in her class said she didn't seem at all well this morning. She told Jennifer that she ought to take a rest, but Jennifer didn't say anything like that to me. She came home to lunch and went back to school to get there for a quarter to two; she likes to be early. I waited at the corner and watched her walk down the street and go into the gate as usual . . . it's a private school, you know, very select,' she added unnecessarily. (Antony was beginning to feel that she

52

had a genius for inessentials.) 'And then she seems to have just disappeared. Nobody saw her there.'

'Was that your usual practice, Mrs Arbuthnot? To let her go the last few hundred yards alone?'

'Yes. Mr Osmond knows all about that. Jennifer has a very independent nature and I think she'd like to do the whole journey by herself. Of course, neither of us thinks that at all sensible, not until she's a little older. But once we get to the corner near the school there's no street to cross and we've always thought it quite safe to indulge her whim as far as that.'

'You see it's all my fault,' Robert almost groaned. 'If I'd told Mrs Arbuthnot last night what had happened she'd have gone all the way with her and Jennifer would be safely home by now.'

'Well, Mr Osmond, I wasn't to know,' said Mrs Arbuthnot defensively. It appeared to Antony, perhaps uncharitably, that she was more concerned for her own situation than the child's. 'And if she's with her mother at least you know she's safe.'

'Is that what you think has happened?' asked Geoffrey rather hurriedly, because he was afraid his client was about to explode into violent speech. 'That Mrs Osmond has taken charge of her?'

'Kidnapped her, you mean,' said Robert bitterly. 'And I don't think Phillipa would do anything herself, she'd get that chap Brodie to do it for her. That's what I think has happened . . . what else?'

'I see. Have you called the police?'

'No, I thought—'

'Unless and until some other arrangement is legally agreed upon between you and Mrs Osmond you're certainly entitled to custody,' Horton pointed out. 'Besides the police have facilities for asking questions, finding out which of her fellow pupils were about when she went through the gate of the school for instance, and what happened after that.'

'I know that's true, but I didn't think they'd be very interested . . . I mean, she's not exactly a missing person if we know where she is.'

'That isn't the point,' said Geoffrey.

53

Antony decided to break his silence. 'I think you've got some other idea in your head, Mr Osmond.'

'I suppose I have,' said Robert doubtfully. 'Suppose she went to Phillipa voluntarily. What then?'

'Did you ever discover what upset her yesterday?'

'No, she wouldn't say a word though she did calm down after a while. This morning she was very quiet – Mrs Arbuthnot will bear me out about that – but I thought she'd be better at school than just sitting brooding over whatever was on her mind. Still, as I say, if she has gone to Phillipa of her own free will what do we do then?'

'It will create an awkward situation certainly,' said Maitland, realising as he spoke that this was the understatement of the year.

'And one that I don't feel myself at all capable of dealing with,' said Robert. 'That's why I called Mr Horton and asked him to bring you along too if at all possible. I thought – I know it's a lot to ask – I thought one or both of you could go and see Phillipa and find out what's happened.'

'Whether Mr Brodie persuaded her to go, or whether it was her own idea?'

'That's right.'

'And then?'

'Deal with the situation as seems best to you. Frankly it's beyond me. On the one hand you might be able to scare Phillipa into giving her up, or on the other, you might be able to persuade Jennifer to come home with you.'

Antony glanced enquiringly at Geoffrey. 'We can do our best, I suppose,' said Horton doubtfully. 'But I don't know that I'm particularly qualified for either of those jobs. What about it, Antony? Don't you think this is one of those cases where one person could manage better on their own?'

'As a matter of fact I do, but—' He broke off, and no one attempted to interrupt him because he was obviously thinking the matter through. 'All right,' he said after a moment. 'I want to talk to Jennifer anyway, and there's just a chance she might be more willing to confide in me if we spoke alone. That is if I have your permission to question her, Mr Osmond.'

'I want to know what's worrying her, and if you can

answer that puzzle for me, Mr Maitland, I shall be only too grateful.'

'I'll try.'

'Have either of you been able to give any thought to the matter since we discussed it yesterday?'

'I hope to get a report from the enquiry agents tomorrow or Friday,' said Geoffrey. 'As things stand, if their stories tally with what Mrs Osmond told us, I have to tell you that I think we should seek another meeting with Mrs Osmond and Mr Begg and try to reach a compromise.'

'That's what I thought you'd say,' said Robert miserably. 'It won't do. You saw what Phillipa's like, she wants Jennifer body and soul.'

'The alternative is a lot of unpleasantness and will perhaps leave you worse off in the end. I'm sure you know, Mr Osmond, that the court's sole interest will be Jennifer's welfare, and if it appears to them that you are an improper person to have charge of her—'

'Yes, I know all that.' He sounded now unutterably weary. 'We'll talk about that again, Mr Horton, but meanwhile my first concern is to know that Jennifer's safe.'

'There's one thing that might emerge from the enquiry,' said Maitland, 'and that is the reason for these three women being willing to give evidence so injurious to themselves. There'd have to be some strong inducement, particularly if they're lying, and if we can find out what it was—'

'Some sort of bribery you mean?'

'More or less. Money perhaps or some other consideration. But that's all conjecture and for the moment we'd better stick to the job at hand. Have you got Mrs Osmond's address on you, Geoffrey?'

Geoffrey had, but before he could find it in his notebook Robert had gone across to the desk, written something and handed the scrap of paper to Maitland, who thanked him, found that the writing was clear enough to decipher, and a moment later left with Horton.

He took the underground to the station nearest to Phillipa's flat in St John's Wood and walked from there. He was pretty certain that Robert's interpretation of the situation was the correct one, but even so there were the two possibilities they had discussed and he was doing his best to prepare what he should say in either eventuality. As things turned out this proved to have been a waste of time.

The building was an old one but it had been beautifully and expensively renovated to give each tenant a maximum of privacy. Phillipa's flat was Number Three, from which he judged it to be on the ground floor, but he was still in a state of indecision as he pressed the bell, opened the main door when a buzzer sounded, and found himself in a lobby which he mentally labelled 'precious'. But before he could register any more definite impression a door almost opposite him, bearing the number 3, was pulled open and he found himself face to face with a man he had never seen before, and whom he presumed for the moment must be Matthew Leighton. This illusion was quickly dispelled by the sight of someone he did recognise, Detective Sergeant Porterhouse, who appeared at the stranger's shoulder. 'Mr Maitland?' said the sergeant in obvious surprise. And then, 'You haven't met Chief Inspector Eversley, have you? He hasn't been at the Yard very long.'

It didn't escape Antony's notice that Eversley had stiffened a little at the sound of his name. The Chief Inspector was a big man with hair that was receding at the temples, a thin face that looked somehow incongruous when coupled with a decided inclination to stoutness, and a beak-like nose. Maitland, concealing his bewilderment as well as he could, started to murmur something polite in response to the introduction, when the detective interrupted him, saying sharply, 'Are you a friend of Mrs Osmond's?'

'I've met her,' said Antony cautiously. He could hear sounds of activity in the flat now and shifted his eyes a little so that his question was addressed directly to Sergeant Porterhouse. 'What on earth is Scotland Yard doing here?' he demanded.

'I might ask you the same question, Mr Maitland,' said Eversley, before his subordinate had a chance to reply. His tone was smooth enough now, but there could be no doubt that for some reason the encounter displeased him.

'Oh no, you mightn't. Not until you give me some good reason for doing so,' Antony retorted.

'You'd better come inside,' said Eversley, backing away from the door grudgingly. 'There's been some trouble here,' he added, stating a fact that must by now be obvious to anyone.

'We can go into the bedroom,' Porterhouse suggested. 'I'm sure Mr Maitland will be only too willing to answer our questions.' He was smaller and slighter than the Chief Inspector, though only minimally so, and normally a silent man; on their one previous encounter Antony had sensed a friendliness in him.

'Let's go into the bedroom by all means,' he agreed. He'd recovered his aplomb by now and spoke almost enthusiastically. 'But your questions for me are going to have to wait, Sergeant, until you've answered a few of mine.'

Eversley said nothing to this but there was something ominous about his silence and Porterhouse smiled deprecatingly. 'After you, Mr Maitland,' he said, throwing open a door on the right of the hall.

If this was Phillipa Osmond's bedroom it was every bit as luxurious as the exterior of the house had led him to expect. 'Right!' said Antony, turning to face the two detectives as Porterhouse gently closed the door on the sounds of activity from the other room. 'What's all this about, and why is this a good place for us to talk?'

'Because Mrs Osmond's dead body is lying in the other room,' snapped Eversley, 'and as I imagine you know, Mr Maitland, there are certain routine tasks that must be performed before she can be moved.'

'Don't bother to break it to me gently,' said Antony with an inflection of sarcasm in his voice.

'You said you'd met her, not that she was a friend of yours,' Eversley pointed out. 'However, if I've offended your sensibilities I'm sorry.' This was quite obviously a lie. 'So now, Mr Maitland, perhaps you'll tell us—'

'You're going too fast, Chief Inspector. My questions are to come first . . . remember?' Eversley's grunt might have been agreement, on the other hand it might not. In either event, Antony pressed on. His anxiety for Jennifer was increasing, but his instinct told him that it might be important to get as much information as he could while he still had something to bargain with. 'How did Mrs Osmond die, and when?'

'The post-mortem—'

'Come now, Chief Inspector, you had your doctor take a look at her before you let your chaps loose in the other room. What did he say?'

'She appears to have died by manual strangulation.'

'My other question?'

'You must realise Mr Maitland that the investigation has only just started. She was last seen alive, so far as we can ascertain, when she came in at two o'clock, probably from a luncheon engagement. There was no sign of forcible entry to the flat.'

'Was she alone when she came in?'

'If it's any business of yours, she was.'

'I want to try to narrow things down a little. I suppose you're trying to tell me that the doctor wouldn't be specific as to the time of death?'

'How on earth did you guess?' said Eversley, sarcastic in his turn.

'At least you can tell me when she was discovered. It's not very late now' – he glanced at his watch as he spoke – 'just past seven. It sounds as if your investigation has been in full swing for some time.'

'She was discovered at about five o'clock.'

'By whom?'

'I think that should be enough to satisfy your curiosity, Mr Maitland. We'll hear from you now.'

At least their talk had given him a breathing space. It was obvious that the police were entitled to some degree of frankness in view of the murder, but there was still the instinct towards discretion which in any lawyer is very strong indeed. 'Her former husband, Robert Osmond, was concerned about his little girl who hadn't come home from school. He thought she might be visiting her mother, and I volunteered to find out.'

That brought a rather hard look from Eversley. 'You say her former husband? How long had they been divorced?'

'I believe about three years.'

'And the child lived with her father?'

'Yes.'

'That seems an odd sort of arrangement.'

'I believe it was of Mrs Osmond's choosing. She was the one who left the family home.'

'Indeed? May I ask if this Robert Osmond is a friend of yours?'

'He's a client of a friend of mine, a solicitor, Geoffrey Horton. You've met him, Sergeant, on one occasion at least.'

'I remember,' said Porterhouse, and permitted himself a smile.

'That doesn't explain—' started Eversley impatiently.

'I got to know Mr Osmond because there was a matter concerning his affairs about which Mr Horton wished to consult me,' said Antony.

Eversley didn't look as though he found this careful explanation satisfactory. 'And how long have you known him?' he asked.

'I met him for the first time yesterday.'

'So your relationship is a purely professional one. But when Mr Osmond thinks his daughter . . . how old is she by the way and what is her name?'

'She's eight years old and her name is Jennifer.'

'Well then, when Mr Osmond thinks she has gone on such a harmless errand as to visit her mother he sends you after her. Don't you think that requires an explanation, Mr Maitland?'

'He was worried—'

'You're evading the point.' This, reflected Antony, not too cheerfully, was only too true. He was still wondering how to answer when Sergeant Porterhouse spoke.

'It might help Mr Maitland to know that Mrs Osmond's solicitor is on his way here. Mr Wilfred Begg, we understand. The name of his firm, Wilkins and Begg, was on the copy of her will that we found in the bureau in the living-room.'

'Thank you, Sergeant.' Antony was genuinely grateful. Once Begg arrived there would be no hiding anything, but still he'd rather evade further questioning if he could. 'If you don't mind telling me, Chief Inspector, whether the child is here—'

'Do you think we should have left her in the other room

with her mother's body while all the routine went on?'
Eversley obviously found the question a stupid one, and
didn't attempt to hide the fact.

'No, but I haven't been here before and have no idea of the
size of the flat. I take it you're telling me that she isn't here,
and that you didn't find her here either.'

'That is quite correct.'

'Then I'd better let Mr Osmond know. Perhaps she's
reached home by now, otherwise he may feel he would like to
institute some further enquiries.'

'Not so fast, Mr Maitland, not so fast. What brought Mr
Horton to you with a question about his client's affairs?'

'That's nobody's business but Osmond's.'

'I think you're mistaken there. I have a feeling it may
become very much my business. What was the relationship
between the couple?'

'I don't believe they'd seen each other since the divorce . . .
until yesterday,' Antony told him. With every word that
passed between them, he was becoming more conscious of
Eversley's antagonism, and now he was torn between a
strong instinctive desire to disoblige the detective and the
realisation that it would be to nobody's advantage to allow
their relationship to deteriorate. This was obviously Sergeant
Porterhouse's view as well for he broke in with a reminder.

'Mr Begg will be able to tell us about that, no doubt.'

'Yes, he was there, and so was I,' said Antony rather
unwillingly. 'Though I only sat in on their meeting, the
conduct of it was strictly Mr Horton's affair.'

'When was the divorce?' asked Eversley suddenly, either
forgetting that he'd already asked that question or hoping to
catch Antony out in an inaccuracy.

'Three years ago, as I believe I told you.'

'And after all this time—?'

'It is my understanding that Mrs Osmond's circumstances
had changed,' said Maitland. 'She's an architect by profession, quite a successful and busy one, I'm told. I'm sorry, I
keep thinking of her in the present tense. And now she was
going to re-marry and felt she was in a position to make a
home for the child.'

'And how did your client – Mr Horton's client – feel about this?'

'He didn't like it,' said Antony. No use denying what could be so easily established.

'Did Mrs Osmond intend to fight for custody?'

'I think she did,' said Antony with less than honesty. 'That was what the meeting was about . . . to see if some compromise could be reached.'

Eversley gave him another of those hard stares. 'I can't help feeling there's more to it than that, Mr Maitland,' he said. 'On the face of it Mrs Osmond hadn't a case, or had she enjoyed extensive visitation rights during the years they'd been parted?'

This was getting worse and worse, but in view of Mr Begg's impending arrival it wouldn't help matters if he evaded the questions any further. 'I don't think she had seen Jennifer at all for five years,' he said bluntly.

And, unexpectedly, Eversley let it go at that. 'You'll be wanting to get back to give your report to Mr Osmond,' he said almost genially. 'We shall have to see him later, of course, but that must wait until our enquiries have proceeded a little further.'

Sergeant Porterhouse went with Antony to the front door of the house. 'I hope you find the little girl's got home safely,' he said, and then paused as though weighing up the wisdom of what he was about to add. 'I expect you'll be seeing a good deal of Chief Inspector Eversley in the future, Mr Maitland, your line of business being what it is. We've been short-handed, you know, and so Sir Alfred Godalming arranged his transfer from some place in Westhampton, the town where he was chief of the CID before he became Chief Constable of that county.'

'So that was why he knew my name!' The Assistant Chief Commissioner (Crime) was no friend of Maitland's, and it seemed likely that a man who might feel himself indebted to him would come to share his views. 'I'm grateful to you, Sergeant Porterhouse, more grateful than I can say,' he added.

Porterhouse's smile had a good deal of understanding as he

backed away sufficiently to allow him to close the front door. It was only when Maitland was half way back to Robert Osmond's flat that it struck him that the reason he'd got off so lightly that evening in the matter of questioning was because Eversley had some motive – and probably a devious one – for not wanting him to encounter Wilfred Begg.

II

'Thank goodness you're here,' said Osmond, opening the door and almost dragging him into the living-room. 'I rang Phillipa's flat about an hour ago to let you know Jennifer is home, and a man's voice answered. I thought, of course, that it must be Leighton, but when I asked, the man at the other end was evasive and eventually produced someone who announced himself as Detective Inspector Eversley. Rather a pompous chap he sounded, and he wouldn't tell me anything except that you were on your way back here. What on earth has been going on?'

'I'm sorry to tell you that Mrs Osmond is dead. Eversley said manual strangulation, so I'm afraid that means murder.'

'Oh my God! What did you tell them?'

'As little as I could,' said Maitland ruefully, 'but Wilfred Begg was on his way there – they got his name from a copy of her will that she had in her possession – so I'm afraid the whole story of the projected custody battle is going to get to the police in double quick time. Eversley said they'd want to see you when their enquiry had proceeded a little further.'

'Yes, I can see that. What a frightful thing. And now there's Jennifer . . . I'm just about at my wits' end.'

'You said she was home.'

'A policeman brought her at about six-thirty. I dare say I should have phoned you right away but I was pretty preoccupied trying to get some sense out of her. The Constable said he found her sitting on a bench in the park shivering with cold. It took a bit of persuasion before she'd tell him who she was and where she lived but as soon as she did he brought her back.'

'And even after he'd gone she wouldn't tell you where she'd been?'

'Not a word. I gathered she'd wandered about the park for quite a long time, and then she was too tired to walk any further so she just sat and got colder and colder, poor kid. But I don't know why she deceived Mrs Arbuthnot like that . . . after all, she pretended to be going back to school. It was quite deliberate. There must be something more to it than she's saying.'

'And she still hasn't told you what upset her yesterday?'

'Not a thing. She's had a hot bath and I warmed some soup for her. I think she's asleep now, absolutely worn out. Do you suppose that things will ever get back to normal again?' he asked rather wistfully. 'At least there isn't that nonsense of Phillipa's hanging over us now, but something has upset Jennifer so badly that I don't know whether she'll ever get over it.'

'I haven't had too much experience,' said Antony, 'but I believe children have a good deal of resilience.'

'That's all very well, but she'd only just discovered that her mother was alive and now I have to tell her that she's dead after all. Can you give me some details about that? It seems unbelievable.'

'I gather the doctors were vague about the time of death, but she was seen alive at two o'clock and her body was discovered at five . . . in her own living-room, so far as I can make out. That's really all I know, but I think you ought to prepare yourself, Mr Osmond, for some fairly extensive questioning by the Chief Inspector once he's talked to Wilfred Begg.'

'You mean he'll tell them all this stuff about the case Phillipa was going to bring to get hold of Jennifer?'

'I'm afraid he will, he won't have much choice in the matter even if he wanted to avoid the question. So it may be as well if you insist on Geoffrey Horton being present when you talk to Eversley.'

'You're telling me I'm going to be suspected?'

'I don't know enough of the circumstances yet to say.

They'll certainly construe what's passed between you in the past few days as providing you with a motive, but I don't know enough about Mrs Osmond's life to know whether there are other people with an equally good reason for wanting her out of the way. And for all I know you have an alibi.'

'Let's see, my last sitting this afternoon was at two o'clock, and afterwards I decided to come straight home. I was still worried about Jennifer after that outburst yesterday. The studio isn't very far away; I expect I arrived here at about two forty-five, something like that. And I was here alone until Mrs Arbuthnot came in about four-thirty. She goes home after she's given Jennifer lunch and taken her back to school, and goes directly there when it's time to fetch her again.'

'So she can't confirm your story.' He didn't add, That's a pity, but the thought was in his mind. 'Did anybody see you arrive?'

'I'm pretty sure not. It was too early for the people with jobs, they wouldn't be coming home just then, and the wives who don't work probably would be having a cup of tea.'

'What time did you say you left the studio?'

'Two twenty-five, two-thirty . . . something like that.'

Maitland, with his recent journey in mind, did a few calculations. 'It could have been done,' he said, 'quite easily. Unless the doctors decide on a time of death that rules you out.'

'Look here!' Robert expostulated.

'I'm only asking you the sort of things Mr Horton will when he talks to you,' said Antony. 'You'll be paying him to think of the worst the police can find to say against you, Mr Osmond, and the sooner you realise it the better. After the post-mortem it may be possible to say more exactly what time she died.'

'But you sounded so—'

'Never mind what I sounded like,' said Maitland irritably. 'They'll ask you what you felt about this custody suit and I already know you well enough to realise you won't prevaricate even if it would pay you to do so. On second thoughts it might be better, less suspicious, if you spoke to the police alone when they come here.'

'You mean that perhaps Mr Horton might not want to be associated—'

'I mean exactly what I say. If you do see them alone, just answer what they ask you and don't volunteer a thing.'

'Whatever you say,' said Robert with uncharacteristic meekness.

'But if they want you to make a formal statement, or start issuing warnings, I think you'd better send for Mr Horton,' Antony went on. 'If you answer their questions frankly there's a good chance that you may convince them of your sincerity, but if things go any further I ought to warn you that it may be serious.'

'I'm just beginning to appreciate that.' He glanced up at the clock on the mantelpiece. 'I can't take you out to dinner because of Jennifer but you must be famished. I can rustle up something here if you like.'

'Thank you, but I think I'd better be getting home. In the excitement about Jennifer I forgot to let Jenny know I'd be late, and she'll be wondering where I am.'

'All right then.'

'And if I may add a further word of advice,' said Antony, 'get some food for yourself and don't try to drown your worries about Jennifer. I don't think Eversley will get around here tonight, but if he does you'll need all your wits about you.'

Robert laughed. It was the first time since he had known him that Antony detected a genuine note of amusement. 'It just struck me as rather comical your sitting there lecturing me as if you were my grandfather,' he said. 'However, I'll take your advice. If the police come they'll find me as sober as a judge.'

'An unfortunate simile,' said Antony, 'but I'm very glad to hear it. I'll phone Horton as soon as I get home and tell him what's happened, so you won't have to make any explanations if you do need to get in touch with him. And if Jennifer seems any more like herself I'd be glad to know about that, I know how worried you must be. But meanwhile I think you ought to get your doctor to have a look at her.'

'There's nothing wrong with her physically.'

'I'm thinking of the possibility that the police may want to see her. I'm sure most doctors would agree, in her present state as you described it, that it would be most undesirable; so for her sake and your own—'

65

'Very well, I'll see to it right away.' Robert hesitated a moment. 'That's one thing I couldn't bear,' he confessed. 'That Jennifer should be involved in this mess in any way.'

III

'I wasn't worried,' said Jenny, when he got home and apologised for his lateness, 'because Willett told Uncle Nick and Uncle Nick told me that you'd gone off in a hurry after a phone call from Geoffrey. I've got the oven turned very low, so you've time for a drink before your dinner spoils any more, but I should warn you that Uncle Nick and Vera are sure to be up later on to find out what was on Geoffrey's mind.'

'I didn't have time to talk to Uncle Nick before I left chambers,' Antony explained, 'as it was rather a crisis and I didn't think of either telling him or phoning you. Osmond's little girl had gone missing.'

'Oh no, Antony! Have you found her?'

'She's home again, but no thanks to my efforts. It's a long story, love, and I'm going to have to phone Geoffrey and tell him how things turned out, so if you listen in to what I have to tell him you'll know as much as I do.'

'Is there something wrong with the child?' she asked with quick concern.

'No, nothing like that. At least, her father doesn't know why she took off or exactly where she was all the time, but physically at least she's as right as rain unless, of course, she's caught a cold.'

'Then . . . oh, phone Geoffrey and get it over with and put me out of my suspense,' said Jenny. 'And then you won't have to explain twice, which I know you hate – until Uncle Nick and Vera start asking questions,' she added.

So Antony went to the phone, explained what had happened when he arrived at Phillipa Osmond's flat, and the advice he had given Horton's client on his behalf. He concluded with an account of Jennifer's return. Replacing the receiver and twisting round to face Jenny he said, 'So now you know it all, love. What I didn't tell Geoffrey, because it seemed to need too much explaining, though I'll have to in the long run, is that this new chap Eversley seems to be some sort of a protégé of Sir Alfred Godalming, and judging from the way he looked at me he's only too ready to share his opinion of me.'

'As if that wretched man being made Assistant Commissioner wasn't bad enough without that!' said Jenny crossly. 'What Uncle Nick will say I can't imagine. What do you think is going to happen?'

'I don't know enough about Phillipa Osmond's affairs to be able to answer that question,' said Antony. He was pouring sherry for himself as he spoke, and then crossed the room with the glass in his hand to join her near the fire. 'I expect you've eaten already have you, love?' he asked. 'Would you like me to pour you a cognac or some other liqueur?'

'No, I'll wait. Mr Osmond has a horribly good motive though, hasn't he?' said Jenny. 'And this will just make things worse than ever for that poor child.'

'Who lives may learn,' said Antony as lightly as he could. Jenny had obviously taken her namesake's plight to heart.

'Do you think he did it?' she asked insistently.

'My dearest love, how can I tell you? He doesn't seem to have an alibi but we don't know the exact time of death yet.' He paused, looking at her. 'For Jennifer's sake I don't want him to be guilty any more than you do,' he admitted. 'But if he is there's nothing we can do about it.'

'If he's arrested Geoffrey will brief you, won't he?'

'I'm pretty sure he will, and when he hears what I've just told you about Eversley Uncle Nick will kick like a mule. And I'll do the best I can for him if it comes to that, but I have to admit to you, love, that when the witnesses Phillipa Osmond was going to produce in the custody suit are brought on to prove motive I think the jury will regard Robert Osmond very unfavourably indeed.'

That was very much what Sir Nicholas said, though rather more forcefully, when the matter was revealed to him later in the evening. 'Even on what you've told me, Antony, a good counsel could make things sound very bad for him indeed.'

To which his nephew, anxious to be rid of the subject for that evening at least, replied, 'My own hope is that six thousand, four hundred and thirty-seven other people will have motives as good as his, which may distract Eversley's attention a little.' At which point their friend, Roger Farrell, dropped in, as he so often did in the evening, which gave Antony a good excuse for turning the conversation in another direction.

THURSDAY, 18th March

I

Maitland was in court the following morning, but it was a simple matter and – as he had known all along – an open and shut affair, which the jury must realise as well as he did. It concluded about mid-afternoon with a Guilty verdict, and after a brief struggle, in which his better nature proved victorious, he went back to chambers instead of going straight home. As things turned out that was just as well; Geoffrey Horton had phoned and wanted to see him as soon as possible. As there was nothing urgent awaiting his attention he phoned his friend and, receiving the assurance that he too was free, went straight round to his office.

As he was so familiar with the place he went first to the clerks' room to say that Mr Horton was expecting him and to ask if there was still any tea going. He received a promise that this would be provided within five minutes, joined the solicitor and sat down to hear what he had to say.

Geoffrey wasted no time in coming to the point. 'It's about Robert Osmond,' he said.

'Somehow I guessed that.'

'The question is, will you act for him?'

'As you've involved me so deeply already you hardly need to ask me that,' Antony pointed out. 'Has he been arrested?'

'No, but I should think it's only a matter of time. And in fairness, Antony, you must admit I was very careful not to force you into anything, but last night you more or less took matters into your own hands.'

'We won't quarrel about that,' said Maitland equably.

'What's happened to make you expect the worst?'

'I'd better start at the beginning. Osmond phoned me quite early this morning to say that the police had interviewed him last night, quite late, and had told him to go round to Scotland Yard to make a statement at ten o'clock this morning. Could I go with him, because you'd told him—?'

'I remember quite well what I told him. Had he taken my advice last night?'

'He said he had, but he didn't seem to have liked this chap Eversley any more than you did.'

'Have you come across him before?'

'No. I rather gathered, Antony, from what you said last night that you'd succeeded in putting his back up already.'

'Not me,' Maitland protested. 'Apparently the new AC (Crime) is filling the vacancies in the CID with men from his old bailiwick. Eversley was bristling the moment he heard my name.'

'That's a pity, but it won't make any difference when they get into court,' said Geoffrey, determinedly looking on the bright side. 'I had to put off an appointment but it wasn't anything that mattered, so I told Osmond to come here and we went together to the Yard. That had the advantage of giving us a chance to talk first, and not surprisingly he started by asking me whether this meant they were going to arrest him. I told him that was a question I couldn't possibly answer at this stage, but I hoped not, and then he explained that what was worrying him mainly was Jennifer. He'd arranged for Mrs Arbuthnot to stay with her all day, as she obviously wasn't fit to go to school, but he'd have to make some other arrangements if he wasn't going back.'

'Did he tell you how the child is this morning?'

'Silent, I gather. He had to tell her about her mother, of course, and that seemed to upset her, but not quite in the way that might have been expected. I pressed him about that, naturally, but he didn't seem to be able to explain himself. He did tell me, however, that she seemed to have forgiven him.'

'And I suppose he told you exactly what happened last night. Had they warned him?'

'Not immediately, but they'd made it quite clear from the first that they knew all about the custody suit and the

70

witnesses that Mrs Osmond threatened to produce if he wouldn't settle out of court. And then one of them – the quiet one, he said, which I suppose was Porterhouse – asked whether it would interest him to know that the journey from his studio to Mrs Osmond's flat took one of their men precisely thirty minutes that evening, and the return journey thirty-five. He protested at that – and wondered afterwards whether he should have done so – that doing the journey in the evening after the rush hour was over was hardly the same as doing it during the day, but the only reply he got was from the senior man who said, rather abruptly, that he didn't see that it would make the slightest difference.'

'I made the journey by underground,' said Maitland. 'Were they postulating a train journey, or one by car?'

'The latter I think, but it doesn't really make much difference as Eversley said. They then spelled out for him what he must have realised already, that as his receptionist said he left the studio at two-twenty-five and he couldn't produce any witnesses to say when he arrived at his flat, that left him two hours and five minutes to play with before Mrs Arbuthnot arrived after her abortive attempt to collect Jennifer from school. Even supposing he'd been at home for no more than ten minutes before that, and even if the journey had taken rather longer than the police's experiment had done, that would still have given him a clear forty or fifty minutes to do what had been done to his wife.'

'They'd already asked him whether he had seen any of his neighbours I suppose?'

'Yes, I forgot to tell you that, and he answered them just as you told me he answered you. That was when they got round to warning him, I suppose they'd been waiting to see whether he could produce some sort of alibi.'

'Seems reasonable.'

'I think,' said Geoffrey, 'that at this point I'd better try to give you what he said to me in his own words as well as I can remember them. He said, "The trouble is I can see their point . . . apparently there was no sign of anyone forcing his way into her flat. Whoever visited her was let in in the normal way. And in the mood I was in I certainly wouldn't have needed anything like forty or even fifty minutes to work myself up to feeling that getting rid of her was the only way out." It could have been done all right.'

'I hope he didn't say that to them,' said Maitland anxiously.

'He says he didn't, he said he decided not to say any more and that was when they asked him to go down to the Yard to make a formal statement.'

'I'm glad he had so much sense,' said Antony. 'Did they give him any idea as to the estimated time of death?'

'No, they didn't say a word about that but if they do proceed to an arrest I'll get to know eventually. I asked him at that point, formally, how he proposed to plead if they did proceed to an arrest, and oddly enough he didn't take offence. He just said, Not Guilty, and then went on to add that, in case I was wondering, he really didn't do it.'

'Did you believe him?'

'We'd better get on with the day's events before we discuss that,' said Geoffrey firmly. 'Having ascertained his wishes I went on to tell him how to deal with the further police questioning. He followed my advice to the letter and really acquitted himself very well, but I judged from Eversley's manner that it was only a matter of time before an arrest was made.'

'That's what I was afraid of. What exactly did he tell them?'

'About Mrs Osmond leaving him and Jennifer, and the fact that they'd been divorced two years later. He didn't go into details as to why he didn't contest it, there was no need for that as I told him. As we knew already that Wilfred Begg must have told them all and more than they needed to know about the custody suit he was quite frank about that. I'd hoped it would make a good impression if he didn't try to hide anything, but I don't think the Chief Inspector is a man to be easily impressed.'

'I'm quite sure you're right,' said Antony fervently.

'He'd already assured me that he knew none of the women who were prepared to testify on Mrs Osmond's behalf, and he said the same thing to the police but I doubt whether they believed him. I'd also advised him to tell them that someone accosted Jennifer as she was leaving school on Tuesday and that up to that time the child had believed her mother to be dead. He did so and explained the misunderstanding.'

'A very natural one, I think,' Maitland put in.

'He then said he was pretty sure of the identity of the man who had spoken to her. I hoped that might give them something to think about, Stewart Brodie's profession isn't a popular one with the regular police force, and – though here I had to prompt him a little – between us we tried to convey that we believed the evidence of immorality might have been faked by him. I hoped that would seem to detract a little from Osmond's motive.'

'And he agreed to all that?'

'I'd the devil of a job to persuade him, he still insists he doesn't want to bring Jennifer into the matter at all. But as he'd had the doctor to see her – on your advice, I believe – and *he* agreed it wouldn't do for her to see the police, that doesn't really arise at the moment.'

'What else had the doctor to say?'

'More or less what Osmond seemed to have decided already: there was nothing wrong with her physically, what's worrying her is all in her mind. She wouldn't talk to him any more than she would to her father, but I don't think she's resenting him any more.'

'That's one good thing at least. What do you think about it now, Geoffrey . . . about the question of Osmond's guilt or innocence, I mean?'

'I haven't quite finished my story yet. Cobbold's report came in about half an hour ago.'

'That was quick work, wasn't it?'

'Yes, but when I spoke to them originally I said it was a matter of urgency because of Phillipa Osmond wanting to know by the weekend whether her husband intended to defend her suit for custody. So they put four men on it, and I have to tell you, Antony, it doesn't look good. About the girls, their enquiries were admittedly extremely brief but nothing whatever emerged to the discredit of any of them. Talking to them had the same result, each one seemed to have an intimate knowledge of Robert Osmond and his circumstances, and though I suppose, people being what they are, you might throw some doubt on the respectability of the one who describes herself as a model, you wouldn't have a hope with the other two. And judging from the impression

73

Cobbold's men got of them – and they're by no means inexperienced, let me remind you – they're none of them the type to be promiscuous.'

'What about Stewart Brodie?'

'From the report I don't imagine either of us would be particularly anxious to make a bosom friend of him, but his story is quite straightforward. Mrs Osmond was an old friend and asked his help over the custody question, as she had done earlier when she wanted to stop Robert denying her a divorce. He undertook the investigation himself, out of friendship for her, and when he finished was in no doubt of what had been going on. I shall get written copies of the report by tomorrow, or Monday at the latest, so we can study them then. If I thought it would do any good to see them ourselves in view of the changed circumstances I'd suggest it, but there really doesn't seem to be any need for that.'

'Which being translated, means that you think their evidence will stand up, and that it's our client who is lying?'

'I'm afraid you're right, though I'd like to think differently. For one thing, I like Osmond; and for another, there's his child to think about.'

'If Eversley does arrest him what's going to happen to Jennifer?'

'The girl Osmond mentioned to us, Amanda Herschell, has promised to go to the flat and stay with her. He thinks, quite rightly, that it would be less strange for the child to be at home. But you haven't told me, Antony, how all this strikes you?'

'I find it depressing,' Maitland told him. 'The one thing I'm sure of is Osmond's devotion to his daughter, and because of that I've been thinking that the evidence of the three young women must be rigged somehow, however convincing it seems. But I don't know, it's asking rather a lot to believe that all three of them are lying. For the rest, I like Osmond, as you do, and I'd very much prefer not to think he killed his wife. But whether he did or not I don't want Jennifer to lose her father for the number of years that would probably be involved if he was found guilty.'

Horton smiled. 'Your usual state of indecision, in fact,' he said in a resigned tone. But privately he was conscious of relief that in this instance at least he wouldn't have to be continually putting on the brakes in order to restrain his more impetuous colleague.

II

When he got back to Kempenfeldt Square Gibbs informed Antony that Mrs Maitland was with Sir Nicholas and Lady Harding in the study, a remark into which it was difficult to introduce a note of disapproval, though he managed somehow to convey that Jenny had taken refuge there in view of her husband's neglect.

From Antony's point of view this couldn't have been better, because he was anxious to unburden himself of the latest developments and this meant that only part of his story must be twice repeated. Unless, of course, Jenny had conveyed to the others the gist of their talk the previous evening without confusing them too utterly; but this was so unlikely as to be practically impossible. When it came to making explanations she was very much an 'also ran'.

So he brought them up to date on the story, at Sir Nicholas's insistence starting at the beginning. His uncle was looking grave when he reached his conclusion. 'You've been letting your sympathies run away with you again, Antony,' he said bluntly. 'You may feel it commendable that Osmond should be so fond of his daughter, but I hardly think your tolerance should extend so far as to cover his murdering his wife, particularly as it seems she must have had good cause for the stand she was taking.'

'I like him,' said Maitland obstinately. 'And you know as well as I do, Uncle Nick, it's not up to me to judge his guilt or innocence . . . of any of these things.'

This was, of course, unanswerable and his uncle made no attempt to do so. 'There is also this man Eversley,' he said. 'My impression is that you did nothing to change his original impression of you.'

'I did nothing to – to exacerbate it,' his nephew pointed out meekly.

75

'That may be, but it seems that you can't come into contact with any member of the police force without – without—'

'Putting their backs up,' suggested Vera in her gruff voice. She was the only person from whom Sir Nicholas would tolerate any deviation from the purity of the English language, and now he smiled at her and said, 'Precisely, my dear.' And then, not quite so amiably, 'Well, Antony? Am I to understand that you intend to involve yourself in this affair over and above the call of duty?'

'I don't know yet whether they'll arrest Osmond,' Maitland pointed out, 'though I should think myself it's inevitable. Geoffrey doesn't seem to think there's much to be done with the evidence of the three girls, though when he gets Cobbold's complete report I'm sure he'll do anything that's necessary to cover any point on which it's deficient. And, of course, we have to see Osmond again, he must know more than he's told us so far about Phillipa Osmond's private life. Arising from that talk I'll decide if anything can be done before the trial comes on.'

'That, if I may say so, my dear boy, seems to me to be eminently – if unexpectedly – sensible,' said Sir Nicholas cordially; but his nephew wasn't under any illusion, as he made his way upstairs with Jenny a little later, that this mood would endure beyond the first move on his part that his learned relative considered to be inadvisable.

FRIDAY, 19th March

I

Geoffrey telephoned Antony in chambers at about eleven o'clock the following morning to report that Robert Osmond was under arrest for the murder of his wife. 'No, I haven't talked to him yet,' he said in response to Maitland's query. 'I thought – well, I hoped – that you'd want to, and that we could talk to him together this afternoon.'

'In that case why don't you lunch with me first?'

'I can't manage that, I'm afraid, I've got a previous engagement. But I'm free this afternoon and could pick you up at three o'clock if that suits you.'

'Yes, of course, I'll be waiting for you,' said Antony. He succeeded well enough in hiding his feelings (though why he bothered, when Geoffrey knew them perfectly well was a mystery), but his spirits sank as he spoke, because of all the tasks that his professional duties involved him in prison visiting was to him by far the most unpleasant.

Robert Osmond had obviously not accustomed himself to his new status and greeted them awkwardly. 'I know you were expecting this, Mr Horton,' he said, when they had settled themselves down at the table in the interview room, 'because my motive sticks out like a sore thumb. And I know this is everyday stuff to you, but to me it's quite unbelievable.'

Geoffrey couldn't resist a glance at Maitland, knowing that he must be shrinking inwardly at this remark. 'I think I can understand how you're feeling,' he said. 'This kind of thing happens only to other people. But it *has* happened, and we've got to consider it. I've already explained to Mr Maitland that the plea will be Not Guilty, but if the prosecution's case is as strong as it seems to be it may be only fair to point out to you the possible advantages of entering a different plea to a lesser charge.'

'I don't quite know what you mean,' said Osmond slowly. 'Unless you think the jury might look favourably on me if I told them Phillipa's behaviour had driven me quite mad, and her death was the consequence of it.'

'Not that exactly,' said Geoffrey seriously. 'Anyway at this juncture we're still a long way from having to think about that. I am not suggesting, Mr Osmond,' he added carefully, 'that you had anything to do with Mrs Osmond's death, but I should be failing my duty if I didn't make you aware of every possibility.'

'Well, you can put that one right out of your mind,' said Robert firmly. 'I didn't kill Phillipa, and even if there was some advantage involved I wouldn't say I did.' In his turn he glanced at Maitland, who so far had remained silent after the initial greetings. 'Not even for Jennifer's sake,' he added.

'Then we must consider the matter of what actually happened,' said Geoffrey, and nothing in his tone could have revealed his doubts to his client. 'Though you'd been out of touch with your wife for so long you must know considerably more about her affairs than we do. For instance, do you know anyone who might have had a motive for killing her?'

'The trouble is I can't think of anybody who might have wanted to . . . except myself.'

'And the fewer remarks you make like that the better,' said Antony, coming to life suddenly. 'What about this chap Stewart Brodie for instance?'

'I've been thinking about him, of course, ever since the meeting at Begg's office. I told you then, I think, that I'd never considered that there was anything between him and Phillipa except friendship, but knowing these girls he produced are lying it seems to me that he must have had some reason for taking so much trouble. Perhaps he *was* in love with Phillipa, I don't know. And if he was, why should he kill her?'

'The consideration might have been money, not love,'

Antony pointed out. Out of the corner of his eye he noted that Geoffrey was now sitting well back in his chair, quite content to have the questioning taken over, as their long association had certainly prepared him to believe was inevitable sooner or later. 'Could Mrs Osmond have afforded that?'

'I should imagine so.' But Robert sounded rather doubtful. 'When we were married we each ran our own show financially, so even then I couldn't have given you a very definite answer. I think she had a little family money, and certainly she was very successful professionally. But to pay off three people would be bad enough, the three women I mean. If a fourth were added that would be a rather big bite out of her capital. The person who could tell you, I should think, would be her partner.'

'I didn't know she was in partnership with someone else.'

'Oh yes, almost since she qualified. And now I come to think of it, that family money I spoke of may have gone into buying into the practice. Her partner's name is Calvin Wheeldon. I don't know too much about him, but I was inclined to like what little I saw of him.'

'There might have been some misunderstanding between them,' said Maitland hopefully. 'But of course you wouldn't know about that either.'

'For all I know he was in love with her too,' said Robert gloomily.

'Do you think that's likely?'

'Not really. She's known him for a very long time, a lot longer than she knew me. Surely if there had been any attraction it would have shown itself before now.'

'It doesn't always follow. Propinquity is responsible for a great many love affairs,' said Antony, 'or so I've always been told.'

'He seemed to me a hard-headed sort of chap.'

'Well, don't let it worry you, we can find out about him. Who else is there who might have a motive?'

'Nobody,' said Robert unhelpfully.

'Money is the root of all evil, or so they tell us. Who had a financial motive for wanting Phillipa – for wanting your wife dead?'

79

'It'll save time if you stick to Phillipa,' said Robert. 'As I've just been explaining to you rather carefully, I don't know too much about her financial affairs.'

'Well, I've seen where she was living, which I think you haven't. There was no lack of money, I can assure you of that. Unless, of course,' he added thoughtfully, 'she was spending every penny she earned.'

'That would be quite like her.'

'Yes, I suppose so. Or someone might have been subsidising her. All the same, just suppose for a moment that she had something to leave. Who would have been the beneficiary? Jennifer?'

'I should think it very unlikely. After all, she took no interest in the child's welfare until this recent craze of hers. And I must say I rather hope that isn't the case, because in a way it would be adding to my motive, wouldn't it?'

'As Jennifer is only a child, I suppose it would. But you still haven't answered my question.'

'Her brother, perhaps. Mind you I don't know.'

'You never told us she had a brother.'

'Why should I? It just hasn't arisen. His name is Rudolph Spencer and he's a playwright.'

'I've never heard of him.'

'I should have said an unsuccessful playwright. I should also explain that that's his own description of himself. Actually when I last saw him he was keeping the wolf from the door by working as a clerk in a shipping company.' Robert smiled suddenly, reminiscently. 'He has his dreams.'

'I get the impression you rather like him.'

'I like him very much as a matter of fact. I meant to keep in touch after Phillipa left me, but somehow it didn't work out that way. But even if he were literally starving in a garret, and Phillipa was rolling in the stuff I can't see him doing anything to harm her. There's no malice in him, and certainly he's the last person in the world to resort to violence.'

'At least he might be able to tell us something about Mrs Osmond's recent associates,' Maitland pointed out. 'The same thing applies to Mr Wheeldon and to Matthew Leighton. Any one of them may give us a lead, which is, I may say, highly desirable. Did Mr Horton tell you that the three young women who agreed to give evidence for Phillipa at the custody hearing are all pretty well word perfect in their stories?'

'I haven't had the chance yet,' Geoffrey put in.

'Is that really relevant now?' asked Robert.

'More relevant than ever. The prosecution will be playing up motive for all it's worth when we get into court, and if we could have shown that Phillipa's case wouldn't have stood up that would have been all to the good.'

'I should have thought Stewart Brodie would have been the first person to approach about that.'

'So he would.'

'But you keep talking of the three women, not mentioning him.'

'Only because he'll be a witness for the prosecution, as they will. Mr Horton was having enquiries made, jumping the gun as it were, but now that you've been arrested it makes a difference.'

'Oh, I see. It takes a bit of getting used to,' he added apologetically. 'Not the sort of thing that happens to people you know, as Mr Horton said, and it seems all the more impossible when one is personally involved.'

'Well, there's nothing more we can do until the Magistrate's Court hearing on Monday. You'll have to take that, Geoffrey, because I have a conference, but in any case we shouldn't be doing anything except reserve our defence.' He turned back to Osmond again. 'Is there someone with Jennifer?'

'Yes, of course, Amanda is there. She's going to stay at the flat until . . . well, I hope until I get home.'

'What about her job?'

'She's going to try and get on the day shift on compassionate grounds for the time being and not work at all on weekends. Then Mrs Arbuthnot can carry on as usual.'

'I'd like to go round and see them. Unless you've any objection, of course.'

'It's all right with me as long as you understand—'

'I know, you don't want Jennifer involved. I should still like to know a little more about her encounter with Brodie, if that's who it was, and what happened when she disappeared the afternoon of the murder. I promise I won't go any further than that without your permission, but do you agree to my asking her that much at least?'

'Yes, if she'll talk to you it may do her good.'

'The question is, what has she been told?'

'I broke it to her yesterday about her mother's death and how she died, and she just stared at me and didn't say anything. So then I went on to explain that because we had had some differences recently the police were beginning to think I might have done it. And then she said, But you didn't, daddy? in such a strange tone, rather as though the answer didn't matter to her either way. Of course I tried to reassure her, and I said if they did arrest me it would only be a matter of time before I was home again and you and Mr Horton would look after everything.' He paused and divided a rather twisted smile between them. 'I wonder if that was true,' he added.

'We'll do our best to make it so,' said Geoffrey briskly, but when they left their client a few moments later neither of them was in a particularly cheerful frame of mind; Geoffrey because he felt that his friend was allowing himself to be persuaded of Osmond's innocence for the wrong reasons and Antony because, though he'd every intention of giving the matter his best endeavours, the responsibility of being trusted was something he could have done without.

II

That evening Sir Nicholas had refrained from kidnapping Jenny to ensure his nephew's joining them as soon as he got home. The study door was closed and it was probable, Antony thought, that Uncle Nick hadn't yet got home. So he exchanged greetings with Gibbs – sour on the butler's part because an early arrival must mean that some duty or other had been neglected – and took himself straight up to his own quarters. Jenny, greeted with the bald announcement that Robert Osmond had been arrested, saw at once that he didn't want to talk about it yet and refrained from questioning him; but neither of them was in the least surprised when Sir Nicholas and Vera arrived almost simultaneously with the after-dinner coffee.

'So your client has got himself into real trouble,' said Sir Nicholas. Antony couldn't make up his mind whether there was more amusement in his tone, or a carefully concealed desire to say, I told you so.

'How did you know that?' he asked. He was rummaging in the cupboard as he spoke for the cognac Sir Nicholas preferred.

'It wasn't really a very difficult sum to do,' his uncle assured him. 'I didn't get back to chambers until fairly late in the afternoon, and when Mallory informed me that Geoffrey had telephoned you this morning and you had gone out to meet him as soon as you came in this afternoon there was really only one construction that could be put on that.'

'You were quite right,' Maitland admitted, straightening up with the bottle in his hand.

'He's under arrest?'

Antony nodded. 'Well, it's only what you were expecting, isn't it?'

'Did he do it?' asked Vera. She was a tall woman, and even in her youth it was improbable that anyone would have called her willowy. Her habit of arraying herself in sack-like garments did nothing to dispel the impression of sturdiness, but at least since her marriage the sacks had achieved a certain elegance of cut and style, and under Jenny's gentle prompting she allowed herself a good deal more latitude in the matter of the colours she wore. She had very thick hair, flecked with grey, which in theory she wore in a bun at the nape of her neck, but which in fact was continually escaping from the pins that should have confined it. She had also a singularly beautiful voice, which had probably been the greatest of her assets when she herself had practised at the junior Bar, though her habit of speaking in an elliptical fashion meant that it was heard a good deal less often than any of her family would have wished.

'I'm not altogether sure about that,' Antony confessed.

'Put it another way then. Are you going to do any work on

his defence besides appearing for him in court?'

'There isn't much I can do. The prosecution has all the witnesses.'

'You mean,' said Sir Nicholas, 'the three young women who were going to give evidence in support of his wife's claim for custody of their daughter?'

'Yes, Uncle Nick, that's exactly what I do mean. It's the biggest part of the prosecution's case, unless there's something we haven't heard about yet. The motive was certainly there, it was pretty obvious their evidence would be accepted by the court. He was going to lose Jennifer, and he's mad about the child.'

'On the other hand,' said Sir Nicholas, 'if he's convicted of murder he'll lose her anyway. What have the police against him?'

'I told you . . . mainly motive.'

'Not opportunity?'

'Well, yes, insofar as he says he was at home and saw nobody. But between the time that he left his studio and the time his housekeeper, Mrs Arbuthnot, arrived back from her abortive attempt to fetch Jennifer from school he could quite easily have got to St John's Wood, done what was done, and been back home again. Eversley made it quite clear to him that one of his men had timed the journey both ways.'

'And how is he going to plead?'

'Not Guilty.' But he added, seeing his uncle about to speak, 'Geoffrey pointed out the other possibility to him but he wasn't having any.'

'That figures,' said Vera. 'Way you described him he sounds an all-or-nothing chap.'

'The question is,' said Sir Nicholas, 'what are you going to do? You said you'd answer that when you'd had some further speech with your client, and I take it your expedition with Geoffrey this afternoon was for that purpose.'

'There doesn't seem to be a great deal I can do, though I have the names of three men who may know something about Phillipa Osmond. I can only hope that what they have to tell me will lead somewhere.'

'I suppose one of them is the man she was engaged to,' said Jenny. 'Matthew Leighton, isn't that his name?'

'Yes, I'm hoping to see him, little as I like intruding on him at a time like this. Also she worked in partnership with a man called Wheeldon, and she has a brother who may be expected to know something about her associates. I can't see the three girls now, of course, or Stewart Brodie, they're the chief witnesses for the prosecution I should think, but Geoffrey's had some enquiries made and he's terribly afraid their stories will stand up. I'd also like to see the girl Osmond was going to marry, who's looking after Jennifer while he's away, or perhaps I should say till there's a verdict one way or the other. And I'd very much like to know what's upset that poor child so much, though I've no idea whether that would help her father or not.'

'Probably not,' said Vera, who was nothing if not blunt. 'And you're doing all this even though you don't quite believe he's innocent?'

'The thing is,' said Maitland, 'I like the man.'

'Which is half way to an implicit belief in his innocence,' said Sir Nicholas satirically. 'May I remind you, Antony, that any action you take is likely to be subject to police scrutiny.'

'You don't have to remind me, Uncle Nick, I'm only too aware of it. But as I don't—'

Sir Nicholas was already leaning well back in his chair and now he closed his eyes as though shutting out some prospect too awful to contemplate. 'How many times have you told me, Antony, that as long as you stick to what you are pleased to call the "straight and narrow" nothing can be suggested against you?' he enquired.

'Several dozen times at least,' Antony conceded, smiling.

'And how many times have things gone wrong, notwithstanding your optimism?'

'About the same, I should think.' Maitland was unrepentant. 'I'll watch my step, Uncle Nick,' he promised, 'and I can't say fairer than that!'

But if he thought to propitiate his uncle he was mistaken. 'If I could only persuade you to forswear the vernacular,' moaned Sir Nicholas, and declined to be consoled.

III

It wasn't too long after that when the house phone rang. This was an instrument originally installed for Gibbs's convenience, but which he had ignored for years, preferring the martyrdom of stumping up two flights of stairs when there was a message to be delivered. Vera's arrival in the household had caused a slight relenting in his attitude, for which they were all grateful.

'A young lady to see you, Mr Maitland, a Miss Herschell,' said Gibbs censoriously, as soon as Antony picked up the receiver.

Antony thought for a moment. 'May I use the study, Vera?' he asked, and when she nodded relayed the message. 'I think Gibbs might be happier if you accompanied me, Uncle Nick,' he added as he turned from the phone. 'Which reminds me' – he glanced at his watch – 'five more minutes and he'd have been in bed, and Miss Herschell probably wouldn't have been admitted at all.'

Sir Nicholas's favourite room was undeniably comfortable, but they found their visitor perched on the edge of one of the chairs looking anything but relaxed. She jumped to her feet as they went in, a tallish girl with bright red hair, green eyes – or as nearly green as eyes ever are – and a creamy complexion. 'Mr Maitland?' she said, looking from one to the other of them. 'It's a dreadful time of day to be intruding on you, but I couldn't get away before because of finding someone to stay with Jennifer. Well, as a matter of fact, Mrs Arbuthnot has been with me for quite an hour, but we both thought it would be better to wait until we were sure Jennifer was asleep, and hope she wouldn't wake up before I get back. She's been dreadfully upset, you know.'

'And no wonder.' Antony came a little further into the room. 'I'm Antony Maitland,' he told her, 'and this is my uncle, Sir Nicholas Harding, who is in the same line of business, if you like to put it that way, and whose advice I always ask about difficult cases. I hope you didn't mind—'

'Of course not.' She took a moment to look Sir Nicholas over with frank interest. 'I'm only too grateful . . . Robert told me about you, Mr Maitland,' she went on, turning back to him. 'And I think perhaps I should have gone to see Mr Horton, but it was so late and he lives out of town so it was really much easier to come here. I hope you'll forgive me.'

'I wanted to see you anyway. Sit down, Miss Herschell, we may as well be comfortable as we talk.' She sat down again, and he took a moment to thank providence that she hadn't chosen Sir Nicholas's favourite chair. 'But first why don't you tell us why you wanted to see me, and why it was so urgent as to bring you here tonight.'

'To find out if there's anything . . . anything at all I can do to help.'

He smiled at her. 'And—?' he prompted.

'And to find out whether you can do anything for Robert,' she said. 'I should have waited until you got in touch with me, I suppose, but I just couldn't.'

'That's very understandable,' said Sir Nicholas. 'Miss Herschell, do you know the details of the story Phillipa Osmond was ready to tell in court and the witnesses she had to back her up in trying to get custody of Jennifer?'

'But it was the murder charge I meant. That other business isn't important any more, is it?'

'I'm afraid it is. Motive will be the main part of the prosecution's case as far as we know at present. So I ask you again—'

'Phillipa said that three women had been having affairs with Robert in the flat and that Jennifer knew all about it. I don't know any more details than that, well I couldn't of course because there wasn't a word of truth in it and so Robert only knew the bare facts.'

'Well, that is one of the first things my nephew will want to ask you about,' said Sir Nicholas. He had obviously, thought Maitland, amused, taken one of his unpredictable fancies to Amanda.

'I have to tell you, Miss Herschell,' he said, 'because I think you'd rather I was straight with you than tried to gloss things over, that Mr Horton had enquiries made which suggest that the evidence of all these women is circumstantial and sounds convincing. No, wait a minute, I didn't say *I* was convinced,' he added hurriedly as she seemed about to interrupt him. 'Mr Osmond tells me you've known each other for two months. How often have you been seeing him?'

'That's a funny question.' She reflected a moment. 'Oh, I suppose one of these women says she was carrying on with him all that time.'

'Something like that.'

'Well, we haven't seen as much of each other as I'd like because I wanted to keep my job until we were married . . . they're so short-handed at the hospital. And if that sounds self-sacrificing it wasn't really, because we didn't mean to wait very long.'

There was nothing for it, he would have to give her some details of the things he had heard. Maitland glanced at his uncle and received a slight confirmatory nod, as though the older man knew exactly what he was thinking. 'One of the women said the affair was over four months ago,' he said, turning to Amanda again, 'and another that she got to know Mr Osmond at about that time. She was seeing him – she said – on odd evenings and occasional weekends, and the dates she gave would overlap the period you knew him by a month.'

'It's awfully difficult to remember exact dates,' said Amanda doubtfully.

'Perhaps your duty roster—?'

'Yes, of course. If I look at that it may remind me. Is that what you want me to do . . . make up a sort of list? Has this woman been asked just when she saw Robert?'

'I suppose the police have asked her, but we've no details of their case yet. And if the prosecution don't bring the question up I shall certainly do so myself in court. The same thing applies to the third woman, whose affair with Mr Osmond – again I'm quoting, Miss Herschell, don't misunderstand me – was shorter and even more recent. The thing is, you see, if we have your evidence on this point it may be possible to trip them up.'

'Well, you can be sure I'm ready to try to remember, because I know Robert wouldn't have done anything to hurt Jennifer, and even if he felt quite hopeless about the custody suit he wouldn't have hurt Phillipa either. Perhaps I can find one of my colleagues to back me up. I mean, if I came back from an evening with Robert I might easily have talked about it, particularly later on when we got to know each other better and it was obvious where we were going.'

'Thank you very much, Miss Herschell, that would be a great help.'

'You're thinking,' she said shrewdly, 'that it will be three against one.'

'Something like that. Is Jennifer still upset?'

'I'm afraid so. She's just as polite as ever, but she won't tell me anything. And of course when she knew what has happened to Robert that just made matters worse. If she – if she comes round again and could give evidence, that might clear all this up. But I know Robert would never agree to that.'

Maitland thought to himself that she must indeed be very sure of Osmond's integrity to be so willing to rely on what his daughter might have to tell. For himself he thought he'd need a very long talk with Jennifer before he agreed to anything like that. But it was no good making the ordeal this girl was undergoing any the worse. 'I shall have to do my best to persuade him,' he said lightly.

'Wouldn't it be a terrible thing to ask of her?' she said with sudden compunction.

'Not so bad as you think. I've tried to explain already to Mr Osmond that the court would be very gentle with a child that age, though that was in regard to the custody suit, we haven't discussed the matter since he was arrested. How do you feel anyway about marrying a man with a ready-made family?'

'If I say I adore Jennifer you'll think I'm being sloppily sentimental,' said Amanda. 'Only it happens to be true.'

'I shouldn't think anything of the sort,' said Antony with some truth. He thought Amanda Herschell was about as unsentimental as anybody he had ever met, and he felt equally convinced that her regard for Osmond was very sincere and that she was telling the truth about how she felt about the child. 'Has she accepted you, do you think?'

'I'm sure she has. To tell you the truth, Mr Maitland, I think she was starved for feminine company. Phillipa was so far right . . . a child needs two parents. And there's one thing I'm determined to do for her . . . for them: to see that Robert, when the time comes, isn't miserable or lonely when she goes on her own way.' She paused there and then added rather drearily. 'If he come home, of course, but I won't think about that. The alternative is too dreadful.'

Time to give her thoughts a new direction. 'Tell me about your association with Robert Osmond,' said Maitland.

'You want to know whether we . . . well, we didn't!' said Amanda. 'Though there were occasions . . . that's why I'm so sure Robert would never have done anything to shock Jennifer.' She grinned at him suddenly. 'A very pure relationship,' she said.

He returned her smile but he hadn't quite finished his questions. 'Tell me then, Miss Herschell – this is something that might be helpful – did Jennifer ever look at you as if she thought there was anything strange about the way the two of you acted together?'

'Mr Maitland, you're not coming round to believe in those women's stories?'

'I'm trying to think of questions you might be asked in court, to which the answers might be helpful in the absence of Jennifer's evidence on the point.'

'Yes, I see. I'm sorry. She was just pleased to see me and we had fun together, the three of us. I'm absolutely certain that no funny business was going on during the time I knew Robert at least, and all I can say is it would be very unlikely for him to have carried on that way before either. Only I suppose they won't believe me about that, the court I mean. They'll think he was intimate with me, just as the others say he was with them, and that I'm hopelessly prejudiced in his favour because in my case he offered marriage.'

'Unfortunately, Miss Herschell, that may be all too true. But I think if you're willing, and if Mr Horton agrees, we'll have to try.'

'Of course I'm willing, that's what I came here to tell you. I wonder what these other girls are like,' she added curiously. 'Do you think my being a nurse might add a note of respectability to the proceedings?'

'It certainly won't do any harm, but I'm afraid we can

hardly call the others disreputable,' said Maitland thoughtfully. 'One is a teacher, another an assistant in a flower shop, and the third is a model.'

'Aha!'

'If you're thinking that for that reason she might be judged to be a person of uncertain morals,' said Antony, 'I think you're wrong. But even if you weren't, don't you see it would only make things worse, lend credence to her story?'

'Yes, I suppose so,' she sighed. 'Do you think it's quite hopeless, Mr Maitland? Robert's case, I mean.'

That was an uncomfortable question. 'It's early yet to give an opinion,' he said evasively. And then, 'Mr Osmond gave me permission to talk to Jennifer,' he added. 'May I come to see you . . . tomorrow afternoon perhaps?'

'Come to tea,' said Amanda. 'That might make Jennifer more at her ease, passing cups and things like that. But I don't know.' She sighed again. 'I'll do my best to get her back to normal, she's so very unlike herself at the moment.'

Sir Nicholas was standing at the bottom of the stairs when his nephew closed the front door behind their visitor. 'That's a very admirable young woman,' he said as Antony came across the hall to join him. 'I only hope that she – and you – aren't deceiving yourselves about this man Osmond's character.'

SATURDAY, 20th March

I

It had been arranged that Antony and Geoffrey should call upon Matthew Leighton together the following morning, and that Geoffrey should subsequently return to Kempenfeldt Square to take part in another family ceremony, lunch with Sir Nicholas and Vera. Mr Leighton's house turned out to be what could only be called a stately home not very far from Eaton Square, a fitting setting for a man whom Antony had come to think of as a tycoon.

Its owner was expecting them. He was a big, grizzled man, still handsome in his late fifties and he had, thought Maitland, a distinctly dazed look, as though things had been happening much too quickly for him. 'It's good of you to see us,' Geoffrey said with obvious sincerity. In fact he was surprised that Leighton had agreed to the interview at all, though probably he was still in a state of shock and didn't yet know quite what he was doing. In that case it was perhaps a shame to take advantage of him, but there was their client to think of as well.

'Why shouldn't I see you?' said Leighton, almost aggressively. 'Anything that makes the time pass—' He broke off there and sat down heavily in one of the armchairs near the fire, waving his visitors to seat themselves in their turn. It was an intensely masculine room, which made Antony wonder what Phillipa would have made of it if she had come to the house as its mistress. 'But I don't altogether understand,' Leighton went on, still addressing Geoffrey. 'You told me that you're Robert Osmond's solicitor. What can you want from me?'

'You must know, Mr Leighton, that the police have arrested my client for the murder of Mrs Phillipa Osmond.'

'Yes, of course I know it.' His tone was a little testy now. 'I came back to town because of Phillipa's death. I'd gone down to my country place on Wednesday afternoon and meant to stay there at least over the weekend.'

At this point Maitland took over, as Geoffrey had been pretty sure he would. 'Mr Leighton, if I seem to be interfering in your personal affairs you must forgive me, but I understand that you and Mrs Osmond were engaged to be married.'

'Yes, certainly we were.'

'She was going to accompany you on this visit to the country?'

'I have no live-in housekeeper, Mr – Mr Maitland. It would hardly have been proper for us to stay there alone together.'

'No, I see. When did you see her last?'

Matthew Leighton sighed and stared at him for several moments without answering. Then he said slowly, 'You and Mr Horton are acting for Robert Osmond, but I'm afraid I don't see how I can help you.'

At least he hadn't said, how I can be expected to help you. Taking some small encouragement from that Maitland attempted to explain. 'Our client was divorced from Mrs Osmond three years ago, and can tell us very little about her life since then or what friends she may have made. In view of the fact that you were about to be married, it seems likely that you must know a little more.'

'You're wondering,' said Leighton, feeling his way, 'whether some other motive may exist for – for what happened than the very obvious one her former husband had.'

'That's it exactly.'

'You don't believe in his guilt then?'

'He's pleading Not Guilty,' said Maitland and hoped that the reply didn't sound too evasive.

'Very well, I'll do what I can to help. You wanted to know

93

when I last saw Phillipa. It was on Tuesday evening, we had dinner together. Do you want the name of the restaurant?'

'No, that hardly concerns us. I only wanted to know how she seemed on that occasion.'

'Her own lovely self.'

'Could you be a little more explicit than that?'

'I don't quite know what to say. You tell me you've met her, at least Mr Horton implied as much.'

'Yes, at the office of her solicitor. I was merely a witness to the meeting. Mr Begg and Mr Horton were hoping to work out a compromise in this custody business.'

'That was wise, I suppose, but in the circumstances hardly possible. Anyway, if you both met Phillipa you know she was beautiful. She was, too, a very loving person.'

'Did she say anything to you about her plans for while you were away?'

'Only that she had to meet a client on Wednesday afternoon and after that she was free. If it hadn't been for that I should have spent the afternoon with her and gone down to the country later. And if you're surprised that I was willing to spend a few days without her it was mainly because I had work to take with me, something that needed doing where I could be free from distraction. Also Phillipa was winding up her affairs at her office and that took up a good deal of her time.'

'Had you discussed financial matters at all, Mr Leighton?'

That brought a frown. 'We discussed the allowance I should give her, of course, and there was one other point. She told me her will was made out in favour of the child, Jennifer, and asked whether I'd like her to change it after we were married. I told her it would be necessary to make a new will . . . I don't need to explain that to you, gentlemen. But naturally I should have liked the arrangement to remain as it was.'

'That brings us to the custody suit.'

'It all seems so pointless now,' said Leighton drearily.

'I know, and I'm truly sorry to be bothering you at a time like this. I know Mr Horton feels the same. But if you'll be kind enough to bear with us there are one or two questions to which I'd like an answer.'

94

'Very well.'

'The first is, why did Mrs Osmond want Jennifer with her after all these years?'

'I think the answer to that must be obvious, Mr Maitland. A single woman with a demanding job isn't in a good position to bring up a child herself. When she first left home – I think I should say when she was driven from her home – she felt that Jennifer would be better with her father. In spite of his failings as a husband he had, she said, a good relationship with the child. But now things would be different, she could devote her time to Jennifer and there'd be no lack of money for either of them.'

'And perhaps you yourself were not averse to having a ready-made family?' Antony hazarded.

'It has been the dream of my life. My first wife – she died only five years after we were married – bore no children, and sometimes I have accused myself of being more grieved by that than by losing her, though I was heartbroken at the time.'

'Mrs Osmond was still of child-bearing age.'

'Yes, indeed, and I hoped we should have been blessed with a family of our own. All the same, how could I deny her what she wanted so much . . . to have her own little girl with her?'

'How long had you known Mrs Osmond, Mr Leighton?'

'About a year.'

'And how long have you been engaged to be married?'

'Four months? Five months? I can't remember the exact date.' He smiled again, rather surprisingly. 'You're thinking, Mr Maitland, that I was rather slow in getting to the point; young people are so impetuous nowadays. Let me ask you a question, are you married?'

'Yes, I am.'

'And how long did your courtship last?'

'I'd known Jenny all my life . . . all her life, I should say. But I admit we were both very young when we married. All the same, you're quite wrong about what I'm thinking. Seven or eight months isn't really a very long time to get to know one another,' said Antony smiling, though the question had taken him uncomfortably near to memories that he preferred to keep buried.

95

'You mean I acted quite quickly for one of my generation.'
Matthew Leighton seemed determined to play the dotard.
'And perhaps I should have been slower if I hadn't discovered
that Phillipa was taking steps to have the child with her again,
to retire from her work and devote her whole time to her. I
knew then that I hadn't been mistaken in her true nature.'

'I see. How did Mrs Osmond feel the custody suit would
go?'

'She was quite sure her former husband would give in
without a court battle. After all the unpleasant facts that
emerged . . . that's why I was a little surprised to receive this
visit from you. I'm very much afraid that the more enquiries
you make the more you will discover to your client's
discredit.'

'Yes, but you see I don't think he did what he's alleged to
have done,' said Maitland, and wondered immediately
whether he had spoken the truth.

'Not the murder perhaps. I should be very sorry indeed to
think that must be added to the rest. But in the matter of his
fitness to look after the child—'

'That's the part I meant,' said Antony firmly, and thought
immediately that the bald statement was too cruel in the
circumstances. 'That doesn't necessarily mean that Mrs
Osmond wasn't deceived too,' he said. 'There were certainly
three witnesses – three young women – produced by Stewart
Brodie, each of whom was willing to testify that she had been
intimate with Robert Osmond and that their meetings had
taken place at his flat, with Jennifer quite aware of what was
going on.'

'Still, you feel there is some doubt about it?'

'I don't just feel it, I'm convinced of it,' said Antony, but he
knew in his heart of hearts it wasn't as simple as that. He had a
profound distrust for instinct, particularly his own, and for all
his momentary certainty he knew well enough that doubts
would creep in later.

'Well, you've certainly given me something to think
about,' said Matthew Leighton.

There seemed to be no answer to that. Maitland asked
instead, 'You guessed our reason for being here. Can you tell
us anything about Mrs Osmond's friends, or even acquaint-

ances? Anybody who might conceivably have a reason for killing her?'

'There's so much evil in the world today that I can't help thinking . . . can't help hoping . . . some stranger perhaps, intent on robbing her.'

'I understand there was no question of forcible entry to her flat.'

'In any case, I can't help you there, I'm afraid. The only two people I know who were close to Phillipa were her partner, Mr Wheeldon, and her brother, Rudolph Spencer. Wheeldon is very much the business man, I'm one myself and I recognise the type when I see it. I'm sure his relationship with Phillipa was purely on that plane. As for Rudolph, I can't say I care for him but that is probably something as much to my discredit as to his. We're such different types.'

'Yes, I see. We won't worry you any further, Mr Leighton, and I'm only sorry to have troubled you at such an unhappy time.'

'Don't think about it,' Leighton said, and sighed. 'As I told you, Mr Maitland, anything that takes my mind off what has happened is welcome just now. And I'll think over what you said. You feel that Stewart Brodie may have been lying to Phillipa.'

'I—' Antony started. What he had said hadn't exactly been an untruth, but had certainly implied one.

'I'd like to believe you,' said Matthew, without waiting for him to finish. 'That would mean the little girl would be safe in future. But you see I don't think you've thought it out very thoroughly. There could be no reason for Brodie to arrange false evidence unless he had been paid for it.'

'No, that's true.' Maitland was anxious to get away now before he committed any further indiscretion. He had taken a fancy to Matthew Leighton and didn't enjoy watching him struggle against disillusionment. Geoffrey obviously felt much the same and they made their farewells rather quickly.

II

They were in good time for their luncheon engagement but Jenny was already with Sir Nicholas and Vera when they got back to Kempenfeldt Square. As soon as he had provided them with drinks and resumed his chair Sir Nicholas demanded, 'How did you get on with your tycoon, Antony?'

'He's a nice chap and very cut up about the whole business,' said Maitland, 'but I wouldn't say he was particularly helpful, would you Geoffrey?'

'Only, as you pointed out to me on the way here, in explaining – perhaps – why Phillipa Osmond had suddenly decided to ask for custody of her daughter.'

'That "perhaps" makes me fear the worst, Geoffrey,' said Sir Nicholas. 'Has Antony been indulging again in groundless speculation?'

'I wouldn't say exactly groundless,' said Horton slowly. 'At least, I think on that one point he may be right.'

Sir Nicholas turned his eyes upon his nephew, but Vera forestalled him. 'Better tell us,' she said.

'It wasn't helpful,' Maitland repeated. 'It only cleared up, to my mind at least, one very small mystery. Leighton was obviously keen to have Jennifer as part of his family, to adopt her I suppose. He'd known Phillipa for seven or eight months before he proposed to her, and he said we must think he'd been very slow about it, which makes me believe he'd been considering the matter for some time. Then he said that it might have been even longer if he hadn't found out that Mrs Osmond was already taking steps to gain custody. He said – I think I've got it right, Geoffrey? – he knew then that he hadn't been mistaken in her true nature.'

'And from that you deduce that she was impatient to get the matter settled, and this was one way of expediting some action on his part,' said Sir Nicholas. 'You may be right about that, because as I understand it Stewart Brodie's enquiries must have begun about six months ago. In any event the first evidence of misconduct on your client's part dates from about that time. Unfortunately, I agree with you both: it doesn't help matters in the slightest.'

'Doesn't it make you think, Uncle Nick, that Antony may be right and the three women are all lying about having known Mr Osmond?' Jenny asked.

'Is that what he thinks?' asked Sir Nicholas, interested.

'Cobbold's report seemed to confirm their evidence,' Geoffrey put in. 'Have you read it yet, Antony?' he added with a sidelong look at his friend. It was a long-standing source of grievance with him that Maitland preferred the spoken to the written word.

'Considering you only gave it to me yesterday . . . not that I think it will help in the slightest because you've told me what it said. What I can't believe – and I know I've said this before – is that Osmond would have done anything to harm his daughter. Whether he had taken them to his flat is the real question, after all, though jurors being what they are even the fact that he had an affair with each one of them would be damaging, if proved.'

'Well, as they will certainly be star witnesses for the prosecution,' said Sir Nicholas, 'that is a matter that can only be dealt with in court.'

'If they aren't telling the truth,' said Geoffrey stubbornly, 'why should they go on with their stories now that Mrs Osmond is dead. Even if they've been paid something already there's no question of their getting any more out of her. If they back out in the Magistrate's Court we'll know you were right.'

'I don't think they'll do that, too many people know what they were going to say and I'm pretty sure Wilfred Begg wouldn't have omitted to get written statements from them. Being prepared to commit perjury isn't as bad as actually doing so, but I doubt if they'd appreciate the difference.'

'That's very true. And about the trial—'

'What about it, Uncle Nick?' Antony prompted him impatiently when he paused.

'Been talking about that,' said Vera. 'Even if you manage to trip one of these girls up it won't make any real difference.'

'I should have thought—'

'You see, my dear boy,' said Sir Nicholas kindly, 'whether they were telling the truth or not, if Osmond thought that the jury, when the custody suit was heard, would accept their evidence and give his former wife charge of their daughter, his motive for murder was still as strong as ever.'

'Yes, I see, I should have thought of that. All the same, I can't leave their stories unchallenged.'

'Might even make matters worse,' said Vera. 'If this man Osmond knew he was being wrongly accused—'

'It isn't like you, Vera, to be a Job's comforter,' said Antony. 'I still say I've got to do what I can. If Phillipa can be made to seem an unsympathetic character—'

'Still no excuse for murder,' said Vera.

'You're quite right of course, my dear,' said Sir Nicholas. 'If Antony and Geoffrey are to get their client acquitted I think they must find some additional line to follow. You've seen Matthew Leighton this morning, what is your next move?'

'I have a date to have tea with Amanda Herschell and Jennifer,' said Antony. 'You can't have forgotten that, Uncle Nick, you were there when I made the arrangement. And Geoffrey has very nobly offered to stay in town and go with me, but if the child talks at all it is more likely to be to one stranger than to two.'

'And what do you think she's likely to tell you?' asked his uncle thoughtfully.

'Damn all, probably,' said Maitland in a gloomy tone. 'And I'm quite as aware as you all are that if she does decide to confide in me what she says may be damaging to Osmond, but I'd still rather know the truth.'

'And if she tells you that he has been entertaining these women at the flat—'

'It still wouldn't necessarily make him a murderer, Uncle Nick. We've taken on his defence, Geoffrey and I, and we're stuck with it now whatever happens.'

Perhaps it was fortunate that at that moment Gibbs appeared to announce that luncheon was served. It was one of the days when he insisted on attending to their wants himself so that no further discussion of Phillipa Osmond's murder

100

was possible until the meal was over, by which time other subjects had come up and kept them busy until they separated again.

III

The visit to Robert Osmond's flat to see Amanda Herschell and Jennifer was not one that Maitland was looking forward to with any pleasure. But a promise was a promise, and notwithstanding what had been said at lunchtime his feeling that it would be a good thing to get to the bottom of the child's attitude was as strong as his feeling about Phillipa Osmond's three witnesses. And just as unreasonable, he thought, as he walked round to the hotel in Avery Street where he was almost sure of being able to find a taxi. The one thing his talk with his uncle and Vera had done, he realised as he gave the driver the address, leaned back in his seat and stretched out his legs, was to clear his mind somewhat about his attitude towards his client. Against all probability he was inclined to believe that Osmond was as innocent of murder as he said he was. There must be other possibilities certainly and it was up to him to find them, but for the moment that would have to wait.

Amanda was pleased to see him and said so. 'I'm just about at my wits' end,' she said, 'and if you can get Jennifer to talk to you it'll be marvellous.'

Antony glanced around him before he replied. 'Where is she?' he asked cautiously.

'In her room. She's . . . I can only say frozen, Mr Maitland. Perfectly polite all the time and affectionate with me but she doesn't volunteer a single word herself about anything.'

'All the same I'd like to see her, if I may. No, just a moment, Miss Herschell' – as Amanda was turning away – 'I'd like to speak to you alone first.'

'That sounds ominous. Come into the living-room then. And you'd better call me Amanda, it may make Jennifer feel more at ease if we seem to be on familiar terms.'

'I'll try to remember. There's one thing I want to ask you first of all: have you been able to make arrangements with the hospital?'

'Yes, I talked to Matron on the telephone. Of course it was hideously difficult . . . explaining what had happened I mean. And I think she'd have liked to be awkward about it but she knows me well enough . . . I'd just have given in my notice if she had been and they're so short-handed . . . That sounds like blackmail, doesn't it?' she added with a half-hearted grin.

'On the way towards blackmail,' Maitland agreed. 'Still, I'm glad you managed to arrange it. The thing I wanted to warn you about was that there'll probably be a visit from some social worker or other, anxious about Jennifer's welfare. You ought to be prepared for that.'

'Do you think they'll make things difficult?'

'As a matter of fact I don't. I think your being a nurse and with the good character references that I'm sure the Matron will give you—'

'I'm not so sure about that after our talk today.'

'Think about it. To do anything else would be to admit that her nurses weren't all paragons of virtue. I'm sure she wouldn't want an idea like that to get about.'

'No, I see what you mean. And you think it will be all right?' There was no doubt about her anxiety.

'Yes, I do,' Maitland assured her. 'Only I thought it was best to warn you. It's not the kind of thing one wants to have sprung on one quite without preparation.'

'All right, I'll think of all the nice things I can find to say about myself,' said Amanda. 'I didn't ask you last night, but what happens now?'

'There'll be a Magistrate's Court hearing on Monday. I can't attend unfortunately because I have a conference, but it doesn't really matter because we'd already decided to reserve our defence. Mr Horton will look after everything.'

'That means that Robert will be – what do you call it? – committed for trial.'

'Yes, I'm afraid it does. But it's after the hearing that we really get down to business, you know. For one thing, though the prosecution may not put on all their evidence in the Magistrate's Court they'll have to disclose it to Mr Horton pretty soon and we'll know much better where we stand.'

'And whatever you do, even if you get him off, there'll always be people who believe he was really guilty.'

'Not if we can find the person who really killed Phillipa Osmond.'

'That means you believe what Robert told you. I wasn't sure. Do you think you can do that?'

'I'm sorry, I shouldn't be raising your hopes falsely.' (Or letting you believe I'm absolutely certain of Robert's innocence.) 'I have to tell you, Amanda, that I just don't know whether we can pull it off. Only I very much hope we can.'

She scanned his face anxiously for a moment. 'I believe you mean that,' she said then, 'and you don't know how comforting I find it.'

'In the meantime, try not to worry too much. We'll do everything humanly possible for Mr Osmond.'

'I'm sure you will, but—' She broke off there, obviously thinking better of what she had been going to say. 'Do you want to see Jennifer now?'

'Yes, if you don't mind.'

'I'll just bring in the tea first, it's all ready.'

She went out and returned a moment later with the laden tray, moved a small table to a more convenient position at his elbow and then disappeared again. He heard a door opening across the hall and the distance was so small that he could hear quite clearly what was said. 'Did daddy come home after all?' asked the child's voice.

'No, darling, I'm afraid we can't expect him home quite yet,' said Amanda. 'It's Mr Maitland. Do you remember meeting him? He's on daddy's side and he's going to help us get him home again.'

'Oh, I see.' It was difficult to be sure, but Antony thought he could detect the faintest hint of disappointment in the child's flat tone.

'He'd like to talk to you, Jennifer,' said Amanda briskly. 'Tea's ready, so come along, there's a good girl.'

'I can't tell him anything.'

'No, he just wants to make sure you're all right,' said

Amanda, improvising hastily, for which Maitland gave her full marks. 'You'll do that for me, won't you, Jennifer?'

'Yes, of course.' They came into the room a moment later hand in hand. The little girl – not so little either – was quite calm now. Ice cold, Antony thought, frozen in her own unhappiness. To his surprise she released her hold on Amanda and marched right up to him, hands behind her back as though she were afraid he might try to touch her. 'Mr Maitland,' she said, 'do you believe daddy killed my mother?'

'No, Jennifer, I don't,' said Antony. Something about lying to a child seemed to him to be particularly repugnant, but she certainly couldn't be expected to understand his own seesaw attitude.

'I didn't think he could have done a thing like that,' she said, as though that were all the assurance she needed. 'But why did those men take him away?'

'Because they don't know him as well as we do. That is . . . you believe now, don't you, that you were mistaken in thinking that your father deliberately misled you about your mother being dead?'

'I suppose so. But now it's true anyway,' she added. It was impossible to tell whether there was any grief behind the words.

'Yes, I'm sorry.' He paused, and was wondering what was the best way to proceed when Amanda interrupted him.

'Come and give Mr Maitland his tea, Jennifer, and get some for yourself.' The child obeyed and then went on unbidden to offer the visitor a choice between sandwiches and scones. She had placed her own cup on the table beside his and came back to stand where she had been before, her eyes fixed on his face.

Small talk seemed out of the question. 'I think I should explain to you, Jennifer,' said Antony carefully, 'that what has happened means I'll have to work very hard to get your father home to you. Will you answer some questions for me?'

He was immediately aware of her withdrawal. 'What sort of questions?' she asked cautiously.

'Quite simple ones. The one your father asked you the day we first met,' said Antony. 'A man had stopped you as you came out of school and told you your mother was alive and

104

wanted you to live with her. What did you feel about that?'

'I don't know!' She turned a pleading look on Amanda. 'Make him believe me, Amanda, I really don't know.'

'Your father asked you something else that day too. Would you have chosen to go to your mother as she wanted?'

'Don't . . . don't ask me that!'

'Is the answer so unbearable?'

'Yes, oh yes! You don't know—'

Amanda came forward and put her arm around Jennifer's shoulders. 'I don't think you'll get anything further out of her,' she said quietly. 'I haven't been able to.'

'We'll turn to something else then,' said Antony, trying to sound cheerfully confident of getting a reply. 'You never told me, Jennifer, what else this man who spoke to you said.'

'And I'm not going to.' She paused, biting her lip. 'I'm sorry, Mr Maitland, that was very rude of me. But really there's nothing to tell.' She sounded, thought Antony sympathetically, at once terribly grown-up and terribly vulnerable.

'Then about the day you disappeared—'

'That was the day my mother died,' she said.

'Indeed it was. Where did you go, Jennifer?'

'I just didn't want to go to school.' Her eyes dropped as she said that. A naturally truthful child, he thought, but she's lying to me now.

'You didn't go to that man, for instance, the one you talked to outside school?'

'No . . . no, I didn't.'

'Had he told you where your mother lived?' He paused for an answer but none was forthcoming and after a moment he went on. 'I've wondered you see, Jennifer, whether perhaps you went to see her. And if you did you might have seen something while you were there that would help your father now.'

'No, no, I wouldn't have done that!' The icy calm was very brittle, he realised that now. 'I can't tell you where I went . . . I won't tell you . . . and it wouldn't help you if I did.' As she finished she shook herself free from Amanda's arm and turned and ran out of the room, very much as she had done on the previous occasion when her father had questioned her.

105

'I'm sorry,' said Maitland, looking apologetically at Amanda. 'I didn't want to upset her, but I did feel she might be able to help. I still do.'

'You think she went to Phillipa?'

'I think it's a possibility. That was the first thing her father thought of when he found she hadn't been at school. And if she was in St John's Wood that afternoon there's a distinct chance that she saw somebody or something that might help.'

'Yes, I suppose so,' said Amanda rather doubtfully. 'But I'm fairly sure she's never travelled about London alone.'

'Do you think it would be beyond her . . . a journey by tube, say? I've been told she's of an independent turn of mind, and I'm quite sure that old-fashioned politeness of hers comes with a good deal of intelligence.'

'You're right about that, she's both clever and resourceful. She could certainly read the maps in the underground,' said Amanda, 'though I wouldn't put it past her to take a taxi if she had any money on her.' Then an idea seemed to occur to her. 'You're not thinking . . .?'

Antony smiled at her. 'No, Amanda, I'm not thinking that a child of eight, even a well-grown child of nearly nine, could have killed her mother by manual strangulation. But I do feel that we ought to get to the bottom of this attitude of hers, if only for her own sake. Something is bothering her and bothering her badly.'

'Yes, that's obvious. I'll work on it,' Amanda promised. 'But you know, I honestly don't see that whatever she has to tell us will help in the slightest degree.'

'I don't know that it will.' He didn't add that it might even prove a hindrance. 'But we have to try everything—' Antony began, and was interrupted by the sharp sound of the door bell.

Amanda gave him a puzzled look. 'I wasn't expecting anybody,' she said, 'unless of course Robert had made some arrangement I knew nothing about. I suppose his arrest was in this morning's papers, but everybody doesn't read them.'

As she spoke she had crossed the narrow hall, reached the front door and was fumbling with the latch. 'Good afternoon, Miss Herschell,' said Eversley's voice. 'Here we are again, you see. May we come in?'

106

As Amanda backed away the Chief Inspector and Sergeant Porterhouse followed her into the hall.

'Haven't you given us enough trouble already?' asked Amanda bitterly. 'There's nothing I can tell you, you know that, except that Robert couldn't possibly have done what you accuse him of.'

'A very natural sentiment.' Eversley sounded almost indulgent, but then his eyes lighted on Antony. 'Interfering again, Mr Maitland?' he asked.

'Doing my job, or rather Mr Horton's as he's otherwise engaged this afternoon,' said Antony tersely, and rather admired the equitable tone he achieved. 'But I'm like Miss Herschell, I can't see what else you want of her.'

'You're both quite right. It's the little girl who was missing for so long on Wednesday that I'd like to have a word with.'

'That's quite impossible,' said Antony quickly. 'I'm sure Mr Osmond told you that.'

'Yes, he did. That's why—'

'That's why, with him safely out of the way, you've come back again. But you know, Chief Inspector, even if I weren't here I don't think you'd find Miss Herschell very easy to browbeat.'

'That's a very unjust accusation, Mr Maitland. However, perhaps you'd better explain it to me. Why can't I see the little girl?'

'She's had a great s-shock.' Perhaps it was the word explain that angered him, but any of his friends would have recognised the slight betraying stammer as a sign of growing anger.

'Did Mr Osmond have his doctor to see her, Miss Herschell?' Eversley asked, turning to Amanda.

'Yes, he did. He said she mustn't be worried. And he only lives downstairs,' she added rather fiercely, 'so I can fetch him in a minute if you won't take No for an answer from me.'

'That's very interesting,' said Eversley in a meditative tone. 'What sort of a shock would you say the child has had?'

'Don't you think it was enough of a shock to hear that her mother was alive? And then so shortly afterwards that she was dead after all, and in such a way?' Maitland interpolated smoothly.

'Yes,' said the Chief Inspector grudgingly, 'but was all that time of hers accounted for? It would have been a still greater shock if she'd gone to St John's Wood and found her mother dead, or if she'd seen her killed, or even if she'd seen somebody she knew entering the flat as she left.'

So obviously he was following much the same train of thought as Antony had done himself, with the distinction that the detective was hoping to find from Robert Osmond's daughter some evidence against her father.

'I can't help your troubles, Chief Inspector,' he said, again taking it upon himself to answer when Amanda sent him an imploring look. 'I'm quite aware,' he added, lying blandly and for once without any conscience-stricken feeling at all, 'that you must feel your case to rest on very shaky grounds. But there's no question of your seeing Jennifer, and if our word isn't enough we can – as Miss Herschell suggested – produce the doctor.'

'Shaky grounds?' said Eversley, with something in his tone that rang a warning bell in Maitland's mind. Before he could say anything, however, the Chief Inspector had turned to Sergeant Porterhouse. 'A waste of time,' he commented. 'However' – as though a sudden thought had struck him – 'there may be something to be gained out of the ruins. I'm sure you've guessed, Mr Maitland, that Mrs Osmond's solicitor, Mr Wilfred Begg, has told us about her suit to obtain custody of the child.'

'You know perfectly well—'

'She was prepared to demonstrate to the court that your client was an unfit father for Jennifer,' said Eversley, steam-rollering over his reply. 'From what I'm told of you, Mr Maitland, I imagine you didn't let the matter rest there.'

'That is hardly your business, Chief Inspector, and as the investigating officer you should certainly not be talking to me.'

'Ah, but we're discussing the custody suit,' said Eversley blandly, 'not the murder. I shouldn't dream of questioning you about that.'

'If you're willing to assure me that you're not relying on what you've learned of the custody suit to provide motive,' said Antony, 'I'd be glad to answer your questions. But I don't think you're going to tell me that.'

'No, I suppose not.' There was obviously no sincerity in Eversley's contrite tones. 'In any case, the three young ladies concerned and the private detective whom Mrs Osmond employed have all told me that they have been visited by agents of your instructing solicitor, Mr Horton.'

'Naturally they would, if you asked them. And at the time the enquiries were put in hand Mr Osmond was not under arrest, and Mr Begg was fully in agreement with the course Mr Horton was taking.'

Eversley smiled at that, in a way that gave Maitland a twinge of uneasiness. 'We'll say no more now,' the detective remarked blandly. 'Miss Herschell, can we rely on you to let us know as soon as the doctor says Jennifer Osmond is fit to be questioned?'

Amanda shot a startled glance at Antony. 'Yes . . . yes, I suppose so,' she said doubtfully. 'But she is really very upset; I can't imagine when that will be.'

'I'm sorry to hear it. Goodbye, Miss Herschell. Goodbye, Mr Maitland.' Porterhouse – that silent man – echoed his superior officer's valedictions, and a moment later the door closed behind them.

Amanda turned a little wildly to Maitland. 'Can he do that?' she demanded. 'Try to make Jennifer give evidence against her father?'

'Take it easy. We don't know yet what Jennifer has to say when – if ever – she decides to talk. But one thing you can be certain of, Amanda, if Robert Osmond is innocent she can't tell them anything to his detriment.'

'No, I see. How stupid of me. He had me rattled for a moment.'

'The thing to remember is that nobody talks to Jennifer until she's talked to us. If that doctor you spoke of stays on our side—'

'He's known Jennifer since she was born. I'm sure he will.'

'All right then, if that happens we should be safe. In any case, if they attempt to force the issue they'll have me to reckon with, not to mention Mr Horton who can be extremely formidable when it's a question of protecting one of his client's rights. You can phone me any time, Amanda, and I'll come, with Geoffrey if necessary. That's why Eversley let things go so easily tonight; it wouldn't have sounded well in court to have proceeded against our protests.'

'I understand. You never had a chance to drink your tea, Mr Maitland, but I think I'd better go to Jennifer now. Will you let me know how the Magistrate's hearing goes?'

'There'll be nothing to tell you beyond what I said to you earlier. Still, I'll call you, of course, or perhaps it would be better to get Mr Horton to do so as he's the one who'll have been there. But if Jennifer shows any signs of relaxing her attitude—'

'I'll be on to you like a shot.' They were neither of them inclined to linger over their farewells and a few minutes later Antony found himself on his way home.

IV

When he let himself into the upstairs hall Jenny was just coming out of the kitchen, followed by a distinctly savoury smell, which made Maitland realise that it was much later than he thought; a realisation reinforced by her asking him, 'Do you want to eat straight away, or will you have a drink first?'

'A drink, if you love me. That is, if dinner won't spoil. I didn't think I'd be kept so long.'

'It doesn't matter, it's only a casserole and I turned the oven down low.' She preceded him into the living-room and went straight across to the writing-table where she started pouring sherry. 'How is my namesake?' she asked, turning with the glasses in her hands.

'I suppose the only answer to that is the standard one the hospitals always give you, as well as can be expected.'

'Oh dear,' said Jenny, not liking the sound of that. 'I haven't met Miss Herschell but she sounded a nice girl from what you said. She's looking after her, isn't she?'

'And doing it very well. But I'm not the only one who's after Jennifer's evidence, love. Eversley and Porterhouse

110

turned up while I was still at the flat.'

'What do they want? I know you said Mr Osmond thought she might have been to see her mother that afternoon, but do they really think that's likely?'

'I just don't know, Jenny. All I can say is that the same idea had occurred to Eversley and I don't suppose Osmond had put it into his head. It was perfectly true what Amanda and I told him, the child is still in a state of shock. If he talked to her as she is now he'd be bound to think it was because she knew something to her father's discredit. I'm pretty sure that isn't the case . . . well, most of the time I'm pretty sure. You know me, love, it would be so much easier if I could just make up my mind one way or the other. But whatever the truth is she's badly upset about something, and for her own sake I'd like to get it out of her.'

'Poor child. Amanda does sound a nice girl. Do you suppose if Mr Osmond goes to prison she'd be able to look after Jennifer herself?'

'I very much doubt it, it's not as if they'd been married already. A single girl, working . . . I'm afraid the courts wouldn't see it that way at all.'

'No, I suppose not,' said Jenny sighing. 'But as far as Mr Osmond's guilt or innocence goes, Antony, you really should know by now that you can trust your own intuition.'

He laughed at that but he protested as well. 'Heaven and earth! You shouldn't encourage me in what Uncle Nick would call idle speculation, love.'

'It isn't anything of the sort,' said Jenny indignantly. '*You* may not know now why you think you can trust him, but when everything's out in the open it'll turn out you have some very good reason.'

'Do you really think so?' asked Antony hopefully.

'I'm sure of it. You like him, don't you, and you're very concerned about the little girl?'

'Both of those things are true.'

'There you are then! You're just afraid of persuading yourself into believing he's innocent merely because you want him to be. And that's silly.'

'I'll take your word for it, love.' He looked at her more closely and saw without surprise that something had disturbed her customary serenity. 'What is it, Jenny?' he asked.

'Nothing really. It's just that I've been thinking about that custody suit.'

'And what was the result of your cogitations?'

'I came up with a few questions,' said Jenny rather hesitantly.

'Ask away, love.' Antony sipped his sherry as though to fortify himself.

'Well, I suppose you've thought of them already for yourself. I don't quite see why, when Phillipa had so good a case against her former husband, she didn't want to take the matter to court.'

'I'm quite sure Wilfred Begg advised her, as Geoffrey advised our client, that the court would be much more willing to listen to her if an attempt had been made at a compromise beforehand. But my version is – since you say I must trust my instinct, love – that that wasn't the real reason at all, or at least not the only one. I think she was paying the witnesses, and that they'd probably want more for committing out-and-out perjury.'

'What a horrible thought!'

'My humble opinion,' said Maitland. 'What are your other questions?'

'The next one follows from the first. Why were these three girls so willing to testify? I mean, it's one thing to have accused Mr Osmond of – of moral depravity, but they were accusing themselves at the same time.'

'That's a puzzle, and I can't answer it.'

'All right, I shall just have to wait. But there is one other thing that bewilders me a bit. I couldn't quite understand at lunchtime when you were talking about why Phillipa Osmond wanted Jennifer back. You seemed to know just what you were talking about and I never got the chance to ask you to explain.'

'Well, even apart from the question of Osmond's guilt or innocence, I'm pretty sure it wasn't the reason she gave at that meeting at Begg's office . . . that her maternal feelings had got the better of her. But it was our talk with Matthew Leighton, love, that gave me the clue to what I think must have been the reason. Did I succeed in conveying to you that

112

he's an intensely respectable old boy with a very strong desire for fatherhood?'

'Yes, I knew you meant he wanted Jennifer. But if he's the sort of man you say he is he'd never have condoned lies being told about it.'

'No, that isn't how I think it was. He said they met about a year ago and had been engaged for four or five months now. Phillipa seems to have set Stewart Brodie to work six months ago, perhaps because her dealings with Mr Leighton weren't going quite as quickly as she had hoped. He said himself – I think I told you this – that it was when he knew she was trying to get her daughter back that he decided he'd been right in his estimate of her character all the time and popped the question without any further hesitation.'

'I'm sure that's not what he said,' said Jenny reprovingly. 'And what *was* his estimate of her?'

'He never told me that, love, as a matter of fact, only that she was beautiful and loving. The beauty I saw for myself that day in Begg's office, but the love, I think, was cupboard love . . . I didn't take to the lady, and what I believe is that she tricked him into feeling they were two of a kind, with a great love for home and family, and that the only thing she needed to make her happiness complete was to have Jennifer with her again.'

'You're making her sound horrid.'

'I think she was. But the trouble is, my dearest love, that if I succeed in conveying that impression to anybody else it only serves to give my client an even greater motive for getting rid of her. But let's not worry about that now. We've all tomorrow free, because there's nothing else I can do until after the Magistrate's Court hearing. So we'll have one more drink and then tackle that casserole of yours.'

MONDAY, 22nd March

I

He got rid of his clients, both lay and solicitor, in good time to meet Geoffrey for lunch on Monday. 'Is the hearing over,' he asked as they seated themselves, 'or have you to go back again this afternoon?'

'All finished, with the result we expected,' said Geoffrey. 'Do you know the stipendiary magistrate, Mr Pender?'

'Not personally, and when I've appeared before him I've found him a quiet sort of chap and very fair in his decisions. Though I agree there was nothing else he could do today but commit.'

'Well, I've heard this and that about him from my revered father-in-law,' said Geoffrey. 'He's a man with a horror of bloodshed and has a particular dislike for murder cases. I believe he'd arranged his list for the day so as to get our unsavoury matter out of the way as quickly as he could.'

'I'm glad about that. Uncle Nick's joining us, and as you aren't in a hurry . . . or are you?'

'I've all the time in the world,' said Geoffrey.

'Then you can tell us both about it at once as soon as he gets here. In the meantime I'll possess my soul in patience, but something tells me,' he added, eyeing his friend critically, 'that I'm not going to like everything you have to tell us.'

Before Horton had time to answer Sir Nicholas had arrived, and as soon as he too had been provided with some liquid refreshment he called on Geoffrey to tell them of the morning's events. The solicitor took a moment to put his

114

thoughts in order and then began.

'The police evidence mostly concerned the murder itself, and the preliminary investigation. Eversley said his piece, and so of course did the policeman who was acting as coroner's officer. A neighbour returning from work had discovered the crime, seeing Mrs Osmond's door partly open and knowing she was normally careful about such things. No fingerprints had been found in the flat that couldn't be quite easily explained. All, in fact, as we expected.'

'I feel sure,' said Sir Nicholas cordially, 'that you have other matters of greater interest to impart to us.'

'I pricked up my ears when they started on the medical evidence,' said Geoffrey, 'but it wasn't really helpful either, neither the police doctor nor the pathologist (whom I strongly suspect of having consulted together) being able to put the time of death any nearer than some time between two-thirty and four-thirty on the afternoon in question.'

'That doesn't help,' said Antony rather morosely.

'As for the cause of death,' Geoffrey went on, ignoring him, 'it had certainly been exactly as they originally said, manual strangulation. I won't go into details, you'll have enough of them presently, but Mr Pender was looking decidedly green by the time the pathologist stepped down.'

'What we suffer in the interests of humanity,' said Maitland unsympathetically. He wasn't looking forward to studying the pathologist's report himself.

'After that there was Wilfred Begg, and you can imagine as well as I can what he had to say.'

'Almost word for word,' Antony agreed.

'The worst thing,' Geoffrey went on, 'which I'd been rather hoping he'd forgotten, was that incautious remark our client made to Phillipa Osmond. I'll see you in hell first . . . do you remember, Antony? And then Begg added gratuitously that the threat had been made in reference to the possibility of her getting custody of the girl, Jennifer.'

'It wasn't exactly a threat,' said Maitland.

'That's something you can point out in court when the time comes, and the best of British luck to you. Begg certainly construed it as such, and equally obviously has his knife into Osmond, because he also mentioned that later in that same meeting I had to restrain him forcibly from making a physical attack on his former wife.'

'That too is not precisely accurate.'

'No more it is. I know we agreed I'd keep my mouth shut, Antony, but at that point I did venture a couple of questions.'

'As I'm sure I should have done in your place,' Maitland assured him.

'The first was to query that last remark, but I can't say it got me very far because it was a matter of opinion after all. But being on my feet I also asked him whether the custody suit was the first time Mrs Osmond had consulted him, and he told me he'd taken care of her affairs for years.'

'Including her will?' asked Antony quickly. 'That was well done, Geoffrey, I've been taking it for granted, I'm afraid, that what she told Matthew Leighton was true and she'd left her money to Jennifer.'

'That was the reply I expected,' Geoffrey admitted, 'but I didn't think it could do any harm because it was bound to come out sooner or later. And I asked Mr Pender's permission, of course, saying that in the circumstances the question of Mrs Osmond's financial affairs and the way her estate was disposed of could not be regarded as irrelevant. He made no objection so I asked Begg what he knew of these matters.'

'Had she been telling the truth?' asked Antony eagerly. But Geoffrey was determined to tell his story in his own way and had no intention of being rushed.

'He started out by telling us that Mrs Osmond could not have been called a provident woman,' he said. 'She was highly regarded in her profession and her income was high but she spent it lavishly and after her death he found that her cash resources amounted to no more than about fifteen thousand pounds on deposit in her bank. There was also her share in the partnership with Calvin Wheeldon, but the agreement was such that the surviving partner had the option of buying out the other's interest at quite a low price.'

'Well . . . well . . . well!'

'You can imagine now, Antony, that I was glad I'd gone back on our agreement. Even if the money had been left to Jennifer, Robert Osmond's financial position is certainly not one that would incline him to kill for the sake of the interest on fifteen thousand pounds during his daughter's minority.'

'No stocks, bonds, or other investments?' asked Sir Nicholas.

'Not so far as he had been able to discover.'

'That's all very well,' said Maitland impatiently, 'but you said, *even* if Jennifer had been the beneficiary.'

'That's quite right, but she wasn't. Phillipa Osmond left her estate to her brother, Mr Rudolph Spencer.'

'Whom we understand to be in poor straits financially,' said Antony. 'There might be a motive there.'

'There might indeed,' said Geoffrey without conviction. 'Stewart Brodie was called next,' he went on, without waiting for any further comment, 'but as far as Osmond's motive is concerned they called it a day when they'd finished with him.'

'I thought they must have done, or you couldn't have been through by now.'

'Anyway what he had to say was quite sufficient for the purpose. His evidence was very brief. It was obvious that the prosecution wanted to keep the details of the witnesses he had unearthed under wraps as much as possible, hoping to make a better impression with them when the case came to trial if they were sprung on the jury completely cold. This time I didn't add any questions of my own. Six months before – he consulted a notebook and gave us the precise date – Mrs Osmond had gone to him concerning the possibility of bringing a suit for the custody of her daughter, Jennifer. She had missed the child all these years but felt it was for Jennifer's own good, until recently some rumours had reached her concerning her former husband's way of life. Mrs Osmond had been an acquaintance of his for a long time and he was only too willing to do what he could for her. As a consequence of his discoveries he advised her that she had a very strong case to take to court if her husband wouldn't agree to a compromise. At this point Mr Pender asked the prosecution whether they intended to produce evidence in support of the witness's statement – I think he was afraid we might have to continue this afternoon after all – but settled down again when he was told there was only one more witness to come, but that full corroboration of Mr Brodie's statement would be forthcoming at the trial. So Brodie stood down and . . . you're not going to like this, Antony.'

'I suppose you're referring to the last witness, whoever he was. I don't like anything about the case, anyway, so you may as well tell me the worst.'

'Another neighbour of Phillipa Osmond's, a retired man who lives in the same building and who saw Robert Osmond loitering on the other side of the street when he returned from picking up his evening paper.'

'Was Osmond previously known to him?' asked Antony quickly.

'No, there was a photograph in the paper he takes, along with the news of the arrest. Of course, he was particularly interested because he knew Mrs Osmond quite well. But if you're thinking he won't make a good witness, Antony, because he saw a photograph first, recognised it and *then* went around to the police I think you're mistaken. He was very convincing.'

'Identity witnesses are notoriously unreliable.'

'I know that but all the same . . . you must admit Robert Osmond is a pretty distinctive sort of chap. Anyway, that's what happened, he saw the photograph, recognised the subject, and went round to the police. And, as I say, I don't think you'll shake him.'

'You're telling me you don't believe Osmond's statement?'

'Is that any surprise to you? No, Antony, what I'm really telling you is that there's no question now that you should leave matters where they are until the trial. I know you, you're all set to go off and interview these two men, Wheeldon and Spencer—'

'I thought it was arranged that I should do so, or that we should do so together.'

'I was willing to go along with you, but I must tell you now – and I think Sir Nicholas will agree with me – that I can see that it would be very inadvisable.'

'I see. Uncle Nick?'

'I think it would do your client no good, and might do a good deal of harm from your point of view . . . and from Geoffrey's,' Sir Nicholas pointed out.

Antony stared at him for a moment, and then turned back to his instructing solicitor. 'I can't argue with that,' he said. Geoffrey looked as if he was about to speak, but stopped when he caught Sir Nicholas's eye. 'I should, however, like the opportunity of talking to these two men in court, so perhaps you will arrange for their proofs to be taken and let me have them when the other papers come along.'

'Yes, of course.'

'Meanwhile we have to see Osmond again. Has he been taken back to Brixton yet?'

'No, because I knew you'd want to see him. He's still at Lennox Street police station, so if you're free I'd suggest we go along as soon as we've finished here.'

'Very well, we can do that.' Sir Nicholas and Geoffrey kept up a fairly continuous flow of conversation throughout the meal, but it cannot be said that Antony contributed his share. In the light of what he had heard he was thinking of what Jenny had said about instinct and wondering whether – just possibly – she might be right.

II

As soon as they had finished their meal Sir Nicholas went back to chambers, but Geoffrey's office being handiest Antony went there with him to phone Amanda before going on to see their client. A difficult business, but at least he had prepared her beforehand for the inevitable committal, and it didn't really cost him many pangs of conscience to refrain from telling her about the new and very damaging witness. He concluded by asking after Jennifer. 'If you think there's been any change and there's a chance of her talking to me now I'll come round later on, of course.'

'I shouldn't do that,' Amanda told him. 'She'd be just as polite to you and just as unhelpful. I wish I could tell you something different but I can't.'

'All right then, but we'll keep in touch.' As he turned from the telephone he found Horton eyeing him in a puzzled way.

'I thought you'd come round to my way of thinking when you agreed so readily to my suggestion that we shouldn't take the matter any further outside court,' Geoffrey said, almost accusingly. 'What do you think Jennifer can tell you anyway?'

'I don't know,' said Maitland wearily. The pain in his shoulder, which was due to an old injury and never quite left him, was always particularly insistent when he was tired or discouraged. At the moment, he was both.

'If Osmond is guilty it can't help matters whatever the child says, and may even be harmful,' Geoffrey insisted.

'But *is* he guilty?'

'He was there,' said Geoffrey bluntly, 'and that's something he's been carefully hiding from us.'

'I know, it doesn't look good. But if he comes up with some explanation and still maintains his innocence, what right have we to judge him?'

'Antony, the evidence is damning!'

'I know, but he's still entitled to a defence.'

'I know that as well as you do,' said Horton impatiently. 'If you still have doubts about his guilt why did you agree not to see Phillipa Osmond's brother and her partner?'

'Because you and Uncle Nick advised against it,' said Maitland with a faint smile. 'In any case, I shall see them in court.'

'You really want me to call them?'

'I said so, didn't I?'

'I don't see that it will do the slightest good, and if you drag out the defence unnecessarily you'll only put the judge's back up.'

'Bear with me, Geoffrey. I've agreed to one of your suggestions, so give me my way in this.'

'I suppose I must,' said Horton grudgingly. And then, as a suspicion suddenly struck him, 'Why did you agree to leave things alone until the trial?'

'You've asked me that once already,' Maitland pointed out.

'Yes, but I'm beginning to think I know the answer. Sir Nicholas said there might be trouble, in view I suppose of the fact that the new Assistant Commissioner is bringing his own men into the CID, people who worked under him before and who presumably will be very willing to take on the colour of his views.'

'And you see how willingly I obeyed him when he backed up your suggestion.'

'Yes, but I don't think for a moment that you'd consider the danger if you were the only one involved. I've seen you in and out of enough scrapes for that, but I think you ought to know me well enough after all this time to realise that if you really feel strongly about this I'll follow wherever you go.'

'Yes, Geoffrey, I do know that, and it would be different if I were absolutely certain in my own mind that my original assessment of Robert Osmond was the right one. Now . . . I just don't know. I may feel differently after we've talked to Osmond, though it's hard to see what excuse he can have for not confiding in us, but in any event, my decision stands.'

'I won't press you to change it because I think it's the right one,' Geoffrey told him.

'Yes, you made that very clear.' Antony smiled at him again, and this time with something approaching genuine humour.

'But you still want to talk to Jennifer?'

'Yes, and I'll admit, if you like, that I don't expect anything to come out of that favourable to our client. But something's weighing on her mind and it will be better for her to talk about it. Amanda may be able to persuade her, but if she can't I shall certainly try again. She's a nice child and doesn't deserve what's happened, and heaven alone knows what will become of her if Osmond is sent to prison. And now, Geoffrey, if you've finished cross-examining me let's get along to Lennox Street.'

The only interview room available at the police station was small, and they were crowded round a table in rather unwelcome intimacy. 'I know why you've come, of course,' said Robert Osmond as soon as they were alone together. 'That chap who says he saw me watching the entrance to the block of flats where Phillipa lived.'

'Are you telling us he was mistaken?' Horton asked.

'Would you believe me if I did?'

'Witness to identity is notoriously unreliable,' Geoffrey told him non-committally.

'Not in this case, I'm sorry to say. I was certainly there.'

'Then we're entitled to an explanation . . . don't you think?' Maitland enquired.

Osmond looked from one of them to the other. 'I can *explain*,' he said. 'Whether you think it constitutes an excuse for not admitting the fact before is another matter. It depends, I suppose, on how well you're able to put yourself in my position.'

'I think you'll find us capable of so small a feat of imagination,' Antony told him, thinking as he spoke that for himself at least imagination would be in no way involved.

'What exactly do you want to know?'

'When you went, why you went, and what you did when you got there.'

'I didn't kill Phillipa, if that's what you mean,' said Osmond quickly.

'In that case there's another question to add to the others: why didn't you tell us about your trip to St John's Wood?'

'I'll take the last one first if you don't mind. If you can find any excuse for me it'll be contained in my answer to that. Quite simply, I was very anxious for you to believe what I told you and I thought if you knew I'd been there there wasn't a chance you would. Even so, I came very close once or twice to admitting it, but when it came to the point I didn't have the nerve. You remember what you told me about the possibility of pleading guilty to a lesser charge. After that I was quite sure it would be fatal to let you know I had opportunity as well as motive.'

'I see. Then perhaps you'll go on to my other questions, Mr Osmond. It might be as well if you told us exactly what happened from the time you left your studio.'

'I didn't even go home. I'd already made up my mind that the only thing to do was to have it out with Phillipa, no holds barred. It was obvious she'd put Stew Brodie up to approaching Jennifer, and I wanted to know exactly what he'd said to her. I thought perhaps it might help me to deal with the situation . . . you remember how terribly upset she was. So I went straight out to Phillipa's place, and since you want the whole truth I may as well tell you, I was still furiously angry. Only somehow on the journey—'

'Your anger faded?' said Maitland dryly. 'Do you know, Mr Osmond, I find that very hard to believe.'

'I'm not surprised, because it wasn't what happened at all. I was going to say I began to have doubts about the wisdom of what I was going to do. You both saw what Phillipa's attitude was like when we met at her solicitor's office, even you, Mr Maitland, though you didn't say a word so far as I remember the whole time we were there.'

'I was there as an observer only,' said Antony. 'I agree Mrs Osmond's attitude wasn't particularly constructive—'

'She was out for blood and she thought she had me just where she wanted me,' said Osmond. 'I knew you, Mr Horton, wouldn't approve of my making a personal approach—'

'You're quite right, I wouldn't,' Geoffrey growled.

'—and I began to question whether I could keep my temper if she started the same sort of thing again. If Jennifer hadn't been involved . . . but she was and I couldn't forget it for a moment. If you want the whole story, I doubt if I could have kept my hands off Phillipa if her attitude hadn't changed.'

'The man who saw you spoke of you as loitering,' said Geoffrey.

'Yes, I heard everything he had to say,' Osmond interrupted with a trace of impatience. 'But don't you think that proves I'm telling you the truth now? If I'd gone there in a rage to murder Phillipa I wouldn't have hung about outside, just asking to be noticed.'

'I'm afraid there's an answer to that,' said Geoffrey, 'as Mr Maitland will agree.' He looked enquiringly at Antony, who obligingly took up the explanation.

'Identification is a tricky business,' he said, 'and if you denied being there – which I'm very glad you didn't because Mr Horton tells me the witness was very sure of himself, and would almost certainly have been believed – I should have done my best to shake his confidence in court. But if I made the suggestion that you have just done, Mr Osmond, I'm afraid the prosecution would have had at least a couple of alternatives to offer. You might have been waiting an opportunity to go in unseen, or you might have observed someone you know going in – any one of your old friends – and were waiting for him or her to come out again.'

'Heads they win, tails I lose,' said Osmond, obviously depressed by this view of things. 'Yes, I can see the force of that. I didn't see anybody I knew, so my vigil wasn't even helpful in that way. I'm not quite sure how long I stood there, I was very occupied with my thoughts and trying to decide what was best to do, but I do know I got back to my own flat about a quarter of an hour before Mrs Arbuthnot came in with the news that Jennifer hadn't been to school.'

'Without having been anywhere near Mrs Osmond's?' Maitland asked. 'Anywhere nearer than the street outside her building that is?'

'No nearer than that. That's true, but I can't expect you to believe it.'

'You don't have to convince us, you have to convince the jury,' Maitland reminded him. 'If you tell your story in court exactly as you've told it to us now—'

'They won't believe me any more than you do.'

'I'm afraid there's nothing we can do but wait and see. You'd agree with my advice, wouldn't you, Geoffrey?'

'Yes, of course. Exactly as you told it to us, with no evasions,' Geoffrey recommended and got to his feet. 'I shall be seeing you again before the trial, of course, Mr Osmond, when Mr Maitland and I have had time to go through the papers the prosecution send us and consider how best to present our side of the case.'

'When will it be . . . the trial, I mean?'

'Not until after the Easter recess, I'm afraid. The first or second week in May at a guess. I'm sorry you'll be kept so long in suspense.'

'What's the odds? Prison is prison whether you're waiting trial or have already been sentenced. The thing that worries me is Jennifer, and Amanda too, of course. Have either of you seen them?'

'I saw them on Saturday,' Maitland volunteered, 'and spoke to Amanda on the phone today to give her the result of the hearing.'

'Did you tell her—?'

124

'About the new witness? No, I didn't. I'd already prepared her for the fact that you were certain to be committed for trial, so at least what I had to tell her didn't add to her worries. As for Jennifer, she's perfectly well, though she still won't talk about her meeting with Brodie in the school playground or about what she did on the afternoon of her mother's death. I have wondered, since Mr Horton told me about the new witness, whether perhaps you had seen her going to her mother's flat, or rather into the building, and that was why you asked me to go there to see what had happened.'

'I'm capable of a certain degree of caution,' said Osmond, 'though in this case it only seems to have made more trouble . . . my waiting outside Phillipa's place I mean, arguing with myself as to whether I should go in or not. But if I'd seen Jennifer I shouldn't have hesitated for a moment. It might have ended in murder unless, of course, Phillipa was dead already which is something we don't know, but fortunately that isn't the way it was. When I asked you to go to St John's Wood it was because I wondered if Jennifer had been there all the time.'

'I see. Well, before your next talk with Mr Horton I shall have done my best to think of all the awkward questions the prosecution are likely to fire at you, and he in turn will do his best to prepare you for them. Otherwise, like him I'm sorry for the delay but try to keep your nerve. I'm bound to tell you, Mr Osmond, that everything is going to depend, as far as I can see, on the impression you make on the jury when we get into court.'

III

Not many more words passed between Antony and Geoffrey before they parted in the street outside, though they had agreed to arrange a meeting for later in the week when their other commitments permitted. Maitland went home, and opted for an early drink rather than a late cup of tea. Jenny supplied him and, having taken a good look at his face as he came in, forbore to ask any questions. But the matter was very much on his mind and it wasn't long before he was pouring out the whole story to her, including the fact that Uncle Nick and Geoffrey had ganged up on him, as he put it, to persuade him to take no further action until the trial. 'And Osmond's explanation of his presence in St John's Wood was . . . specious,' he added. 'Geoffrey doesn't believe a word of it.'

'Do you?'

'I don't know, I just don't know, love.'

'It doesn't sound as if you've had a very pleasant day,' said Jenny in a deliberately neutral tone, and Antony smiled at her.

'You're quite right, my dearest love, I didn't. But I think I was right to agree not to meddle any further. Geoffrey – good chap that he is – told me when we were alone later that he'd agree to anything I wanted to do. If I were sure—'

'What then, Antony?' she asked him when he hesitated.

'I'd have taken him up on the offer. But in my present state of indecision . . . I'd take a chance if I was the only one involved, love, but I can't risk getting him into trouble.'

'No, I see that.'

'I did persuade him to call two more witnesses, though. Phillipa's partner, and her brother. Her brother – his name is Rudolph of all things, Rudolph Spencer – inherits what she had to leave, and for all I know she may have been making difficulties for her partner. I shan't make any – any deleterious suggestions, of course, but there's just a chance that the fact that there's at least one other person around with a sort of motive may make the jury think twice.'

'But you're not very hopeful?'

'How can I be? Osmond had motive *and* opportunity, he'd threatened her in the presence of witnesses, and she died. That'll be quite enough, and though the judge will certainly tell the jury that they aren't there to consider the prisoner's morals, the stories of the women I always think of as Phillipa's witnesses won't help either.'

'From what you told me he didn't . . . exactly . . . threaten her,' said Jenny.

'He said he'd see her in hell before he gave up Jennifer,' said Antony, 'and in the circumstances I don't know what else

126

you'd call that except a threat. There's also the fact that Wilfred Begg was under the impression that Osmond had to be restrained from assaulting Phillipa at the meeting in his office. I can probably confuse him about that, but it's so little, so damned little.'

'It may turn out better than you think,' said Jenny. 'In fact, if you're right about Mr Osmond's innocence I'm sure it will.'

'I've been trying to tell you, love, I just don't know.'

'We've had all that out already,' Jenny told him. 'Trust your instinct, Antony, and do your best. That's all anyone can do.'

If anyone but Jenny had said that to him he would probably have flared into anger. As it was, 'The trouble is, somebody else's best might be better than mine,' he said glumly.

'Don't be silly, of course it wouldn't. The man who never loses a case,' said Jenny, hoping to make him laugh at that old and very nonsensical story. It did raise a small smile, but perhaps it was better not to harp on it. 'Will Uncle Nick be waiting to hear what Robert Osmond had to say?' she asked instead.

'Tomorrow will be time enough. He's got enough of his own way today, we mustn't spoil him.' He reached for his glass and raised it to her in a silent toast. 'Are we expecting Roger this evening?' he asked. 'It's a pity Meg didn't know any more about Robert Osmond than the fact that he'd taken several publicity photographs of her.'

'And that he's good at his job,' Jenny added. 'At least, the picture of Meg that Roger carries in his wallet is – what's the opposite of enlarged? Anyway, it's taken from one of them and it's certainly very good.'

'I've never seen it,' said Antony intrigued.

'He's probably afraid you'd think him sentimental. But the thing is he's caught Meg's likeness as *we* know her, not the face she shows to all the world.'

Which was interesting, but not – when Maitland came to think about it later – exactly helpful.

REGINA *versus*
OSMOND, 1976

THE CASE FOR THE PROSECUTION

THURSDAY,
the first day of the trial

I

Mr Justice Conroy was short and inclined to stoutness, neither of which fact detracted in the slightest from the impressive figure he made when seated on the bench, though if his manner had been less dignified his cherubic cast of countenance might have done so. On the morning when the trial of Robert Osmond for the murder of his former wife was to begin he took his place as usual, placed his pocket watch on the bench in front of him (a habit which newcomers among counsel were apt to find unnerving), glanced sharply towards the gallery where the spectators were accommodated as though warning them that any acts of indecorum on their part would be immediately suppressed, and finally – while the preliminaries which were now so familiar as to be boring were going on – turned his attention to the body of the court where the opposing counsel were presumably prepared to do battle.

On the whole he was inclined to approve of Paul Garfield, QC, who, with his junior Mr Wicken, was appearing for the prosecution. A man very well aware of the difference between right and wrong and famous for his careful mastery of detail, he had in the judge's view only one fault . . . having apparently no great opinion of the collective intelligence of

131

juries he was inclined to repeat himself, sometimes even to the extent of assuming the character of a schoolmaster instructing a rather dimwitted class. But this, in view of his extremely correct attitude towards the court, was a small fault and could easily be forgiven.

Antony Maitland, appearing with his learned friend, Mr Stringer, for the defence, was another matter altogether. He had been known to Mr Justice Conroy since he was a schoolboy, and though the judge had many times since then seen him in action on behalf of one client or another he'd never been able to rid himself of a feeling that counsel's attitude was a frivolous one, unworthy of the dignity of his profession. He had in addition a well-deserved reputation for dealing with his cases in an unorthodox way, which his lordship could not but deplore. Still, Conroy was confident of his own ability to keep things running smoothly, and looked forward with mild interest to the coming contest.

The accused now, a society photographer or something of the sort, though it had to be admitted from his appearance that no one would have suspected him of so useless an occupation. He had listened apparently unmoved to the reading of the indictment, and in a firm voice made the response 'Not Guilty' to the inevitable question as to how he proposed to plead. That could be, and probably was, mere bravado and it was impossible to predict how it would go over with the jury. An undistinguished-looking group in the judge's opinion, but he prided himself that he would be able to guide them on to the right track when the time came. Whatever that might be, he had certainly no intention of pre-judging the issue, but listening to Garfield – now well-launched into his opening address – it seemed that the defence would have some difficulty in countering the charge.

Meanwhile Maitland, who could have told you beforehand with very few errors exactly what his opponent was going to say, was to all appearances asleep. Derek Stringer beside him was taking the note, but both he and Geoffrey knew him too well to be worried by this apparent lack of attention. Maitland knew – who better? – how wellnigh unanswerable Garfield's case was, unless some miracle intervened and he was past the age of expecting miracles.

Except for the inevitable conferences, when he and Geoffrey and Derek had hammered out the best way of presenting the defence, he had had little time to spend in the intervening months on Robert Osmond's affairs. Now his client's appearance shocked him. The judge might consider Osmond calm, but to his counsel's eyes, when they talked for a few moments before the court convened, the signs of strain were only too obvious, and his first eager question, 'Have you seen Jennifer? How is she?' had put the seal on his despondency. He had seen the child several times but made no further attempt to question her, so while he could give her father a good report of her health he still hadn't a clue as to what was going on inside her mind.

Geoffrey had been inclined to be worried over the fact that the trial would be held before Mr Justice Conroy, not the easiest of men. Maitland himself, however, was well enough aware that the majority of the Queen's Bench judges were apt to look on his methods with a jaundiced eye, a possible exception being Mr Justice Carruthers, who seemed to derive some amusement from them. Failing him, Conroy would be no more difficult to deal with than half a dozen others he could think of; the real obstacle, to his mind, was Garfield, a man of puritanical disposition and – what was almost worse – as completely without a sense of humour as it was possible for a man to be. The witnesses called to prove motive would shock him, and inevitably, Maitland thought, prejudice him against the defendant. And from a strictly personal point of view there would be the added annoyance of the fact that the press would dig up that old story, dating from their first appearance as adversaries – in the first case, as a matter of fact, that he himself had handled as a QC – when his client, a man who found quotation irresistible, had greeted Garfield's cross-examination with the sad comment, '*The words of Mercury are harsh after the songs of Apollo*'.

But none of that could be helped now. He turned his head a little and opened his eyes to look up at counsel for the prosecution: a tall man almost handsome in spite of a bony, prominent, enquiring nose. He was discoursing now with obvious distaste on the custody suit, and there was nothing whatever for the defence to learn from his discourse. Nor was

133

he likely to give utterance to any remark that could conceivably be regarded as prejudicial, but even if he did it would probably be an unpopular move with both judge and jury to raise any objection. By the time he had finished repeating himself (and that brought another memory, of Kevin O'Brien's whispered remark on an occasion when they had appeared together, *what I tell you three times is true*), Robert Osmond's infamy would be fairly fixed in the jury's mind, and what had the defence to offer against it after all? Only the prisoner's own denial, and however convincingly he might make it, it was unlikely to turn the tables in his favour.

But all things come to an end and at last Garfield seated himself again. Mr Justice Conroy consulted his clumsy timepiece and evidently decided that there was time to call one witness before the luncheon recess. This proved to be Phillipa Osmond's neighbour, the one who had found her body, a man called Joseph Bilton who described himself as an investment consultant, a job at which Maitland thought, rather enviously, he must be pretty successful; that is if he gave his clients the same advice as he gave himself.

He was a smallish man with the beginnings of a paunch, beautifully tailored, and with an air of undeniable prosperity about him. His flat, he said, was next to Mrs Osmond's, he had to pass her door to get to his own. It was only later, when the police questioned him, that he tried to make an estimate of the exact time he had returned from work, but as far as he could judge it was about five o'clock. Mrs Osmond's door was slightly ajar, which surprised him. As a woman living alone she was naturally very careful about such things. Still standing in the corridor he called out to her but received no reply, so he pushed the door further open and stepped inside, still calling her name. As soon as he reached the sitting-room door, which was also open, he saw her body lying in the middle of the room and telephoned the police, asking them to bring a doctor in case he was wrong in his diagnosis that she had been dead for some time.

'To go back a little, Mr Bilton,' said Garfield. 'When you noticed Mrs Osmond's door was open did you see any signs that entry might have been effected by force?'

'No.' For the first time the witness sounded a little

doubtful, as though this wasn't something he'd thought about before. 'I suppose you mean signs of splintering of the wood or scratches round the lock. I think I should have noticed if there had been but I wasn't looking for anything of the sort. I wasn't really worried when I went in, just thought she'd forgotten to close the door and felt I should draw it to her attention.'

'And when you looked into the sitting-room, where was she lying?'

'Almost in the middle of the room. I should explain that she had one of the one-bedroom apartments, and none of the rooms were very large.'

'Thank you, Mr Bilton. Your lordship, I should like to introduce this plan into evidence; it shows the layout of the deceased's flat in detail, and will be sworn to in due course by the draughtsman who drew it up.' There was a slight delay while the exhibit was produced and labelled, and then Garfield turned back to the witness again.

'I'm sorry to keep you waiting, Mr Bilton. You were telling us that Mrs Osmond's body lay almost in the centre of the room.'

'Yes, you see, because it was so small, the furniture was mostly along the walls, keeping a clear space in the middle.'

'And how was she lying?'

'On her back.' The witness paused there and shuddered, though whether he was genuinely distressed by the recollection or whether he felt this was the proper thing to do Maitland was unable to decide. 'I can see it all as clearly as if it was yesterday,' he said. 'Her left arm was lying beside her, but her right was thrown out at an angle, and her legs were bent as though they had buckled up and she had fallen backwards when she was attacked.'

'You formed an immediate opinion that she was dead?'

'I'm afraid that it was only too obvious. The marks on her throat, and the way her head was lying. I'm not accustomed to violent death, but it seemed to me there could be no doubt about it.'

'Thank you, Mr Bilton, I'm sorry to distress you by making you go back over such an unpleasant experience. From your own observation then, you would say that Mrs

135

Osmond had herself let the murderer into the flat, and was standing facing him in her sitting-room when she was attacked?'

Was that worth an objection? Probably not, Eversley would certainly be asked the same thing, and would claim the status of an expert to justify his reply. 'That was certainly my impression,' said the witness firmly.

Nothing much to be made of that. It was Derek Stringer who rose to cross-examine. 'How long had you been a neighbour of Mrs Osmond's?' he asked.

'Almost five years. I was already in residence when she moved in and tried to be a good neighbour by offering her whatever assistance she needed. I understood she had been recently divorced, or at any rate was separated from her husband.'

'Was *she* a good neighbour?' asked Stringer, smiling.

'I don't quite know what you mean by that, but in the sense that she caused no disturbance of any kind certainly she was. We were never on visiting terms, perhaps that was natural as we both lived alone, but I met her a number of times at parties given by other people in the building.'

'That's very interesting. Perhaps you can give me some of their names.'

'A Mr and Mrs Wellbury, but they moved away about a year ago. He was retiring and they had decided to live in the South of France.'

'Anybody else?'

'Only Michael and Stella Ringfield. They are brother and sister not husband and wife.' Maitland, all his senses alert now, saw his junior stiffen and if it had been anybody else he'd have shoved a note under his nose, *Leave it!* But he thought he could trust Derek and as it turned out he was perfectly right. Stringer immediately left the subject, and after a brief enquiry as to whether the witness could tell them anything about Mrs Osmond's visitors – to which the answer was an unequivocal No – sat down. As Garfield did not wish to re-examine the witness was allowed to go.

At this point, Mr Justice Conroy took pity on the assembly and adjourned for lunch, with a stern reminder that the court would reconvene at two o'clock precisely.

II

After the recess boredom set in, while various necessary but dull witnesses were called: the man who had prepared the plan that had become Exhibit A, to swear to its accuracy; and a fingerprint expert who took a good deal of time to explain the steps he had taken to identify each set of prints he had found as belonging to someone who had a perfect right to have been in Phillipa Osmond's flat. It seemed that whoever did the cleaning there had been thorough, because no clues emerged from his evidence as to Phillipa's friends, except that Michael Ringfield had been in the sitting-room at some time recently, and his sister both there and in Phillipa's tiny kitchen. There was really no need for cross-examination, though Derek in each case asked a few desultory questions, but when Detective Chief Inspector Eversley was summoned Maitland immediately called his wandering thoughts to order.

It was probably the first time Eversley had appeared as a witness at the Central Criminal Court, but he was obviously no stranger to the Crown Courts in his own part of the country, and his answers to the preliminary questions were given with a speed that argued familiarity with the procedure. His department had been called in almost as soon as Phillipa Osmond's body had been found. Nothing had been touched when he arrived on the scene, only the doctor had been in the room to confirm the fact of death. The witness described the position of the body in greater detail than Mr Bilton had done, produced a number of rather gruesome photographs which had also to be entered as exhibits, and went on to enumerate the contents of the flat in detail, so that both judge and jury had constantly to refer to the copies of the plan that had been provided for them. Nothing appeared to have been disturbed, there was money in Mrs Osmond's handbag, and a detailed scrutiny of the front door had revealed no signs of breaking-in. In his opinion (Garfield had glanced in

137

Maitland's direction as he put the question) Mrs Osmond had let her murderer in herself, preceding him to the sitting-room, and then, instead of seating herself which would have been more natural whether her visitor was a woman or a man, had turned to face him. How long they had talked together it was of course impossible to say, but it seemed a fair deduction to draw that it was the killer who had left the front door open on leaving.

'Thank you, Chief Inspector, that is all quite clear,' said Garfield, 'and we have already heard from some of your experts. Perhaps you would describe for us the course your investigation took.'

'The pathologist arrived and while he was making a more detailed examination of the deceased I took the opportunity to interview Mr Bilton and to look round the flat, whose contents I have already described. But while I was engaged in this latter occupation the bell rang, and my assistants being occupied I went to the door myself.'

The pause there, Antony thought, was probably for effect. Garfield put it to good use by enquiring smoothly, 'And who was the visitor, Chief Inspector?'

'A man with whom I was at that time unacquainted . . . except by reputation,' said Eversley, putting a faint stress on the last words that immediately aroused Antony's ire. 'However, Detective Sergeant Porterhouse, who was with me, came up at that moment and was able to enlighten me. It was Mr Antony Maitland, who is leading the defence in this case.'

Conroy leaned forward then and peered suspiciously over the top of his spectacles, first at the witness and then at counsel for the defence. 'There seems to be some need for explanation here, Chief Inspector,' he said. 'If there is any question of Mr Maitland's testimony being required—'

Eversley turned slightly to face the judge a little more directly. 'No question of that, my lord.'

'If your lordship will permit the witness to explain what passed between them,' said Garfield, 'I think it will become evident that the matter does not directly concern us.'

'Very well. As Mr Maitland is present I suppose there can be nothing against this course of action. Unless, of course,' he added, turning to Antony, 'the defence itself should have some objection.'

'My learned friend is quite correct, my lord, my visit to Mrs Osmond's flat has nothing whatever to do with the case now being heard, except very indirectly. But you would perhaps prefer to hear what transpired from the witness himself.'

'Very well, you may proceed, Chief Inspector.'

'I asked Mr Maitland, not unnaturally, whether he was a friend of Mrs Osmond's, and upon receiving a negative reply enquired why he wished to see her. I think I should add, my lord, that the information was forthcoming only after I had given an account of what had happened—'

'To which I had a perfect right,' said Antony, on his feet again.

'Nobody is disputing your rights, Mr Maitland,' said the judge. His air of patient courtesy had never been more marked or more deceptive. 'But as you have made no objection to the court hearing the witness's evidence on this point perhaps you will allow him to give it . . . without interruption.'

'If your lordship pleases.' The meaningless phrase had a faintly mutinous sound.

Eversley took up his story without any further prompting. 'Mr Maitland informed me that he had called to see Mrs Osmond on behalf of her former husband, the accused in this case, with whom he had become acquainted over another matter to which I shall be referring presently. I should explain that the prisoner and the deceased, who were separated five years ago and divorced two years after that, have one daughter, Jennifer, now aged eight. The child had been living with her father, and he was anxious when she was not brought back from school at the usual time and it transpired that she had not attended at all that afternoon. He felt that it was possible she might have visited her mother, and Mr Maitland – purely, he assured me, in a friendly capacity – had offered to make an enquiry that might have proved embarrassing to the person most concerned. I was able to assure him that Jennifer had not been in the flat at the time her mother was discovered dead, though of course the possibility of an earlier visit existed.'

139

'Then perhaps you will tell us, Chief Inspector, what was this mysterious matter in the course of which Mr Maitland had become acquainted with the accused.' For the moment Conroy had taken over the questioning.

'I was about to do so, my lord. Mrs Osmond, who was a professional woman, an architect, had felt it better for her daughter's sake to leave the child in her father's charge when they separated.'

Antony was on his feet again. 'My lord!'

'Yes, Mr Maitland?' said the judge, with a benign air that came very near to unnerving counsel.

'I'm afraid the witness, unwittingly I'm sure, is in danger of misleading the court. The facts are that a little over five years ago Mrs Phillipa Osmond deserted her husband and child, and when at the end of two years she applied for a divorce she expressed herself as being quite willing to leave Jennifer with my client. In the circumstances, had custody at that time been in dispute, I have no doubt that the court would have made an order to that effect, which was no doubt what she had in mind when she consented to the arrangement.'

'Is that correct, Chief Inspector?'

'The facts are not in dispute, my lord, but I cannot necessarily agree with Mr Maitland's interpretation of them.'

'We must hope then that the evidence we are to hear in the course of the next few days will prove enlightening,' said Mr Justice Conroy, heavily sarcastic, but it was a moot point, Antony considered, at whom the sarcasm was directed. 'Perhaps,' the judge added to the witness, 'you will proceed with your evidence.'

'With the greatest of pleasure, my lord. Mr Maitland left, and a short time later Mr Wilfred Begg, the deceased's solicitor, arrived. I'm quite sure the court will wish to hear his evidence at first hand, but in view of what has just passed I may perhaps be permitted to explain that a suit concerning the custody of the child, Jennifer Osmond, was in course of preparation and it was in that connection that Mr Maitland became acquainted with the man for whom he is now acting. He was not this time directly concerned—'

'That's the second time the word directly has been used,' said the judge, leaning forward and peering at counsel for the defence in an interested way. 'Perhaps you could explain it to us, Mr Maitland.'

'With the greatest of pleasure, my lord. My client's solicitor, Mr Geoffrey Horton, who has instructed me in this case, had asked me if I would be willing to deal with this custody question if the matter finally went to court. I agreed, and was introduced to Mr Osmond so that I could hear his side of the story. Your lordship will understand, I am sure, that I could not deal with the matter without having heard that.'

'Yes, Mr Maitland, that makes the matter very clear. You may proceed, Mr Garfield.'

'I am obliged to your lordship.' Commendably, there was no sarcasm in his tone. 'You are quite right, Mr Eversley, Mr Begg's evidence is extremely important and must be heard from him. I think, however, as the matter has already been mentioned, that it would be in order for me to ask you whether he informed you at this point of the fact that Mrs Osmond wished to regain custody of her child.'

Eversley's eyes flickered for a moment in Maitland's direction. 'He informed me of that and of a number of other things that will be of interest to the court,' he said. 'These matters also will be better heard from the people more nearly concerned. Briefly, however, the prisoner was determined to retain custody of his daughter, while Mrs Osmond had obtained evidence that would certainly have resulted – had the case gone to court – in that arrangement being reversed. As a result of what Mr Begg told me I questioned the accused later that evening. His replies were evasive and I asked him to attend at Scotland Yard the next morning to make a statement. This he did, in the company of his solicitor, whom he insisted should be present.' ('Very properly,' muttered Maitland rebelliously under his breath.) 'Meanwhile our enquiries were proceeding, and as a result of what came to light Robert Osmond was arrested the following morning.'

'Thank you, Mr Eversley. We have agreed, my lord,' said Garfield, turning to the judge, 'with your lordship's permission, of course, that the very distressing facts revealed by these enquiries will best be brought out at first hand by the later witnesses.'

'That is as it should be, Mr Garfield,' said Conroy graciously.

'There is just one other question, which cannot be answered by anyone but the present witness. Have you talked to Jennifer Osmond?'

'No. I have made several attempts to do so, but each time I have been confronted with the fact that her doctor would not allow her to be questioned by the police. She's said to be too upset,' said Eversley, in a tone that conveyed accurately enough his disbelief.

Maitland was on his feet again. 'The doctor has given a certificate to that effect, my lord, which can be produced if necessary. He is also quite willing to be called to give evidence as to Jennifer's state of mind following the shock she received on learning of her mother's death, but unless my friend for the prosecution insists I should prefer not to interrupt his rather busy schedule.'

'What have you to say to that, Mr Garfield?' asked the judge.

'There seems no reason to go to such extremes, my lord,' said Garfield rather disdainfully. 'As I think I indicated in my opening address, our case is quite capable of proof as it stands. I can quite understand, however, that Chief Inspector Eversley must find it annoying to have unnecessary obstacles put in the way of his doing what he conceives to be his duty.'

'I am quite ready to concede the Chief Inspector's sense of duty, but I must object to the word "unnecessary",' said Maitland.

Garfield rather too obviously ignored the remark. 'I have no further questions for this witness, my lord,' he said coldly.

'Do you wish to cross-examine, Mr Maitland?'

Antony was still on his feet. 'Certainly I do, my lord,' he assured the judge.

'Well' – again the watch was consulted – 'I think you must restrain your ardour, Mr Maitland, until tomorrow morning. Do you think you can wait till then?' Which immediately put Antony in mind of the Mikado and his relish over the idea of boiling oil (*something humorous, but lingering*); though it was a different operetta he was humming when he left the court a few minutes later with his colleagues. *Barristers, and you,*

142

attorneys, set out on your homeward journeys.

Jenny, and certainly Vera, would have put words to the tune immediately, but Geoffrey only thought it seemed vaguely familiar and said irritably, 'I can't see what you're feeling so cheerful about.'

'I was just thinking,' said Antony meekly, 'how very unlikely it was that old Conroy would ever offer to marry the plaintiff in a breach of promise case.'

'Of course, if you're going to talk nonsense—' said Geoffrey, unappeased.

III

For the first time in living memory Gibbs wasn't in the hall when Antony got home. The study door was standing ajar invitingly, and when he looked in he found that Jenny was there already so he promptly joined the party, pausing on his way to the fireside to pour sherry for himself, uninvited. 'Is Gibbs ill?' he asked.

'Caught a cold,' said Vera, 'and I got him to keep to his room. Not easy,' she added, which they could all well believe, the colds being a frequent occurrence and generally being spread with indiscriminate generosity throughout the household.

'That explains it then. You needn't have kidnapped Jenny, you know,' he added, crossing the room as he spoke.

'A way of ensuring the pleasure of a few minutes of your company, my dear boy,' said Sir Nicholas benevolently.

Antony had a grin for that. 'It's a good thing that's all you wanted,' he said. 'There's absolutely nothing to report about the Osmond case yet.'

'Nothing?' queried Sir Nicholas in an unbelieving tone.

'In his opening address Garfield hammered all his points home *ad nauseam*,' Maitland told him.

'Which I agree is hardly newsworthy,' his uncle murmured.

'That's exactly what I meant. After that it was all dull stuff, nothing that amounted to a row of beans,' said Antony, perhaps in revenge for being made to give what he considered an unnecessary account of his activities. Sir Nicholas closed his eyes briefly in protest but made no further comment. 'And then we got to Eversley, and I'll say this for Garfield he didn't make him repeat every bit of the coming evidence that he'd already promised in his opening address, but contented himself with the minimum. Conroy, of course, had a few questions about my visit to Phillipa's flat soon after the police arrived there—'

'Only natural,' said Vera in her gruff way.

'No more than I expected,' Antony agreed. 'Anyway, Garfield wasn't being awkward about that, and though I had to pull Eversley up once or twice over his interpretation of what had been said it went over well enough with the judge, I think. After all, when I was already all set to act for Osmond in the custody suit it was only natural I should take on his defence on the more serious charge as well.'

'Quite natural,' said Sir Nicholas. 'Has the Chief Inspector finished his evidence?'

'Yes, but I haven't cross-examined yet,' said Antony, knowing well enough that that was the point at which they would really become interested. 'I'll tell you all about that tomorrow evening,' he promised. 'Unless I can get away in time to join you for lunch, Uncle Nick, but I should think that's unlikely. And nothing that's happened so far has given me any inspiration, Jenny love, so you needn't look at me hopefully, like a bird with its beak open waiting for a nice, juicy worm.'

'Ugh!' said Jenny, grimacing, but she was not to be distracted from her point. 'Perhaps not yet,' she added, 'but before we're any of us very much older—' She relented then and broke off her teasing, and allowed Sir Nicholas to steer the conversation in another direction.

144

FRIDAY,
the second day of the trial

I

There could be no denying that Detective Chief Inspector Eversley had a complacent look when he resumed his place in the witness box the following morning. Maitland, getting up to face him, wished very much that it was within his power to change that, but though he had sat up late on Thursday he didn't feel that he had come up with any questions likely to disturb the witness unduly. Start with something unexpected then. 'I wonder, Chief Inspector,' he said, and was quite unaware that the dulcet tone he used might well have been a deliberate mimicry of his uncle's manner in a similar situation, so that Mr Justice Conroy – who thought him not half the man Sir Nicholas was as an advocate – peered at him suspiciously for a moment over the top of his spectacles, 'whether it is the prosecution's intention to call Mrs Phillipa Osmond's cleaning woman to give evidence.'

'That question, Mr Maitland, should surely have been put to Mr Garfield,' said the judge before Eversley could reply.

'I'm a little puzzled, my lord. There is nothing in the papers that were sent to my instructing solicitor to indicate such an intention, in fact I don't even know the lady's name.'

'I'm sure if you wish to call her, her name could be supplied.' Conroy looked enquiringly at the witness, but Maitland broke in quickly before he could reply.

'Your lordship, I am sure, would not have allowed anything in the nature of cross-examination of one of my own witnesses.'

'Certainly I should not, Mr Maitland. What exactly is it you wish?'

'My learned friend has been careful not to weary the court with too much repetition of evidence, a fact for which I am sure we are all grateful. Nor should I wish to delay matters in any way, but I'm sure that a statement was taken from this anonymous woman, and I should like your lordship's permission either to have this statement sworn to and produced in court, or to allow the present witness to answer a couple of questions about what she told him.'

'Hearsay, Mr Maitland?'

'In the interests of dealing expeditiously with a very small matter, my lord. I am sure if I'm willing – as I am – to accept Chief Inspector Eversley's word in this matter the court can have no objection to doing so.'

'It's extremely irregular,' said Conroy doubtfully.

'Two very small matters, my lord,' Maitland repeated in an unashamedly coaxing tone.

'Mr Garfield?'

'I have no objection, my lord. The evidence – if you can call it such – to which my learned friend refers can be of no help either to the prosecution or the defence, which is why no previous reference has been made to it.'

'Very well. Ask your questions, Mr Maitland.'

'I am obliged to your lordship. As I said, Chief Inspector, they are very simple.' Eversley had been quietly fuming all this time and was now, Maitland thought, suitably softened up. 'Mrs Osmond lived alone, did she not?'

'She did.'

'And had no housekeeper?'

'In such a small place? No, only – as you surmised – a charwoman.'

'Then I am sure you asked this woman to look around the flat and see if she could tell whether anything was missing.'

'I did, of course. As far as she could tell nothing was out of place, nothing had been removed.'

'From the evidence that has been given about fingerprints it is obvious that she did her work very thoroughly. When had the flat last been cleaned?'

'On Tuesday, the sixteenth of March,' said Eversley. 'The

146

day before Mrs Osmond's death.'

'Thank you for the reminder, Chief Inspector. Now to turn to your investigation. When did it first occur to you that my client might be the guilty party?'

'Within a few hours of my arrival at Mrs Osmond's flat.'

'So soon? I know there is a convention to the effect that in a case of murder the principal suspect must always be the husband or wife of the deceased, but in this instance that was hardly applicable. They had been divorced for three years, and hadn't lived together for two years before that.'

'When I heard that Mrs Osmond had desired to regain custody of her daughter, and with the evidence she had to support her claim,' said the witness, 'my suspicions were naturally aroused.'

'To the exclusion of all other possibilities?'

Eversley's answer did not come quite so quickly this time. 'Naturally if there had been any signs indicating the possibility that some other person was guilty they would have been examined,' he said at last.

'How hard, I wonder, did you look for anything of the sort?'

'The matter was investigated thoroughly in the usual manner.'

'Was it? I suggest to you, Chief Inspector, that you very quickly made up your mind as to my client's guilt, and being – I'm sure sincerely – convinced of that you looked no further.'

'If there had been any indication whatever of some other person's guilt . . . but the evidence that the accused was actually in St John's Wood on the afternoon of Mrs Osmond's death was very quickly forthcoming.'

'Was it at that point or earlier that you decided to question him?'

'Before. I went to see him on the evening of Mrs Osmond's death.'

'Yes, we're coming to a point that interests me very much. What did you mean when you told the court that my client's replies to your questions were evasive?'

Eversley's patience was running thin already. 'Exactly what I said,' he snapped.

'Come now, Chief Inspector, my client is not a fool. Nor are you, if I may say so, very good at concealing your thoughts, and when you burst in on him positively bristling with suspicion what did you expect?'

'His wife had been murdered—'

'His former wife,' Maitland corrected him gently.

'If you prefer it. Of an innocent man I should have expected some concern at least, and a desire to be helpful.'

'Are you telling me your own attitude was not antagonistic at that point?'

'No more, I think, than was natural under the circumstances.'

'The court, of course, will make what it likes of that statement. Did he refuse to answer any of your questions?'

'Not exactly. But he did refuse to amplify any of his replies, or to make a formal statement except in the presence of his solicitor.'

'I'm sure you will agree that was his right, Chief Inspector.'

'It may be, but an innocent man—'

'Chief Inspector!' That brought Eversley up short. 'Perhaps his lordship will permit me to tell you that your attitude reminds me of a verse of Lewis Carroll's,' Maitland went on. He knew it was inadvisable but he couldn't help it. *'I'll be judge, I'll be jury, said cunning old Fury. I'll try the whole cause, and condemn you to death.'*

'Really, Mr Maitland,' Conroy protested, 'this is neither the time nor the place for reciting poetry.'

'I must apologise to your lordship in that case. For myself, I felt that it conveyed the witness's attitude very accurately.'

'That, Mr Maitland, is a matter of opinion.'

'Precisely, my lord. May I continue with my cross-examination of this witness?'

'If you must,' said Conroy grudgingly.

Maitland turned back to the witness again but Eversley spoke before he had time to frame a question. 'I'm sure I didn't mean to convey the impression that I had pre-judged the matter.'

'No, Chief Inspector, that is the jury's prerogative not yours or mine. You will agree, then, that my client's actions were perfectly within his rights.'

'He was following your advice, I suppose,' said Eversley viciously. His intention of being conciliatory obviously didn't go very deep.

'You seem to forget, Chief Inspector, Mr Horton who instructed me is Mr Osmond's solicitor. But as you still seem to feel that his attitude was unreasonable, perhaps you would care to enlarge on what you have told us.'

This was clearly the opening Eversley had been waiting for. He answered without hesitation, 'An innocent man would have had no reason not to be open with me.'

'There you go again!' said Maitland sadly. 'If you're not careful, Chief Inspector, you will encourage me to incur his lordship's wrath again by some appropriate quotation. You really mustn't pre-judge the issue you know, and I'm sure it's as obvious to the jury as it is to me that Mr Osmond, confronted by a hostile interrogation, adopted – very sensibly – a cautious attitude. You're not disputing that he was within his rights to do so?'

That hadn't gone quite as the witness had intended. 'Of course not,' he said. 'I'm only saying—'

'I think his lordship – and perhaps even my learned friend for the prosecution – will agree with me that you have already said too much on this subject.'

Conroy smiled his tight, impartial smile. 'You really must not usurp the privileges of the court, Mr Eversley,' he said.

Maitland carefully restrained a desire to cheer, and schooled his features into impassivity. 'I am grateful for your lordship's assistance,' he said, and turned back to the witness again. 'You also complained, Chief Inspector, that you had not been permitted to see the little girl, Jennifer Osmond. I can't help wondering why you should have wished to do so.'

'She was missing, as you yourself told me, on the afternoon of the murder. There was some question as to whether she had gone to visit her mother.' He paused, obviously considering another indiscretion, but then thought better of it. 'In the circumstances, I think it was natural that I should wish to see her.'

'It was impossible, Chief Inspector. You do understand, don't you? Mr Osmond told you – did he not? – that Jennifer had been badly upset by a man who accosted her in the school playground the day before the murder. Her doctor did not wish her to be subjected to any further annoyance.'

Perhaps it was his choice of words that roused Eversley to anger again. 'That's all very well, but—' he started incautiously, and then broke off, eyeing counsel in a resentful way.

'You were about to assure us that you would have dealt with her very gently,' said Maitland. 'I'm sure that is true, but it is equally true that talking to her would have done you no good. Perhaps I should explain, your lordship, that Miss Amanda Herschell, who is looking after Jennifer Osmond during her father's absence, will be appearing as a witness for the defence, and will be able to explain to us that though she and Jennifer are on very good terms, she has been unable to persuade the child to tell her what the stranger said to her, or where she went on the afternoon she played truant from school. I'm sure your lordship will agree that in face of this determined silence her doctor's instructions are reasonable.'

'As far as I can tell it will be some days yet before Miss Herschell gives her evidence, Mr Maitland,' said Conroy rather coldly. 'I'm sure that when the time comes we shall all be interested in knowing whether the situation remains as you have outlined it.'

'I can only speak for matters as they now stand, my lord. I'm afraid it has been a very traumatic experience for Jennifer, first to learn that her mother was alive when she had believed her dead, and then so soon after to be told of her murder.' Perhaps it was Conroy's sceptical look that prompted him to add recklessly, 'If her attitude changes, and with her doctor's permission, I should be only too glad to call her as a witness myself.'

'Thank you, Mr Maitland, that seems a very fair offer,' said Conroy, heavily sarcastic. 'Have you any further questions for this witness?'

'No, my lord, I think we have clarified all the matters that my friend's direct examination left obscure.' He sat down as he spoke and as Paul Garfield did not wish to re-examine Eversley was allowed to stand down and the next witness was called.

This was the doctor who had first pronounced Phillipa

Osmond dead, and neither his evidence nor that of the pathologist who followed him gave the defence much opportunity in cross-examination. It would have been nice, of course, to pinpoint the time of death more exactly, but neither witness would commit himself to anything nearer than some time between two-thirty and four-thirty on the afternoon in question. It was obviously of no use to query the cause of death . . . manual strangulation. The pathologist gave a brief lecture on the simplicity of this, but gave it as his opinion that on this occasion it had been the work of a man, and not a particularly small man at that. 'The thing is,' he explained earnestly, 'people don't realise how simple it is to do. There were no signs of other injuries to the body; the murderer must have felt quite confident of his ability to achieve his end without difficulty. Besides,' he added, leaving his theories aside for a moment, perhaps because he saw out of the corner of his eye that Maitland was half way to his feet, 'there were signs of bruising on the neck that indicate that the murderer had large hands.' At which point, of course, every eye in the courtroom turned towards the dock, but to point out that Robert Osmond was not the only man in the world to whom this description would apply would only have been to draw attention to the remark. The witness then proceeded to go, unasked, into a certain amount of rather unpleasant detail as to what the post-mortem on Phillipa Osmond's body had revealed, but there was nothing there to help either the defence or the prosecution, and it is probable that nobody in the court was really unhappy to see him stand down. Mr Justice Conroy took the opportunity of calling the luncheon recess.

'If anybody has any appetite left after all that,' Maitland grumbled, as soon as the judge had left the bench.

II

However that might have been it cannot be said he enjoyed the interval. Horton and Stringer had joined him at Astroff's that day – Sir Nicholas had left a message that he couldn't manage to be there after all – though the time at their disposal was too short to allow much conversation. It was long enough however for Geoffrey to speak his mind freely on the unwisdom of certain of Antony's remarks that morning.

'Eversley annoys me,' said Maitland shortly in reply.

'That,' said Geoffrey, 'was only too obvious. You realise, I suppose, that you've committed us to calling that child if she decides to talk to Miss Herschell after all.'

'At this stage it seems unlikely.'

'Perhaps it is, but you must remember, Antony, that Miss Herschell will be on oath, and if one thing is sure in this uncertain world it's that Garfield will ask her about it now. We may well end up with Jennifer herself in court.'

'Would that be so very terrible?'

'It might be,' said Geoffrey rather grimly. 'What if she did go to St John's Wood and saw her father there, perhaps in circumstances that were very incriminating indeed. That would explain her determined silence, wouldn't it?'

'If that's what's keeping her quiet I imagine it will go on doing so,' said Maitland, and though Geoffrey came as near as he ever did to losing his temper at that point and told him he was being deliberately stupid he declined any further discussion of the matter. Unfortunately he was even more annoyed with himself than was his instructing solicitor, but as Derek said, when he decided that Geoffrey's strictures had gone far enough, it was no good crying over spilled milk.

When they got back to court the first witness to be called that afternoon was Stewart Brodie, and Maitland needed only one look at counsel for the prosecution to decide that he found the business of examining him extremely distasteful. Brodie was a man of medium height, with thick black hair and a neatly trimmed beard, but in spite of what might easily have been classed as good looks there was still something undeniably shifty about him, which obviously Garfield sensed too. However, it was extremely improbable that either the jury or the spectators had any idea of this, and perhaps not the occupants of the press box either. Garfield was too old a hand to allow his opinion to become obvious, except as a matter of policy, and took his witness through the preliminaries with practised ease. Brodie gave an address in Ruislip and described himself as a private enquiry agent. 'And it was in that capacity, I understand, that Mrs Osmond consulted you when she wished to regain custody of her daughter?'

'That's right. Not that this is my line of business nowadays. Any type of investigation handled, but that's mostly industrial stuff lately, if you know what I mean.'

'I think, perhaps, it will be as well if we stick to the matter at hand, Mr Brodie,' said Garfield, allowing a little coldness to creep into his voice. 'You weren't averse, I take it, to involving yourself in more domestic affairs.'

'All bread and butter, isn't it?'

'I take it, Mr Garfield, that that should be construed as agreement,' Mr Justice Conroy enquired.

'I believe so, my lord. Mr Brodie, you are telling us, are you not, that you agreed to look into the matter for her.'

'Certainly I am. It wasn't the first time I'd helped her, there was the divorce too. When that came up I was able to find her just the evidence she needed to bring Robert to heel. So naturally she came back to me when she wanted to get custody of Jennifer.'

'We are not at present concerned with the divorce proceedings, Mr Brodie. About the other matter, she came to you—?'

'About six months before she died.'

'And she told you—?'

'That she wanted Jennifer back,' said the witness, as though the matter were perfectly simple. 'Well, we both knew that Robert would kick like mad, so something had to be done.'

'I really think that is a point we should clarify, Mr Garfield,' said Conroy. 'The witness is telling us, I believe, that both he and Mrs Osmond were well aware that the prisoner would object to her attempts to gain custody of her daughter.'

'Is that right, Mr Brodie?'

'Absolutely right.'

'Then perhaps you will tell us how you set about your investigation.'

'It·wasn't too difficult to work out,' said the witness in a rather patronising tone. 'I knew Robert, you see. But in the circumstances I didn't think that simple evidence of immorality would be much good. So I had the flat watched. Robert's flat, I mean.'

'By one of your employees?'

'No, I thought this was a job that I could handle better myself. And I soon began to realise that everything wasn't on the up and up as far as he was concerned. After that there wasn't much to it; when the girls appeared I followed them home, it was just as simple as that.'

'Yes, we shall be hearing from each of them in due course. What gave you the idea of watching the flat?'

'I know Robert,' said Brodie simply, as he had done before.

'I see. This investigation went on over a period of six months you say?'

'More or less.'

'I gather from what you've told us, Mr Brodie, that you were acquainted with both Mr and Mrs Osmond.'

'During the time that they were married, yes. I hadn't seen Robert since they separated, but Phillipa and I remained good friends.'

'Perhaps you'll be kind enough to tell us, Mr Brodie, how many women you recommended Mrs Osmond's solicitor to *sub poena* if the custody suit was actually brought?'

'Three in all. But it wouldn't have come to court.'

'I imagine, however, that you took statements from each of these women.'

'Certainly I did. But the signed originals are in Mr Wilfred Begg's possession.'

'Then we must ask him about them. That is all I have to ask you, Mr Brodie.' Garfield sat down again with an air of relief but Maitland was on his feet before the judge had time to question him as to his intentions.

154

'From what you have told us, Mr Brodie, it seems that you knew Mrs Osmond well?'

'Knew her? I knew her very well indeed. She was one of the – one of the most wonderful women.'

'You know my client too, I believe.'

'Better than I like.'

'I see. You were her friend more than his, even during the period when they were married.'

'That's exactly right, and as I said I haven't seen him since.'

'Since she left him?'

'Not since then . . . until I had to give evidence in the Magistrate's Court.' He shot a venomous glance towards the still figure in the dock.

'And when she wanted a divorce she came to you?'

'Of course she did. Not that there was any need for what I could do for her, Robert gave in like a lamb once he knew she didn't want to keep Jennifer with her . . . just then.'

'Did I detect a slight hesitation there, Mr Brodie? You were going to say merely that Mrs Osmond didn't want the child with her, weren't you?'

'That's what I said, wasn't it?'

'Yes, but you added the words "just then".'

'Well, she wanted her now, didn't she? I mean she did before she was killed.'

'That's one of the things I should like you to enlighten us about, in rather more detail than you've already done. She came to you for help again, didn't she?'

'Certainly she did . . . good old Stewart! And as I said there was no doubt Robert would have given in again.'

'There still remain a number of things of interest to me about that, Mr Brodie. For instance, you told my friend that you watched Robert Osmond's flat. There are a number of other tenants in the building; do you mean you actually stationed yourself on the – the seventh floor, I believe? The one on which his flat is situated at any rate.'

'I do.'

'Was that not to make yourself a trifle conspicuous?'

'Not at all. Each floor has its own miniature lobby, with large banks of greenery. Concealment was quite a simple matter.'

155

'If rather boring. Now, Mr Brodie, have you any idea why Mrs Osmond changed her mind and wanted custody of Jennifer after all?'

'Mother love . . . natural, wasn't it?'

'If you forget the fact that Phillipa Osmond left her husband and child, and had made no attempt to see Jennifer for five years . . . then I suppose you could call it natural. However, as you knew Mrs Osmond so well perhaps you wouldn't mind telling the court how long you had known her and what made her, in your eyes, such a wonderful woman?'

'I've known her for ever, ten years or so I daresay. As for being wonderful, handsome is as handsome does . . . that's my motto.'

'Are you trying to tell us that your opinion about her had changed?' asked Maitland after a moment's hesitation while he tried to disentangle this rather obscure announcement. To his surprise, though not to his displeasure, the question aroused a streak of aggressiveness in the witness.

'Trying to trip me?' he asked. 'She's dead, isn't she? Murdered? And I know you lawyers, up to every trick in the book.'

'That would be gratifying, if true,' said Maitland, with a touch of ruefulness in his voice. 'But you didn't answer my question, Mr Brodie.'

'*I* didn't kill her, you know.'

'Nobody suggested that you did. But are you telling us that there was any reason—'

'Of course not!' said the witness sharply. 'But if you're interested I can tell you just where I was . . . out on an investigation. It's all confidential, of course, but I can produce my records . . . no difficulty at all. And if you're going to ask me if anybody saw me during that time, I wasn't there to be seen.'

Maitland reverted into vagueness. 'Nobody is questioning your movements, Mr Brodie,' he said. He turned for a moment towards the bench. 'I must apologise to your lordship, my questions were not intended to make any implication or to elicit any such denial on the witness's part.'

'I suppose, Mr Maitland, we must give you the benefit of the doubt.'

'I am obliged to your lordship. Let us turn to this investigation of yours into my client's conduct, Mr Brodie. It went on over a period of six months, you say?'

'Quite six months.'

'An expensive business,' Maitland commented.

'I didn't say I spent every night outside his flat. Weekends were a good time, and once I was pretty sure they were bedded down for the night I could go away till the morning. After all, all I needed were a few addresses. It was the girls who were going to give evidence of what had been going on, if it was necessary.'

'All the same, it makes me wonder a little about Mrs Osmond's financial resources.'

'A wealthy woman. At least, by my standards.'

'How much was the final bill for your services?'

'I don't remember offhand, not without my records.'

'Ah yes, those records. You seem to rely on them a good deal,' Maitland commented dryly. 'But at least I daresay you can remember this, had the account been paid?'

Brodie frowned at him, obviously working out the pros and cons of what his answer should be. 'Not yet,' he said finally.

'But you have claimed against her estate, I expect. Have you any idea how things were left?'

'Why should I have?'

'You seem to have known her very well. But you didn't tell us, have you put in a claim?'

'I don't know that I shall bother.'

'Oh, I should if I were you. Do you know Matthew Leighton?' he added, but in spite of his casual tone the sudden change of subject seemed to bewilder the witness.

'No, I don't.' Brodie's mood was definitely ugly now. 'How should I know a man like that?'

'I thought perhaps you might have done some work for his company. Some of this industrial work you mentioned to my friend.'

'And if I had – which I haven't, mind you – it wouldn't have been at his level. I'd have been dealing with some underling.'

'I see. But we still haven't got back to the question, Mr

157

Brodie. What reason did Mrs Osmond give you for wanting custody of Jennifer after all this time?'

'Did she need one? The child was hers,' said Brodie abruptly.

'After five years in which she showed no interest in Jennifer's welfare?'

'She had no reason to explain herself to me.'

'But surely, to an old friend to whom she turned for help in trouble?'

'Well, if you must have it, she said she was tired of working. She'd made some good investments and would have plenty to live on, and besides that there'd be child support that Robert would pay her if she won the case.'

'That could hardly have been the only reason.'

'Motherly love!' said Stewart Brodie, and – perhaps forgetting where he was for the moment – laughed aloud. But the laugh had more than a touch of bitterness about it. 'And I was fool enough to believe it . . . then.'

'But not now?'

'I didn't say that,' said the witness quickly.

'I must have misunderstood you. One last thing, Mr Brodie. You've told us how you found the young women who were prepared to give evidence in the custody suit, and now I understand will be giving evidence in this court. How did they strike you?'

'As completely honest and very good witnesses.'

'I'm sure you are right on the last point at least.'

'Are you calling me a liar?' (Garfield must have decided that the witness was more than capable of dealing with the question, or else his own distaste for the man made him unwilling to intervene.) 'I saw each one of them leaving Robert's flat in the early morning, and could have backed up their testimony myself if there had been any need.'

'Yes, I see.' The fact that this was untrue could hardly have been made more explicit if he had said so in so many words. 'There's just one other thing that puzzles me, nothing to do with the truth or otherwise of their statements, about which the court will be able to decide for itself in due course. It would have done none of them any good to have the whole

158

story come out. Why do you think they were willing to testify?'

'Phillipa's lawyer – Wilf she calls him – could have *sub poena'd* them, couldn't he, if they refused?'

'But I gather there was no question of that. Each of them was quite willing to appear.'

'Well, there are some people who think fair's fair,' said Brodie, 'and I expect that each of them felt the little girl would be better off with her mother. Sentiment, of course, you and I know that' – he was making a belated attempt to be friendly – 'but I daresay that was the thing that influenced them most.'

'Do you really think so? Well, as I said, we shall have the opportunity of judging that for ourselves. I won't trouble you any further, Mr Brodie. Thank you for your help.'

Garfield had a few more questions to ask on re-examination, but it cannot be said that they brought much in the way of enlightenment. He gave it up at last and called Miss Loretta Kinsman to take the stand.

As he had done with Stewart Brodie, Maitland eyed this new witness with a good deal of interest. From the beginning Brodie had shown an antagonistic attitude towards the defence, which hadn't been a bad thing as it had led him into more than one indiscretion, but this time it was different. When it came to the defence's turn a conciliatory attitude would be in order.

Funnily enough the first thought that occurred to Antony as she gave her name ('but everyone calls me Laurie'), address in Golders Green, and her occupation as a model, was that in some strange way she reminded him of Phillipa Osmond. Not that they looked at all alike – this girl had dark, straight, silky hair falling almost to her shoulders – but perhaps the resemblance lay in the fact that each, he was convinced, was quite certain in her own mind that she was completely in command of the situation. Later he was to add a bantering manner to his list of resemblances, but this, naturally enough, was not apparent during the preliminary questioning.

Garfield's puritanical air was now more marked than ever. He too, however, was obviously determined to treat his witness with kid gloves. 'I'm sure you appreciate, Miss Kinsman,' he said, 'that my questions may prove a trifle embarrassing.'

'If I don't mind, why should you? Tell the truth and shame the devil, that's my motto.'

'Then I needn't hesitate in getting straight to the point.' Garfield was stiffer than ever, so that Antony felt a momentary pang of sympathy for his opponent. 'How long had you known Phillipa Osmond?'

'I didn't know her at all until Mr Brodie introduced us. And that was the only time I met her.'

'You had no special interest then in seeing her get custody of her daughter?'

'None at all, except a vague feeling that Robert isn't really a proper person to have charge of the child. That's what you want to know about, isn't it . . . my relationship with him?'

Counsel for the prosecution was silent for a moment, obviously taken aback by the suddenness of the question. Taking pity on him, 'You mustn't ask counsel questions, Miss Kinsman,' Conroy admonished her, leaning forward and peering at the witness in an interested way.

'I only wanted to help,' said Laurie, with obvious sincerity, 'because that's what I'm here for, isn't it?'

'Just answer Mr Garfield's questions,' Conroy told her.

'All right then, but it does seem a waste of time,' said the witness irrepressibly.

Conroy leaned back, obviously defeated. Garfield said coldly, 'Perhaps we could approach the subject in a rather more roundabout way, Miss Kinsman. This Mr Brodie you mentioned—'

'You must know all about him. They shouted for him to come into court just before me. In fact, that's him right over there,' she added, pointing to the bench where the witnesses who had already given their evidence were seated.

'Yes, Miss Kinsman, but we must take everything in order. What do you know of him?'

'He's a private detective and I think he's a friend of Mrs Osmond's.'

'When did he first approach you?'

'About four months ago, and I don't mind telling you I'd

160

have thought twice about talking to him if I hadn't felt rather sore with Robert at the time. So out it all came, and then he asked me if I would meet Phillipa and I did and it seemed too unkind not to agree to give evidence for her.'

'What had Robert Osmond done to offend you?'

'Why he dropped me . . . for somebody else, I suppose. At least I expect that's what happened. He isn't the sort of man to be without a woman for long.'

'How long did your acquaintance with him last?'

'I love that word,' she said, and laughed. Garfield became more poker-faced than ever. 'Six months or so, I suppose,' she added.

'And during that time your relationship became intimate?'

'That was the whole point, wasn't it?'

'Thank you, Miss Kinsman,' said Garfield bleakly. 'Now I'm sure you realise that the court is not concerned so much with Robert Osmond's morals as with the effects of his actions on his daughter.'

'Well, I understood that about the custody suit, but this is different, isn't it? This is murder.'

'All the same I should like an answer to my question, Miss Kinsman.'

'It wasn't exactly a question,' she said, having taken a moment to think that over. 'I suppose it's motive you're worried about, if Robert was quite sure Phillipa would win.'

'My lord!' said Maitland, coming to his feet in a hurry. 'The interpretation of the evidence is a matter for my learned friend, Mr Garfield, when he addresses the jury.'

'In this instance, I must agree with you, Mr Maitland. Perhaps you will explain to your witness, Mr Garfield, that she should confine herself to answering your questions.'

'I'll endeavour to do so, your lordship. Miss Kinsman, the court really cannot allow you to indulge in speculation.'

'I only wondered . . . oh well, if you say so, I don't want to argue. And I realise what you want to know all right even though it wasn't a proper question you asked. You want to know if Jennifer knew about our affair.'

'Yes, Miss Kinsman, that is the point on which we should like enlightenment.'

'Well, that was the one thing I didn't like about the whole

deal,' said Laurie frankly. 'I don't pretend to be a saint, but a kid like that should be allowed to keep her innocence for a little while at any rate.'

That was indeed to come to the heart of the matter, rather nearer to it than Antony liked if the truth were told, but there was no way he could stop this line of questioning. The trouble was, every word the witness spoke carried conviction, her manner of treating the matter was so completely casual. 'What is Jennifer Osmond's age, Miss Kinsman?'

'She told me once she was eight, but of course, she may have had her ninth birthday since then.'

'And where did your meetings with Robert Osmond take place?'

'Why at his home, of course. I thought you knew that.'

Garfield ignored that, and Mr Justice Conroy had obviously decided there was no point in intervening any further. 'At what time of day did you go there?' Garfield asked.

'In the evening or at night, of course. I've even had to wait outside until that sour-faced Mrs Arbuthnot left. Sometimes I'd just go later and spend the night with him.'

'There was no question of his getting a baby-sitter and taking you out?'

'No, he wouldn't do that. I think he liked to be looked upon as a doting father who employed somebody during the day when he had to be at business but otherwise devoted himself to the child.'

'I'm afraid I'm going to have to ask you to be a little more plain with me, Miss Kinsman.' Again Maitland was aware of a stab of sympathy for his adversary. The witness might not suffer from *gêne*, but counsel obviously did.

'I've admitted we were intimate, haven't I?'

'Yes, but I'm afraid the how and when are important too, and from your earlier remarks it's obvious that you realise why. For instance, if you went in the early evening just as Mrs Arbuthnot left—'

'We'd have dinner together and then Jennifer would go to her room to do her homework. And if you think Robert was one to leave a girl alone while that was going on, you're quite mistaken. There's a comfortable sofa in the living-room, one of those very long ones. The kid came back once or twice and caught us at it.'

In spite of the fact that he didn't like what he was hearing Antony's thoughts were again a mixture of amusement and compassion for his opponent. As counsel for the prosecution Garfield was getting exactly what he wanted to underline Robert Osmond's motive, but what he was hearing revolted his every feeling, as was quite evident in his voice when he went on with his questioning. 'If you disliked the situation so much, surely you could have suggested an alternative.'

'Of course I did, but Robert wasn't having any. He said it would do Jennifer good to know how many beans made five. If I stayed the night it was all right because we went to the bedroom and she never came in there. But I'd see her looking at me at breakfast-time all goggle-eyed. She knew what was going on all right.'

'And on those occasions you would leave before Mrs Arbuthnot came?'

'Certainly I did.'

'So you never met her?'

'Never.'

'Thank you, Miss Kinsman, that is all I have to ask you. Perhaps, Mr Maitland—'

'Certainly I wish to cross-examine,' said Antony, getting to his feet promptly.

The witness turned a little to face him, eyeing him as speculatively as he had looked at her when she first came into court. 'Are you Robert's lawyer?' she asked abruptly.

'His counsel,' Antony told her.

'Was that why you didn't want me to say—?'

'I couldn't allow you to speculate on a matter that is outside your province, Miss Kinsman. Perhaps you have never been in a court of law before?'

'No, I haven't, and I don't like it now.'

'Then perhaps his lordship will permit me to explain to you that no one is allowed to attempt an explanation of the evidence except counsel. His lordship will explain matters of law to the jury before they retire to consider their verdict. It is then the jury who are the sole judges of the facts.'

163

'I'll take your word for it,' said Laurie Kinsman, and shrugged.

'Really, Mr Maitland,' Mr Justice Conroy interposed. 'Have you any questions for this witness, or do you merely wish to indulge in a dialogue with her?'

'I have several questions, my lord. If your lordship will permit me.'

'I see no way of stopping you, Mr Maitland, but I should like you to get on with them, and refrain from wasting the court's time.'

'If your lordship pleases. Now, Miss Kinsman, you have told the court that you met Mrs Osmond only on one occasion, and had no personal reason for wanting her to get custody of her daughter. But don't you feel that your evidence displays some bias against Mr Osmond?'

'No more than he deserves.' Garfield, who had half risen, sank back into his place again. 'Perhaps I don't care much for him after the way he dropped me,' Laurie Kinsman went on, 'but I wouldn't be telling lies because of that.'

'For some other reason perhaps?'

'Really Mr – Mr Maitland did he call you?' She jerked her head in the direction of the judge. 'How can you suggest such a thing?' The teasing note was very evident at that moment.

'Very easily. You are here under *sub poena* no doubt.'

'I got a paper saying I had to come.'

'Exactly. But previously, when it was merely a matter of the possibility of a custody suit, you were willing enough to give evidence.'

'That was different.'

'Because you had a motive for giving evidence on Phillipa Osmond's behalf?'

'I don't quite know what you mean by that.'

'You intimated to my friend that it was out of consideration for Mrs Osmond that you were telling your story.'

'That's true.'

'But now my client is accused of murder.'

'I can't help that, can I? My motives don't matter, only the truth. And you're not trying to suggest that I should change my evidence now?'

'I'm not trying to suggest anything, Miss Kinsman, except

that you should tell us what really happened. You're under oath remember.'

'Considering all the fuss they made about it with a Bible and all, I'm not likely to forget it. But I should have been in the other case as well.'

'Describe Jennifer Osmond to me.'

If he had hoped to confuse her by the sudden change of subject he was to be disappointed. 'I was surprised when I met Mrs Osmond, the child isn't much like her. She's fair, of course, but not nearly so good looking. A nice enough little thing, but quite plain really.'

That was probably as good a description as anybody could expect. 'Then I've only one more question for you, Miss Kinsman. Would you mind telling us about Robert Osmond's flat?'

'It's quite a while since I was there,' she said, more doubtfully than she had previously spoken.

'Anything you can remember . . . the layout, some of the furnishings,' Maitland suggested.

'There's the big sofa I told him about.' Again there was that jerk of the head, though this time in Garfield's direction. 'I couldn't forget *that*. It's a very large living-room on the right of the hall and the kitchen is behind it. Both the bedrooms are on the other side, with a bathroom and lavatory in between. There's a hall stand, or rather a rack for hats and coats . . . I believe what used to be called a coat-tree. You fall over it as you go in, really the hall is much too narrow.' She broke off there and eyed him quizzically. 'Will that do?'

'If that is all you can remember.' But it was as much and more than was necessary as he knew perfectly well. 'One last thing, Miss Kinsman—'

'You said that before,' she pointed out.

'Well, this really is the last question. Do you still maintain that when Mr Brodie approached you about the possibility of giving evidence on Mrs Osmond's behalf in the custody suit no consideration was offered or accepted?'

'Certainly not! I told you it was only after I met Mrs Osmond and felt sorry for her . . . a girl should be with her mother,' she added sententiously.

Maitland bowed to the inevitable and let her go, and as

Garfield did not wish to re-examine her place was soon taken by the second of the witnesses Stewart Brodie had found to champion Phillipa Osmond's cause.

This was Mrs Ella Boyd, who worked in a flower shop in the West End and lived with her husband in Putney. Antony, again observing her carefully, saw quite soon that she wasn't quite as young as she first appeared, though certainly not more than thirty. She was slim and of medium height with curly hair and gentle manner. The thought crossed his mind that the flower shop must make a perfect, if exotic, setting for her. He took a moment to glance at Garfield, whose austerity of manner seemed momentarily at least to be tempered by bewilderment. And no wonder really. Even apart from the fact that she was married she looked the last person . . .

Again Garfield started with an apology for the embarrassment his questions might cause her, which this time sounded quite sincere.

She greeted his words with a slight, not unattractive grimace.

'I can't say I find it the most attractive subject in the world,' she admitted.

'That I can understand. Perhaps I had better ask you first, Mrs Boyd, whether you recognise the accused?'

She turned to look at the man in the dock. 'Yes, of course, that's Robert – Robert Osmond. Somehow he isn't one of those people you'd ever want to call Bob.'

'When and where did you meet him?'

'He came to the shop where I work. He wasn't the only one of course, men often do ask for a date. But I liked the look of him . . . found him attractive.'

'And when was this?'

'I don't remember exactly but I'd say about six months ago. And if you want to know when I told him I wouldn't see him any more that must have been three months ago now.'

'And when did you meet Mr Stewart Brodie?'

'Just two days after I broke with Robert. I remember it very well. And I was doubtful, of course, about what he wanted . . . who wouldn't have been? But he took me to see Mrs Osmond and then I made up my mind that the truth was the only thing.'

166

'Did Mr Brodie tell you what made him approach you?'

'Oh yes. Mrs Osmond had been thinking of a custody suit for a long time . . . five or six months I think he said. So she'd employed Mr Brodie to find out—' She broke off there looking embarrassed.

'To find out something about her former husband's way of life,' Garfield prompted her. 'You have told us where you met him, and that you found him attractive. Did you tell this to Mr Brodie?'

'Yes, he seemed to know so much there didn't seem to be any point in denying it.'

'You went on to admit to having had a liaison with Robert Osmond?'

'Yes, I did.'

'For the purpose of the custody suit the point at issue was where your encounters took place, and perhaps I should explain to you that that question is just as important to us here today.'

'It was always at his flat. Mostly in the evening, but sometimes at the weekends too.'

'Was Jennifer present?'

'She was in the flat, yes. But if you mean when what you've called our encounters took place, not if I spent the night. But I didn't often do that.'

'On the other occasions?' Garfield prompted her.

'It's – it's not easy to explain.' She paused, but then seemed to make up her mind to a measure of frankness. 'You must understand that as far as Robert was concerned, I was there for one thing and one thing only, and the living-room was just as suitable as the bedroom. Oh, he'd send Jennifer out on some pretext or other, but she quite often came back again. Looking back on it I'm not proud of that, but as I told you I found him very attractive. But finally it was the realisation that I was just – what's the word the feminists use? – a sex object to him that opened my eyes. It just wasn't good enough.'

'So you put an end to the affair?'

'Yes, I did.'

Garfield hadn't quite finished with her, though that was really all she had to say to him. Perhaps he felt that she was a more sympathetic witness than Laurie Kinsman had been, in any case he wasn't content until the matter had been thrashed out at sufficient length to impress the dullest intelligence. As Maitland got up at last to cross-examine Mr Justice Conroy was consulting his watch, and it seemed expedient to start with a comment which his lordship might find soothing.

'I shall not need to detain you long, Mrs Boyd.' Then, casually and in seeming contradiction to his opening remark, 'A flower shop must be a nice place to work.'

'I love flowers,' she said simply, so that Antony was able to congratulate himself that his gambit was setting her at ease. 'I'm learning to arrange them quite well,' she added confidingly. 'Mrs Binns, who I work for, is wonderfully artistic.'

At this point, Mr Justice Conroy uttered a warning cough, which went unnoticed probably by the witness but was enough to put counsel for the defence on track again. 'You've admitted to my learned friend, Mrs Boyd, that you do not find the subject we are here to examine today a particularly attractive one. Why, when Mr Brodie approached you, did you agree to give evidence if you dislike the thought so much?'

'Because it's true,' she said, as though it explained everything.

'But your husband—'

'We're modern people. And my mother used to say, what the eye doesn't see the heart needn't grieve over.'

'You were counting at that time on my client being scared off before the custody suit got into court?' said Maitland, smiling at her to take any sting there might be out of the words.

'He's very devoted to his daughter,' said Ella Boyd, 'but he hadn't a hope of winning that case if his goings-on had been brought out into the open.'

That was not exactly what Antony had wanted to hear, and he had an uncomfortable feeling that his next questions would be no more helpful. 'Tell me something about Jennifer, Mrs Boyd,' he suggested.

'She's eight years old, Robert told me, though she might be more because she's quite tall for her age and certainly very intelligent. And she's fair like her mother but not a bit like her otherwise. Mrs Osmond was very good looking, you know, and one has to admit that Jennifer's nose is decidedly snub. She has very good manners – the child, I mean – but they're rather spoiled by a habit of staring that I found disconcerting, though Robert didn't seem to mind.'

'You mean staring at you when something happened that she didn't understand?'

'I think she understood all right. Believe me, she'd have been better off with her mother, and that's why I agreed to help Mrs Osmond.'

'The case is different now. Mr Osmond is on trial for murder. I can understand you feeling this way when it was only the custody of his daughter that was at stake, but it's very different now.'

'Are you trying to persuade me to change my evidence,' she asked, exactly as the previous witness had done.

'I only want you to tell us the truth,' said Maitland rather hastily.

'I've already told you that,' she snapped. Suddenly she was angry, and his mind formed the unlikely image of a kitten spitting its defiance. 'You're going to remind me that I'm under oath, so let *me* remind *you* that that would have been the case in the custody hearing as well. I know exactly what I'm doing.'

'That may be so.' (How long would it be before old Conroy intervened?) 'A great many people nowadays will swear to tell the truth quite lightly, but the law happens to take the matter of an oath very seriously indeed.'

'It's called committing perjury, I know that. But the question doesn't arise because what I've told you is nothing but the truth.'

'All right then, Mrs Boyd, we'll leave it there. Have you met Norma Martin or Loretta Kinsman since Mrs Osmond was killed?'

'I've never met either of them though I've heard their names, and when Miss Kinsman was called to give evidence of course I knew then who she was. What makes you think I know them?'

'Only that Miss Kinsman used almost exactly the same

169

argument a little while ago as you have just done for not changing your evidence.'

'I won't change it because it's the truth,' she said stubbornly.

'I see. Just one other thing then, Mrs Boyd. Could you tell us something about Robert Osmond's flat?'

'Yes, of course, it's not so long ago that I've forgotten.' As Laurie had done she described the layout and gave a little more detail about the way the furniture was arranged. But what interested her most was obviously the colour schemes of the various rooms.

When Maitland let her go his depression was deeper than ever and he wasn't sorry when the judge said briskly, 'It's getting late. If you wish to re-examine, Mr Garfield, I suggest that we leave it over until Monday morning.'

Garfield agreed, with what almost amounted to enthusiasm, and the court promptly adjourned. Geoffrey obviously would have liked to talk over the day's events at length, but Derek was, as usual, in haste to be gone and Antony only said wearily, 'You don't need to tell me, Geoffrey, I know just as well as you do how badly every answer I received sounded. But do me the credit of admitting that all those things had to be asked.'

'Yes, I know,' said Horton, a little conscience-stricken when he saw how tired Maitland was looking. 'Do you want to see our client again?'

'What's the use? He'll only tell us all over again that it's a wicked plot, and quite frankly, Geoffrey, I'm not in the mood to listen to him.'

SATURDAY,
the weekend recess

Perhaps it was as well that Sir Nicholas and Vera had been out the previous evening, and Jenny was always willing to postpone her questions when she saw that her husband wasn't in the mood to talk. But there was no hope of avoiding the matter at lunchtime the following day and, as Gibbs – still sniffing occasionally – decided to absent himself once the various dishes had been placed on the table, there was nothing to stop it from being brought up immediately. Sir Nicholas who, when at all possible, vetoed all discussion of legal affairs at the dinner-table, was quite prepared to talk shop over lunch.

'Halloran tells me,' he said, as soon as they were alone, 'that your defence of Robert Osmond cannot be said to be going very satisfactorily from your point of view.'

'Of course, Halloran would have heard,' said Antony bitterly. 'That man Brodie wasn't so bad. It's quite obvious he knew Phillipa Osmond very much better than he admits, in fact I'd be very much surprised if they hadn't had an affair, probably an on-and-off one for years.'

'Your crystal ball in operation again, Antony?' asked his uncle languidly.

'Perhaps, but I had the distinct impression that before he knew Robert Osmond had been arrested for her murder he wondered whether the police might look on him with suspicion. He was antagonistic from the start and I got him to lose his temper—'

'You amaze me,' Sir Nicholas murmured.

'—and he denied in so many words that he killed her.

Which was unnecessary to say the least.'

'Come now, didn't you find that encouraging?'

'I might have done if we'd come across even the slightest proof that he had a motive. We know already that Phillipa was lying when she told Leighton she'd made her will in favour of Jennifer, but it seems that when she said he knew Brodie by reputation that wasn't true either. I think that when Brodie undertook to supply the evidence she needed to get custody of Jennifer he'd no idea of Leighton's existence and thought he'd be rewarded by some permanent relationship with her, if not marriage. He obviously felt some resentment towards her, but though I may regard his defensive attitude as suspicious – he went so far as to indicate that he could provide a sort of alibi, which may or may not be true – the evidence against Osmond is far more compelling. And if I'd been feeling at all elated by the impression he made, the first two girls that Robert Osmond was embroiled with would have put a stop to that.'

'You'd better tell us,' said Sir Nicholas, and between mouthfuls his nephew proceeded to oblige him.

'Phillipa Osmond wasn't my type,' he concluded, 'and I admit to having had my doubts about our client's guilt, but these young women – the two who were in the court this afternoon – if they'd been coached in their stories someone had done an excellent job of it. In fact, I don't believe it could have been done. They speak of Osmond with complete familiarity and can both describe the flat – different aspects of it, as you might expect – in a completely convincing way.'

'Phillipa Osmond used to live there,' said Vera casually.

'So she did, but that was five years ago. If she described it to them don't you think she was taking rather a chance that Robert might have changed things?'

'A chance, yes, but not a very big one,' said Vera and glanced at her husband who took up the explanation smoothly.

'What your aunt is trying to tell you, Antony, is that if Robert Osmond had left her she'd have had the whole place turned upside down in an instant, just as Jenny does whenever you go away; but most men are only too thankful to leave things as they are.'

172

'That's very unfair, Uncle Nick,' Jenny protested. 'It's only—'

'Yes, I know, my dear, it's only consideration for your husband's feelings. Let me understand you, Antony, you felt that yesterday afternoon's witnesses were telling the truth?'

'Yes, I did, and everything I asked them just underlined that. I'd no choice, I had to put certain things to them, but their answers just made things worse. And then another thing; the one I haven't seen, Norma Martin, will be called, I suppose, on Monday morning. She's a teacher, who stands to lose her job when she gets up in court and describes her affair with Osmond. Would she risk that if she weren't telling the truth?'

'Might,' said Vera.

Sir Nicholas exchanged a smile with her down the length of the table. 'I must say, my dear, I'm inclined to agree. Think about it for a moment, Antony, think of the position as it was when the only concern was the custody suit. She could have refused her testimony, and Mrs Osmond's lawyer wouldn't have wanted a hostile witness. It's different now, she's been *sub poena'd* to appear, and I doubt if she wants to admit that she was quite ready to commit perjury.'

'What exactly are you suggesting, Uncle Nick?'

'That some consideration may have been offered to these women to make them willing to perjure themselves. The question is, what?'

'Do you really think so?' For the first time that day Antony showed some signs of animation. 'But even if they are all lying in their teeth, or whatever the phrase is,' he added gloomily, 'I don't see how it helps us. They're convincing, and there isn't a court in the world who'd have given custody to Robert Osmond after hearing what they had to say. Which gives him a first-class motive for disposing of Phillipa; he's really wrapped up in that child of his. If she hadn't gone all to pieces – and I wish I knew why that had happened – she could have told the court herself that she'd never set eyes on any of these women before . . . if you're right about that.'

'I've only been trying to suggest to you, Antony, that what you have heard so far is not conclusive so far as the charge of immorality is concerned. But don't you think you're in

173

danger of losing sight of the issue? Your client has been charged with murder, after all.'

'Yes, and he might be as pure as the driven snow in other ways and still guilty of that,' said Maitland despondently.

'In that case,' said Sir Nicholas in a bracing tone, 'let us turn to a more cheerful topic. How did our friend Paul Garfield take all this?'

'That's the one bright side of the proceedings,' Antony told him, cheering up a little. 'The poor chap is stricken to the core by these goings-on, but his sense of duty forces him to elicit all the gruesome details. It's a good thing he's not on the jury though,' he added thoughtfully. 'Conroy might talk until he was blue in the face about Osmond's morals not having anything to do with the case, but Garfield would be quite incapable of separating the two aspects of the matter. And you know, Uncle Nick, the wretched man did go out to St John's Wood that afternoon, which puts him right on the spot as far as opportunity goes. Personally I don't think we've the chance of a celluloid cat in hell.'

For once Sir Nicholas gave no outward sign of the fact that this casual manner of speaking displeased him. 'That being so we can drop the subject with a clear conscience,' he said firmly. 'Unless you care to tell us what is really bothering you, Antony.'

'Jenny's namesake. I agree with you, Uncle Nick, there isn't positive proof of Robert Osmond's immorality, or that he's a murderer for that matter, though I'm rapidly reaching the conclusion that both things are true. But there's one thing I'm not in any doubt about and that's his devotion to his daughter. And what's going to happen to the child when he's sent to prison for years?'

'Don't take the troubles of the whole world on your shoulders,' said Vera. 'Thought you said you liked Osmond,' she reminded him.

'I do, that's the worst part of it. And there's that nice girl, Amanda Herschell, too.'

'Wouldn't they let her keep Jennifer,' Jenny asked.

'Not a hope, if by "they" you mean the social service people. Oh well, there's no use thinking about it,' he said, making an obvious effort to throw off his gloom. 'Do you

174

mind if I refill my glass, Uncle Nick? I've a strong feeling I should like to get absolutely plastered.'

That had at least the advantage of diverting Sir Nicholas's attention. He had been prepared to give his nephew a certain amount of latitude, in view of his depression, but enough was enough, and that last remark was altogether too much for him to bear.

MONDAY,
the third day of the trial

I

Norma Martin was a small girl, neatly dressed, rather plain really, though with a pleasant smile and an attractive voice. She told Garfield that she lived at a boarding-house in Ealing and taught English to the third form at a nearby school. Garfield started very much as he had done with Miss Kinsman and Mrs Boyd, regretting the embarrassment that must be caused her, but her reply differed a little from the others in style if not in content.

'It's rather odd really, this question of sexual morality,' she said. 'I mean, so many people are quite promiscuous nowadays. Everybody knows but nobody cares . . . so long as they aren't found out.'

'Yes, Miss Martin, that's quite true but—'

'Well, it seems so unfair that just one lapse . . . that's all it was, I do assure you. I shall have to leave my job, of course, but it can't be helped. The eleventh commandment, you know.'

'I'm afraid—' Garfield was obviously out of his depth.

Again she didn't let him finish. 'What I said just now, Thou shalt not be found out. But I thought it was more important that Phillipa Osmond should have her daughter with her and that's why I agreed that if she had to bring a suit to obtain custody I'd give evidence for her. Now, of course, everything's changed and I can't help myself.'

Garfield seemed to be struggling visibly with himself as to how best he could regain command of the situation. 'Perhaps you will tell us first of all, Miss Martin, how long you have known Mrs Osmond?'

'I only met her once when Mr Brodie took me to see her.'

'Then you could have no special reason for wanting her to win her case for custody of her daughter?'

'No reason at all, except that I felt it was the right thing.'

'That brings us to the question of your feelings for Robert Osmond.'

To Maitland's surprise she took her time before answering and blushed in a way that he thought had gone out of fashion. 'I think I have to admit,' she said at last slowly, 'that my deeper feelings were never involved. Robert is a pleasant companion, amusing, but I didn't fall in love with him . . . not what I mean by love. On the other hand, physically he did rather sweep me off my feet. I was lonely, I suppose – my home is in the North of England – and I thought perhaps he was too and we could help each other. But Mr Brodie told me there'd been many others.'

'This relationship with Robert Osmond, when did it take place?'

'We met about three months ago and we were still seeing each other until Mr Brodie came to see me. After that I couldn't face Robert again.'

'Didn't he try to get in touch with you?'

'I just didn't answer the phone.'

'He didn't come to see you or try to get in touch with you at the school by any chance?'

'No, he knew I wouldn't like that and I think he had enough feeling for me not to do anything that would hurt me.'

'Where did you meet him?'

'I'm ashamed to say he picked me up.' She smiled a little at that, though Antony thought she was very near to tears. 'I know it's hopelessly old-fashioned to put it like that, but I can't think of any other way to describe it. I hadn't any classes that afternoon so I went into town for lunch and by chance I picked a restaurant very near to his studio.'

'Can you remember its name?'

'I think it was the Three Dukes, something like that. Robert told me he'd never been there before.'

177

That was a neat touch, it meant the story couldn't be checked. On the other hand, Antony thought, in her own way she sounded as convincing as the other two girls had done. 'And after that?' Garfield prompted.

'He asked me to spend the weekend with him at his flat.'

'And you agreed?'

'Yes, I'm afraid I did.'

'Did you tell anyone else where you would be?'

'No, I was too ashamed. Only it didn't seem like that at the time. If he'd said an hotel I'd have been horrified, but his own flat was another matter. Of course I didn't know then that Jennifer lived there too.'

'And when you did find out?'

'I don't want you to misunderstand me, Robert is very good to his daughter indeed. But he's also a man completely without inhibitions, he didn't care if she saw us making love or that she knew I spent the night sometimes . . . well, two nights on that first occasion.'

'Didn't her being there worry you?'

'It did in a way, of course, but I was too happy, I think, to worry very much. And I said to myself, she's only eight years old, she can't possibly understand. Only I'm afraid she did, I think I knew that really all the time. If you were as much with children as I am, you'd know they're far more aware of what is going on than we give them credit for. Even quite small children.'

'How did Mr Brodie get in touch with you?'

'He's a private detective,' she said, as though that explained everything.

'Yes, but he must have found out about this affair somehow.'

'This alleged affair would be more accurate, my lord,' Maitland put in, again unconsciously imitating his uncle's languid manner.

'If you feel that would be preferable. Perhaps you would re-phrase your question, Mr Garfield.'

'If your lordship pleases.' But before he could say anything Norma Martin was looking from him to Maitland accusingly. 'You don't believe me,' she said.

'Nothing was further from my thoughts, Miss Martin,'

178

Garfield assured her. 'But I'm afraid when the time comes my learned friend for the defence may have some difficult questions for you. But in the meantime, I should like to have an answer. How did Mr Brodie get in touch with you?'

'He was having Robert's flat watched, and one morning – I stayed overnight only at the weekends – someone followed me home.'

'Yes, I see. How did Jennifer take this association of yours with her father, Miss Martin?'

'I hate to say this but I think she was used to it,' said Norma. 'A nice child,' she added firmly, 'but sadly in need of a mother's care.'

When Garfield had impressed all this on the collective mind of the jury to his own satisfaction Maitland began his cross-examination by questioning the witness as to Jennifer's appearance, with which she was apparently quite familiar, and asking for a description of the flat. If she had stayed the night only at weekends there was no question of her having encountered Mrs Arbuthnot, and if Osmond had indeed been conducting a series of clandestine affairs, it wasn't surprising that he should have taken care to avoid this. Unfortunately Norma had a much more detailed memory than either of the other two girls had shown. She could describe in detail the bedroom furniture, the way things were arranged in the living-room, and – obviously being of a more domestic turn of mind – had also penetrated into the kitchen so that she could give the name of the maker of the electric stove, refrigerator, the dishwasher.

Antony listened with growing dismay, knowing that the questions had to be asked and disliking the answers he was getting very much indeed. 'You've told us, Miss Martin, that you are likely to lose your employment as a result of the evidence you have given. Can you tell me why you didn't refuse?'

'I couldn't, they issued me with a *sub poena* to say I had to attend.'

'But before that the police had questioned you, hadn't they?'

'Yes, certainly.'

'What did you tell them?'

'Why, what I've just told the court.'

'You could have avoided appearing today by saying that your previous statement had been . . . mistaken.'

'Even if it had been true, how could I have admitted to having been ready to perjure myself?'

'Yes, I agree that would have been difficult.' Nothing changed in Maitland's tone, but an echo of what had been said on Friday afternoon was insistent in his mind. 'So when you talked with Mrs Boyd and Miss Kinsman you arranged to persist with your stories?'

'I don't . . . what makes you think that?'

'I think you compared notes with them at least once since Phillipa Osmond was killed, and one of you – I don't know which – pointed out to the others that it wouldn't be good policy to admit that you had been ready and willing to commit perjury.'

That brought another flush, but her tone was even enough when she replied. 'You're calling me a liar.'

'I'm afraid I am.' In spite of himself he sounded apologetic, and perhaps it was his tone that reassured her.

'I understood you would have some questions for me, not just insults,' she said in her quiet way.

'I'm sorry that you take what I've said like that.'

'How else can I take it?' she asked with a flash of anger.

'You haven't denied that you know the other two ladies who have admitted to being involved with Mr Osmond at various times.'

'I haven't denied it and I haven't confirmed it, and there's nothing more to be said.' She hesitated for a moment, but when Maitland didn't continue with his questions she burst out as though she could no longer bear the silence, 'But you're going to say it, aren't you?'

'It doesn't amount to very much, and I have no way of making you answer. But I'd like to remind you, Miss Martin, that it isn't just a matter now of restoring the custody of a child to her mother. My client is on trial for murder.'

'You heard what I said.'

'Yes, but it worries you, doesn't it?'

'You want me to change my story?'

'My lord!' said Garfield.

180

'I should like to hear Mr Maitland's answer to that question,' said the judge.

'I only want the witness to tell the truth.'

'Then I think we must hear what, if anything, she has to say, Mr Garfield. Will you go on Miss Martin?' he added courteously to the witness.

'Would it do any good? Even if I deny knowing Mr Osmond there are still the others.'

'Even so—' said Maitland encouragingly, and left it at that.

There was a long silence. It occurred fancifully to Antony that everyone in the room must be holding their breath. 'I think I knew all along that I couldn't go on with it now,' said Norma with a distinct break in her voice. 'Only I thought . . . I'd taken money already for telling this story and if I went back on it now it would get other people into trouble besides myself.'

'I see.' Maitland's tone was gentle now, the sympathy he had felt for this girl from the beginning very evident. 'I don't want to distress you any further, Miss Martin, but I'm afraid I must ask you to spell it out for us, if not in words of one syllable, at least so that we can all understand you beyond any shadow of doubt. Are you acquainted with my client, Robert Osmond?'

'No, I never met him before, or went to his flat, or saw the little girl.' She turned so that she was facing the man in the dock directly. 'I'm sorry,' she said. 'I'm so very sorry.'

Maitland's voice recalled her attention. 'I think that will suffice, Miss Martin,' he told her, though he was very sure that his learned opponent would have something to say about that. 'You made this statement in the knowledge that you have taken an oath to tell the truth, and not wishing the record to show that you lied?'

'I did lie, and I'm more sorry than I can say, but it's the truth I'm telling you now. Will it help at all?'

'You must leave me to worry about that, Miss Martin,' Maitland told her. 'That is all I have to ask you, and I must thank you for your frankness. But I'm afraid—' His gesture towards Garfield was unnecessary. Counsel for the prosecution was already on his feet.

'You have told the court under oath a very circumstantial

story, Miss Martin,' he said coldly, 'and now you tell us it was all a lie. What made you change your mind?'

'I was worried from the beginning—'

'Naturally enough. You mentioned, I believe, that you felt it possible you would lose your employment as a consequence of giving evidence here.'

'Yes, but that wasn't the reason. I'd been telling myself that if Mr Osmond did kill his wife my story couldn't harm him. But then suddenly I saw that I hadn't the right to judge him, and if I felt he'd been convicted because of the lies I told about him I'd never be able to face myself again.'

'That,' said Garfield, at his most sarcastic, 'is a very affecting sentiment. But I'm afraid we can't just leave it there. You are telling us that you accepted a bribe to give evidence injurious to the accused at the custody hearing that his wife – I should say his former wife, now deceased – was proposing to bring against him. I'm afraid I must ask you to give us a few more details of this – this transaction. You told us, for instance, that Mr Brodie approached you. If this was not in consequence of his having followed you home from Robert Osmond's flat, how did you come to know him?'

'I don't have a telephone . . . too expensive,' said Norma. And added quickly, seeing Garfield's affronted look, 'And that isn't an inconsequential remark, it's quite relevant to what you asked me. And I can't explain how I met Mr Brodie without telling you a little first about why I was willing to accept money to do such a dreadful thing.'

'You are about to tell us, no doubt, that your motive was in some way unselfish.'

'I'm afraid I don't quite know where to draw the line between selfishness and unselfishness,' she told him. 'If it's unselfish to care desperately what happens to one's parents, then, yes, that was what I was about to tell you.'

Maitland was finding himself torn between his own curiosity, and sympathy for the witness. Perhaps he should intervene . . . but his mind had hardly formulated the thought before Derek was thrusting a note in front of him. *Don't!* He glanced at his junior enquiringly and caught Stringer's low voiced murmur, 'If she's telling the truth now

182

it would be better for her to get it out of her system.'

Meanwhile Garfield was continuing his examination. 'I think perhaps you had better explain that to us, Miss Martin.'

'If I must. My father lost his job and my mother needed an operation. They haven't many savings . . . enough to keep them going, we hope, until he finds something else to do, but nothing beyond that.'

'I was under the impression that the National Health Service had been instituted to help in just such cases,' said Garfield.

'Yes, of course it is, but the trouble is that you can't choose your surgeon and there's a particular man in Leeds who's noted for being successful in cases like my mother's. Also I wanted her to have a private room, or at least a semi-private one, and dad's hospital insurance didn't cover him for more than three months after he left work. So you see I was wide open to temptation, and I'm afraid I succeeded in persuading myself at first that the little girl would be better off with her mother. But now it's different, you must see that.'

'And you must realise, Miss Martin, that you are asking us to disregard the evidence that Mr Brodie has given us—'

'And the others as well. Laurie Kinsman and Ella Boyd,' she explained, seeing his deliberately incredulous look.

'That does not exactly incline me to give any ready credence to your present story,' Garfield told her.

'I'm doing my best to explain.'

'I asked you how Mr Brodie got in touch with you and you informed me you had no telephone. You also said that was not an irrelevant remark, but I'm afraid I don't see—'

'I've told you why I needed money, and I tried to get a bank loan. I knew dad couldn't, but after all I have a job. Only they turned me down, and I was using the telephone box on the corner to call home to let them know. I live in a boarding-house, and the only phone there is in the hall, much too public, but I can't have pulled the door of the telephone box properly closed, or perhaps the latch was defective and it slipped open again. Anyway, Mr Brodie was waiting to make a call himself and he'd obviously heard everything I said. He was very polite when he spoke to me . . . he said he hadn't

183

meant to overhear but as he had done perhaps he could help me. And he asked me to go to his office the following Saturday morning.'

'And you went?'

'Yes, I did. I didn't see how there could be any harm in it. And Ella Boyd and Laurie Kinsman were there. Mr Brodie explained what he wanted of us and offered us all quite a large sum of money to be paid immediately and I honestly didn't think it would ever get as far as court and having to give evidence under oath. I don't know what the others said here on Friday, but at the time they agreed quite readily, and I'm ashamed to say that after I'd thought it over for a while – all that money! – I did too. So then Mr Brodie went out of the room and came back with Mrs Osmond. And they rehearsed us one by one in our stories and she gave us some particulars of the flat, and said her husband would certainly not have changed anything around, he wasn't that sort. And it had been re-decorated just before she left, and she was quite sure he'd have left everything just as it was. And Mr Brodie said it was important when we were questioned that we mustn't all remember exactly the same things and . . . well, I suppose you could say we shared what Mrs Osmond had said between us. That's all really, except that I got the impression that Mrs Osmond and Mr Brodie knew each other very well.'

'That hardly concerns us, Miss Martin.'

'No, of course not. I'm sorry, I expect I'm telling this very badly. Phillipa Osmond was very persuasive about how badly she wanted her little girl with her, and I think if I hadn't agreed already I would have done after I'd talked to her. Only later Laurie Kinsman said she didn't believe a word of it.'

'You are telling us now that, far from never having met Miss Kinsman and Mrs Boyd, you encountered them that day, and perhaps on other occasions?'

'Well, we all left Mr Brodie's office together, and Laurie suggested that we should have lunch. I felt so miserable about the whole business that nothing seemed to matter so I agreed. But we didn't meet again until after Mrs Osmond's death.'

'You are telling us that you had some conversation over lunch that first day, however?'

'Yes, indeed we did, rather a frank conversation if you

want to know. Laurie is a very forthcoming sort of person. She said we were all in it together and ought to get to know one another. I didn't really want to, but the other two may have met again, I don't know.'

'You have told us about your ostensible motive for taking part in this – in this—'

'Conspiracy,' said Maitland helpfully and far from inaudibly.

'My lord, I really must protest my learned friend's interventions. We have no proof—'

'I might just as well complain, my lord,' said Maitland, coming to his feet, 'that my friend is cross-examining his own witness.'

'I could always ask for permission to treat her as hostile,' Garfield flashed back, forgetting for a moment to address his remarks to the judge.

'As she is answering your questions so willingly that would, indeed, be unreasonable,' Maitland adjured him. 'However, if the word conspiracy seems to you to be premature, I will withdraw it.'

'If you gentlemen have quite finished,' said Conroy coldly, 'perhaps, Mr Garfield, you will continue with your examination of your witness.'

'If your lordship pleases.' He waited rather pointedly until his opponent had seated himself again. 'I should like you to understand, Miss Martin, that I shall be recalling Mrs Boyd and Miss Kinsman after your evidence is concluded.'

'So that you can check up on me,' said Norma Martin. 'That's reasonable, I suppose, but I am telling you the truth now.'

'Then let us have your version of that talk you had together over lunch. Did anything emerge of a personal nature, or concerning their reasons for agreeing to what my learned friend is pleased to term a conspiracy.'

'Laurie was quite open about her motive, it was just for the cash. She smiled at us and said she didn't care about the money really but she did like the things that it could buy. It was different for Ella Boyd, I don't think she cared about the money at all, though when Laurie pressed her she did admit it would come in useful. She wanted a divorce and her husband was unwilling to give her one and she thought if it all came out about her affair with Mr Osmond her husband would believe it and be so disgusted that he'd agree to what she wanted. And both of them would have preferred the matter to go into court, because we'd been promised extra money if that happened. I mean, that was Laurie's reason, Ella just wanted the publicity.'

'Did they also tell you at this hypothetical meeting how they met Stewart Brodie?'

'Laurie said she'd known him for some time. They had mutual friends and used to be asked to the same parties. I did say to her that I thought it was rather risky for him to have approached her out of the blue like that, but she just looked at me in surprise and opened her eyes very wide and said, "Why?" I tried to explain, but she interrupted me and said, as if it was the most natural thing in the world, "Everybody knows I'm a gold-digger. I make no secret of it. I think it was quite natural that Stew should think of me." '

'And Mrs Boyd?'

'That was quite different. She'd talked to her lawyer about getting a divorce and I think he told her it would be difficult to obtain one quickly if Mr Boyd didn't agree and if she couldn't produce any evidence that he was an unsatisfactory husband. I gathered he gave her Mr Brodie's name, and she went to see him and told him the whole story. It was after he reported to her that there was nothing to be found against her husband that he suggested this course to her. Mr Maitland called it a conspiracy, and he was quite right about that, but I think the idea was Mrs Osmond's in the first place. After all, she was the one who'd walked out on her husband and child, though what Mr Brodie said about that was that she'd found it quite impossible to live with Robert . . . with Mr Osmond. You see how well he had us trained. I had several more sessions with him and I suppose the others did too. And after I talked to Laurie, who was so certain that Mrs Osmond's story about missing her little girl was a pack of lies, I began to think about it and wondered if she wasn't right. Perhaps it wasn't so much that Phillipa Osmond wanted custody of Jennifer as that she wanted revenge on her husband for something. She talked as if she hated him.'

186

'Thank you, Miss Martin.' Garfield's tone turned a conventional phrase into an insult. 'That is all I have to ask you. My Lord, I should like—'

'One moment.' Maitland was beginning to feel like a jack-in-the box. 'Before my learned friend calls or recalls his next witness, my lord, I should like your permission to ask Miss Martin one – no, two – further questions.'

'If you must, Mr Maitland,' said Mr Justice Conroy in a long-suffering voice.

'I shall not delay matters long, my lord. Miss Martin, all this happened some time ago. How is your mother now?'

'She's very well,' said Norma with a suddenly radiant look. 'The operation was a complete success.'

'And has your father found another job?'

'He's been promised one soon. But I've been feeling for a while that I ought to go home and look after them as well as I can. So you needn't worry about my losing my job here because perhaps nobody up north will read about the trial. I don't know what the headmaster of the school will feel about giving me a reference, but he's a nice man. He may just say I'm a good teacher and leave it at that.'

'Then we must just hope for the best.' Privately he felt the whole country would eventually hear about the case. But as he sat down again he was realising only too vividly how little he had gained.

Garfield, as was only to be expected, asked and obtained permission to recall the three previous witnesses. Laurie Kinsman was the first, but she had of course heard what Norma Martin had said and must have made up her mind that nothing of it could be proved, as far as she was concerned at least. So she stuck to her story about her affair with Robert Osmond and even embellished it a little. Maitland did his best to shake her, but was unable to do so. Ella Boyd started in the same way, denying everything that had been said, a position which Garfield naturally was only too willing to accept. In her case, however, the defence was able to bring up the matter of her prospective divorce, asking the name of the solicitor, and suggesting that enquiries made of him would confirm Miss Martin's story at least in part, to which she assented readily enough, though still maintaining that the rest

187

of her story was true. The fact that she had wanted a divorce had really nothing to do with the case, and after all, she added defiantly, her objective had been achieved and there had been quite as much publicity as she could have wished. 'You mean, I suppose,' said Maitland rather dryly, 'that perjury will prove quite as offensive to your husband as adultery would have been.' And sat down while she was still protesting that that wasn't what she meant at all.

'But it won't really get us much further forward,' he agreed with Geoffrey as they and Derek were lunching together. 'Whatever Phillipa's reasons were for wanting Jennifer, I'm convinced they weren't unselfish ones. But Robert was desperately fond of the child and he must have realised he wasn't going to be able to keep her when those three told their stories. The fact that he knew it was a frame-up would just add to the bitterness he felt towards his former wife. As Garfield, when he comes to his closing address, will no doubt make very clear to the jury.'

'Now don't start blaming yourself for bringing out one small section of the truth,' said Geoffrey. 'The jury aren't lawyers, and for all we know the fact that one of the prosecution's witnesses didn't come up to proof will have a disproportionate effect on them.'

Antony shook his head. 'Not when Conroy and Garfield are finished with them,' he said gloomily. 'Still, it had to be done.'

'There was one chap among the spectators who seemed to be taking a particular interest,' said Derek, so casually that Maitland immediately suspected an attempt to distract his attention. 'He was in the front row, and leaning so far over the railing I thought he might fall.'

As an attempt to change the subject – if that was what it had been – it was a dismal failure. 'He'd more right than most to be interested,' said Geoffrey shortly. 'Matthew Leighton,' he amplified in response to Antony's enquiring look. 'He was there last week too.'

'Poor chap. This morning's evidence wouldn't make good hearing for him,' said Maitland. 'If he believed Norma Martin, of course,' he added. 'I daresay he didn't.'

II

The luncheon recess had obviously given Stewart Brodie an opportunity to think over his position, and this had obviously led him, as Maitland put it later, to adopt a course of stout denial. However circumstantial Norma Martin's story may have been the parts of it that could be proved did nothing to contradict his previous evidence, and the same might be said of the fact that Ella Boyd admitted to having wanted to shock her husband into granting her a quick divorce. Garfield naturally didn't press him very hard when he re-examined; whoever was believed, Robert Osmond's motive was there for all to see, a fact upon which he would be only too ready to elaborate in his closing address. Meanwhile, the whole affair only too obviously offended him, there was nothing to be said as far as he could see in favour of any of the people concerned. He relinquished the witness to renewed cross-examination with obvious relief.

Maitland, however, in consultation with Horton and Stringer, had decided there was nothing to be gained, and might even be something to lose, in trying to shake the witness's story. He had, however, a couple of questions to ask, and shot the first at Brodie almost before he was fully on his feet.

'I have been wondering, Mr Brodie, why you accosted Jennifer Osmond when she came out of school the afternoon before her mother's death, and what you said to her on that occasion.'

There was a pause. Maitland could almost see the wheels going round . . . how much can be proved? 'I met her at her mother's request. Phillipa felt it kinder to prepare the way for a meeting. I gave the child a – a loving message, and that was all there was to it.'

'Thank you. Would it surprise you to know that this innocent encounter upset Jennifer very much?'

'It certainly would.'

'The court will remember Chief Inspector Eversley's evidence in this connection.' He had gathered his gown about him and started to sit down when his second question took the witness unawares. 'Mr Brodie, how long had you and Mrs Phillipa Osmond been lovers?'

Stewart Brodie was still stuttering his denials while Garfield objected vociferously to the question, when counsel for the defence actually seated himself and allowed the battle to rage around him. Was anything gained? He didn't know, but there was a chance perhaps that some small seed of doubt might be planted in the mind of the jury.

Wilfred Begg's evidence held no surprises for the defence, and was obviously everything that the prosecution could have hoped it to be. He described his first meeting with Phillipa Osmond, when she consulted him about getting a divorce from her husband. 'She'd been separated from him,' he told the court, 'for two years, and hoped her application would go through uncontested, but that was something to which Robert Osmond would not at first agree. Mrs Osmond had previously been reticent about the reason for her leaving her husband, and as it seemed that he was, to a degree at least, the aggrieved party, I was doubtful of the outcome of the action. But when she broke down and told me he had been consistently unfaithful to her, as well as treating her with great unkindness at times, I realised that we could cite constructive desertion.' At this point, he obviously remembered that the phrase might not be familiar to the jury and added, 'In other words, that Mr Osmond's behaviour had been responsible for her leaving him.'

'And did the case in fact go to court?' Garfield asked.

'No. I got in touch with Mr Osmond's solicitor and arranged a meeting between the two parties at which we would also be present. I should tell you that Mr Osmond denied her allegations, though he seemed to be taken aback when she asserted that they were capable of proof, at least as far as his conduct with other women was concerned; but I still think that if she had not consented to leave the child, Jennifer, in his custody he would have fought the case.'

'You would say then that he is devoted to his daughter?'

'Oh yes, indeed, that was quite obvious.'

'So now we've come to more recent events. Mrs Osmond decided that she now wished to have her daughter to live with her?'

'Yes. Perhaps I should tell you that I had in the meantime acted for her in a number of business matters, so it was natural she should consult me again.'

'Did she give you a reason, Mr Begg, for her change of mind?'

'She was a professional woman, an architect, and she had told me previously that she felt in the circumstances it would have been unfair for her to insist on having the child with her. The decision, of course, had been a very difficult one to make, but she felt that in Jennifer's best interests she should leave her with her father. But now her position was such that she was able to retire, and devote her full time to bringing up her daughter. Also she was to re-marry, a wealthy and respected man, who was as eager as she was for this arrangement to be made. She was aware however of her former husband's obsession with the child, and knowing of his previous behaviour had thought it as well to make enquiries about his present way of life. She was horrified to find that he had not only continued his extra-marital affairs, but had conducted them in his own home . . . a small flat which he shared with his eight-year-old daughter.'

'And then?'

'She provided me with the names of the witnesses, three women and the enquiry agent who had looked into the matter for her. Naturally I interviewed them, and satisfied myself that our case was sound.'

'But there was, I understand, a meeting between the two parties on this occasion also.'

'Yes, this time at Mr Osmond's insistence. The meeting was, I'm afraid, conducted in a somewhat acrimonious spirit, at least on Mr Osmond's part.' He went on to describe in detail what had been said, including what he called Robert Osmond's threat to his former wife, and the fact that he had had to be restrained from physically attacking Phillipa.

'You had no doubts yourself,' asked Garfield when he had finished, 'that if the case went to court your client would be successful in regaining custody of her child?'

'No doubt at all. In my own mind I felt that Mr Osmond's anger was proof enough of that.'

That brought an objection from Maitland, though he was well aware that it was too late to do much good. Naturally Garfield went through the details of that last interview several times . . . he was the only counsel Antony knew of who was able to do this without apparently wearying the jury, or bringing out any signs of impatience on the part of the judge. But at last he sat down again and the defence was able to take over the cross-examination.

Again it was Maitland who rose to face the witness. 'I wonder, Mr Begg, whether you would agree that it was a strange arrangement for Mrs Osmond to agree to . . . that her husband should be left to look after her daughter for five years after she left him.'

'In the ordinary way I should have done so, and I realise that Mrs Osmond found the arrangement distressing, but she felt that it would be better for Jennifer, as she herself would have had so little time to devote to her care.'

'It seems to me that the same difficulty must have been experienced by my client, perhaps to an even greater degree. He also had his professional duties to attend to.'

'Mrs Osmond's point – which I may say I felt quite reasonable – was that it was easier for a man to obtain housekeeping assistance than it was for a woman.'

'Even though both were equally able to pay for it?'

'She felt that a – a motherly woman would be more likely to take a man and child in that situation . . . shall we say under her wing?'

'We will put it whatever way you please, Mr Begg, but I still feel it was an odd arrangement. You told my friend in the course of his examination that you had taken care of Mrs Osmond's affairs for at least the last three years.'

'That is so.'

'Did she make a will during that time?'

'Yes, certainly. She had, I understand, previously left everything to her husband, but in the new circumstances that was quite unsuitable.'

'I think, my lord,' said Maitland, turning towards the judge, 'you may consider that the matter of Mrs Osmond's financial affairs and the way her estate is disposed of is not irrelevant.'

'I take it, Mr Maitland, you wish to question the witness on these matters.'

'Yes, my lord, I do.'

'In that case, I shall make no objection.'

'I'm obliged to your lordship.' Antony turned back to the witness. 'Perhaps you will tell us what you know of Mrs Osmond's financial situation, Mr Begg.'

'Enough to tell you that she could not be called a provident woman,' said Wilfred Begg slowly, and it seemed regretfully. 'She was, I believe, highly regarded in her profession and certainly her income was a high one. But she spent lavishly, and on enquiry I have found that her cash resources amount to no more than about fifteen thousand pounds on deposit at her bank. There is also, of course, her share in the partnership, but I believe the arrangement was such that the surviving partner had the option of buying out the other's interest at quite a low price.'

Almost, if not precisely, the same words that Geoffrey had reported him as using in the Magistrate's Court. Antony remembered his uncle's query on that occasion. 'No stocks, bonds or other investments?'

'Not so far as I have been able to discover.'

'Let us suppose, Mr Begg, that Mrs Osmond had wished to make certain large payments in cash, so that they would not be traceable to the recipients—'

The witness did not even let him finish. 'It would be a difficult if not impossible thing to prove. She was in the habit of drawing cash for expenses that seem to have been considerable.'

'You have examined her bank accounts, Mr Begg. I am referring to a period shortly before her death.'

'Nothing out of the ordinary, I assure you.'

No help there then, in confirming Norma Martin's story. 'To whom did she leave her estate?' Maitland asked.

'To her brother, Mr Rudolph Spencer.'

'Thank you, Mr Begg. May we now return to the meeting between my client and Mrs Osmond which took place at your office on the sixteenth of March last? What was your

193

impression of Mrs Osmond's attitude at that meeting?'

'She was extremely self-confident.'

'Because she felt she could prove that my client was not a proper person to have the care of a child of Jennifer's age?'

'Yes, of course. There was no doubt about it, hearing the evidence no court could have failed to feel as she did and to give her custody.'

'Would it surprise you to know, Mr Begg, that one of these witnesses you speak of, giving evidence in this court this very morning, has denied categorically having ever even met Robert Osmond?'

'It would surprise me very much indeed,' said the witness sharply.

'Nevertheless, I assure you it is true. Now you have told us that at this meeting Phillipa Osmond seemed completely confident that she would be able to get her own way. Would you agree that she taunted her husband repeatedly with the hopelessness of his situation?'

Wilfred Begg thought about that for a moment. 'I suppose I must agree to that,' he said. 'There was obviously a good deal of ill-feeling between them.'

'So that when she asked him whether it would not be better to give in gracefully and he replied he'd see her in hell first, wouldn't you also agree that this was a very natural response for him to make in the heat of the moment?'

'He was certainly very angry, but I took the remark as a threat.'

'That, of course, we must leave for the jury to decide. If we are to take it literally . . . but I wonder if there is one person in this courtroom who has not at some time in his life made a remark in a fit of anger to which it would be unfair to give a literal interpretation.' He flashed a quick smile in the direction of the jury box and then turned to address the judge. 'I'm excluding the ladies from this speculation of mine, my lord. In my experience they're far less likely than we are to give vent to sudden irrational bursts of anger.'

'I'm sure you're right, Mr Maitland,' said Conroy with an air of benignity which quite unnerved counsel. 'The question is, does Mr Begg agree with you?'

'I'm afraid I must still say I took it for a threat, my lord.'

'There is also the question,' said Conroy, obviously enjoying himself, 'which I am sure Mr Maitland is going to bring up at any moment, as to whether the prisoner was actually about to attack the deceased or not.'

'I can only say, my lord, that he made a movement towards her which I construed as threatening, as also I believe did his solicitor, Mr Horton, who grabbed his arm to hold him back. The accused denied any violent intention, of course, but that was only to be expected.'

'Very well. I think that covers the matter very adequately, Mr Maitland, would you not agree?'

'Except that I should like to ask Mr Begg, my lord, whether he warned his client—'

'She had had every opportunity of observing the prisoner's attitude for herself,' said the witness rather huffily.

'All the same—'

'No, Mr Maitland,' said Conroy firmly.

It was obviously hopeless to persist. 'If your lordship pleases,' said Antony, with a meekness which was only too obviously assumed. 'I have no further questions for this witness,' he added abruptly and sat down with a swirl of his gown.

For once Garfield seemed ready to let the witness go without re-examining, and Mr Justice Conroy, after consulting his turnip of a watch, decided it was a little too early to adjourn.

Michael Ringfield, the next and last of the prosecution's witnesses, looked young to be retired, though that was how he described himself. He and his sister had a flat on the third floor of the building where Phillipa Osmond had resided and had known her since she came to live there five years before.

As far as Garfield was concerned the witness was there for one purpose and one purpose only, and he lost no time in coming to the point. 'I must ask you, Mr Ringfield, to cast your mind back to the afternoon of the seventeenth of March last.'

'The day Phillipa was killed? That's easy because it's not a thing you're likely to forget, whereas I must admit I take very little notice of what day it is now.'

'I'm glad it is so clear in your mind,' said Garfield. 'That

195

should make it easy for you to describe for us what happened.'

'Nothing happened exactly.'

'What you did and what you saw that afternoon,' explained Garfield patiently.

'I went out as I always do to pick up an evening paper.'

'At what time was that?'

'Now, there I can't help you, not for certain. I never go before three o'clock, because there's always a chance the chap on the corner won't have got them yet, but I don't suppose it was much after that that I went along.'

'Did you notice anything in particular as you walked to the corner?'

'No, I didn't. There was a cold wind blowing, and it was in my face as I went. I bought the paper and had a word with the chap who sells them, which I always do because I'm a regular customer of his, but when I turned to walk back it was different because the wind was behind me and I took my time to look around.'

'And what did you see?'

'Robert Osmond standing across the road from the building I live in. He seemed to be watching the door.'

'Now we must get this very clear, Mr Ringfield. Is the man you saw in this room?'

'Yes, certainly. The – the accused,' said the witness as though the description embarrassed him.

'There must have been a number of people about. How did you come to notice him so particularly?'

'Well, it wasn't the sort of day for standing about, but there he was. I think it was his stillness that caught my eye. There isn't a bus stop there or anywhere near it, and though there's a row of shops he didn't seem to have any interest in them. In fact, he was standing with his back to a bookshop window. But what made me notice him particularly was that I recognised him.'

'Was he in the habit of visiting Mrs Osmond? Had you met him there?'

'No, nothing like that. I know there are people who have what they call an amicable divorce and still stay friends, but from what Phillipa said it hadn't been like that at all. But she showed us a photograph of him one day.'

'Are you telling us that in spite of what you just said she had one on display?'

'Oh no, that wasn't what I meant at all. We were talking . . . I think it was about the time she got her divorce, and I don't remember exactly what was said except that it wasn't complimentary . . . to her husband I mean. And then she said something like, "One look at him would prejudice the court in my favour," and she went to a drawer and took out this photograph and showed us. She laughed then and said, "Look what I had to put up with!" And it happened that she left the photograph on the table near me after she'd handed it round, so I got a good look at him. I admit I was curious.'

That wasn't the end of the examination of course, each point had to be repeated until Garfield was quite sure it was imprinted on the mind of each of the jurors. But at last it was over and Maitland was at liberty to take over the questioning.

'There is just one thing that puzzles me, Mr Ringfield,' he said slowly, 'and before I mention it I should perhaps make it clear to my learned friend for the prosecution that the defence does not deny Robert Osmond's presence in St John's Wood that afternoon. The court will hear his explanation when he himself gives evidence. But you told us – did you not?—' he added, turning to the witness, 'that you saw the photograph from which you recognised my client at about the time of his divorce.'

'That is as I remember it.'

'Yet from this one occasion three years ago you were in no doubt that it was he you saw.'

'No doubt at all. I thought, that chap looks familiar, and I took a second look. It isn't the sort of face you can forget easily, and of course I wondered what he was doing there. But naturally it was only when I knew what had happened that I realised the significance of what I'd seen.'

'Naturally,' Maitland agreed smoothly. 'You tell us you had known Mrs Osmond for five years. Did you know her well?'

'My lord,' said Garfield, puzzled, 'is this relevant?'

'I must leave Mr Maitland to tell us that,' said Conroy.

'My lord, we have heard very little about the lady whom

my client is accused of killing. Surely my learned friend would not grudge the court some further information about her.'

'Would you, Mr Garfield?'

'Not if it was relevant, my lord.'

'All the same I think . . . I'm sorry, Mr Garfield, I cannot sustain your objection. You may proceed, Mr Maitland.'

'I'm obliged to your lordship. Should I repeat my question, Mr Ringfield, or do you remember what I wanted to know?'

'How well we knew Phillipa.'

'We, Mr Ringfield?'

'I'm speaking of my sister as well as myself. At first it was just a matter of exchanging greetings if we encountered one another in the lobby, but after a while we began to know her better. I believe my sister extended the first invitation, when we were having a get-together with some of our neighbours, but after that we began to visit one another more frequently and to know her better.'

'Well enough, after two years, to discuss her divorce?'

'Phillipa was not at all – not at all a reticent woman. The subject caused her no embarrassment, and I think she was glad to have someone she could speak to about it.'

'Yes, very understandable. On that occasion at least she spoke of her husband disparagingly?'

'Yes, as I remember it that was how she came to show us his photograph.'

'And yet she had left her daughter in his custody.'

'I'm sure she felt it was best for the child.'

'Is that what she told you?'

'No, I wasn't at the time aware of the child's existence.'

'Indeed? When did you learn it?'

'I suppose about seven or eight months ago.'

'At the time she wanted to obtain custody?'

'She told us that was what was in her mind.'

'And did she explain her previous indifference to what was happening to Jennifer?'

'She said she had felt it was best for her. Single-parent families were always difficult, but even more so for the woman than for the man.'

'Didn't that strike you as rather an original point of view?'

198

'Not at all. She spoke of little Jennifer so lovingly that I could be in no doubt it had been a grief to her to be apart from her for so long.'

'Did Mrs Osmond have many friends?'

'I believe so. I'm not in a position to say for certain.'

Garfield was on his feet. Mr Justice Conroy inclined his head in his direction. 'You need say nothing, Mr Garfield. I had already reached the opinion that this line of questioning has gone far enough.'

'My lord, I fail to see—' Maitland began, but the judge interrupted him ruthlessly.

'It seems you wish to show that Mrs Osmond was an unnatural mother,' he said. 'I'm in complete agreement with Mr Garfield that that has nothing to do with the case, unless you are preparing the ground for a change of plea.'

'No, my lord.'

'I should have said, a qualification, by claiming that your client was suffering from diminished responsibility at the time of the crime.'

'Nothing of the sort, my lord.' Antony achieved a tone of scandalised incredulity. 'My client's plea of Not Guilty is quite unequivocal.'

'I am pleased to hear it, Mr Maitland. Have you any other questions to put to this witness?'

'No, my lord, not if this line of enquiry is barred to me.'

'Mr Garfield?'

'I do not wish to re-examine, my lord.'

'Then we will adjourn.'

The routine instructions as to when they would assemble the following morning were lost on Maitland, who twisted round urgently to speak to his instructing solicitor. 'You said you'd had a word with – what was her name? – that chap's sister.'

'Stella Ringfield. Yes, I spoke to her briefly.'

'Do you think it will be the slightest use calling her?'

'If Conroy won't permit questions on anything to do with Phillipa I see no reason at all,' said Geoffrey. 'She'd be in and out of the witness box in two minutes flat, and the only result would be to irritate the judge.'

'Yes, I suppose so. The thing is, if the flat was cleaned

thoroughly on Tuesday and the fingerprint evidence means anything, they were with Phillipa the evening before she died. Did her opinion of her correspond with that of her brother?'

'No, not at all. She said Phillipa led a rackety sort of life, and when she finally told them about Jennifer she – Miss Ringfield – didn't believe a word of her story of being devoted to the child. But I have to add that it was quite obvious that Ringfield had shown some signs of being smitten by Phillipa's charms, so her opinion could hardly be called unbiased. She has probably become completely dependent on her brother's company . . . after all, they're neither of them exactly young.'

'Why did she continue the friendship then?'

'At a guess because she thought Ringfield would do so with or without her.'

'I see.'

'But you can't call her, Antony, it would be worse than useless.'

The court was beginning to clear by now. 'You're right, of course, Geoffrey,' said Antony rather wearily. I'd like a word with our client though before they take him away, if that can be arranged. Do you want to join our discussion, Derek?'

'No,' said Stringer firmly. 'I've a very good idea of what you want to say to him, but I don't envy you the job.'

The three men met a few minutes later in one of the small interview rooms below the court. 'I'm glad to have the chance of thanking you,' said Osmond by way of greeting, 'for getting that girl to tell the truth this morning. They can't say now, can they, that Phillipa would have won the case?'

Antony, having been only too well aware of a sort of simmering excitement on the part of his client throughout the afternoon's proceedings, exchanged a rueful look with Geoffrey. 'I'm afraid you mustn't rely too much on Miss Martin's change of evidence,' he said.

'But why not? And I think it was damned clever of you—'

'It wasn't anything of the sort, she was obviously only too ready to come out with the true story, it wasn't anything to do with me.'

Robert Osmond was suddenly very still. 'Are you saying

you still don't believe me?' he asked. 'And why shouldn't I think it will make a difference?'

'To take those two questions in turn, I should perhaps explain to you once again that what Mr Horton and I believe doesn't matter at all. But if it's any consolation to you, I do believe Miss Martin was telling the truth at last. The trouble is you're being tried for murder, not for immorality.'

'But they've been citing that as my motive.'

'Not exactly. I hate to dash your hopes, Mr Osmond, but there are a number of different ways that Garfield can deal with this when he makes his final speech to the jury. You see, when we first met, when the custody suit was the only thing we were worried about, after hearing the evidence I don't see how Mr Horton could have advised you except to try to come to some compromise with your former wife. If you'd insisted on going to court you'd have lost, so what difference does one of the witnesses telling the truth *now* make to your motive *then*?'

'I hadn't looked at it that way.' He was silent for a moment and then looked up and achieved a smile. 'I admit I was hoping . . . but I'm grateful to you for putting me straight.'

'At least that was the last of the prosecution's witnesses,' said Antony. 'I shall be opening the defence in the morning, and I shan't say much in my first address so don't think I'm giving up. It's much more effective to hit them with everything we've got at the end than to weary the court with a twice-told tale.'

'No, I understand that. What a queer chap that Ringfield is.'

'What did you think of him?'

'He seemed to be ready to take Phillipa entirely on her own evaluation. Do you really think he could have recognised me from seeing my photograph three years ago?'

'The question is purely academic, as you don't deny you were there.'

'No, but I might have done if I'd thought I could have got away with it. Well, you know that, of course, because I lied to you in the beginning. I've had a good deal of time to think lately and I've been wondering whether, if you'd gone on believing me, I'd have been able to bring myself to repeat that lie under oath.'

201

'Did you come to any decision either way?' asked Antony lightly.

'I don't know. I kept thinking of Jennifer, you see. I'd have proved myself a coward, willing to say anything to save his own skin, and I don't want her to have a father like that.'

'There is every likelihood that you will see Miss Herschell in court tomorrow,' Geoffrey put in. 'If her evidence is reached, as I should think it will be.'

'Have you talked to her? Is Jennifer well?' The questions came so eagerly that it was obvious he had been reining himself in not to ask them before.

'One or the other of us has been in touch with her constantly,' Geoffrey assured him. 'Jennifer is quite well . . . but missing you,' he added, though he had as a matter of fact no idea whether that was true or not.

'I wonder,' said Osmond thoughtfully. 'Has she ever spoken yet about what upset her so?'

'Not a word,' said Maitland. 'But there have been no more upsets, Miss Herschell assures me, only a continued silence about what happened to her on those two days.'

'Poor child. And now what sort of a life will she have while I'm in prison?'

'I've taken away your last hope, haven't I?' asked Maitland roughly, and jumped to his feet and began to pace up and down the narrow room behind his chair.

'It was a very small hope, and it didn't last very long,' said Robert, almost humorously. 'I suppose there's no chance of Amanda being able to keep charge of her?'

'She asked me that herself and I had to tell her I didn't think there was the faintest hope of it.'

'Then at best Jennifer will be brought up among strangers, and Amanda will be lonely. Oh God, how I've let everyone down!' He slammed his hand down on the table.

'Easy does it!' said Maitland, coming to stand with his hands resting lightly on the back of his chair and looking down at his client. 'I have a feeling – a very strong feeling, Mr Osmond – that no action of yours brought this situation about.'

That brought a moment's silence. Geoffrey did his best to look non-committal, but Robert was frankly staring. 'I've

202

made a complete mess, not only of my own life but of theirs,' he said at last. 'And you tell me I'm not to blame.'

'Yes, I do. I think if there's been any letting down in this business it's I who have failed you.' He stood a moment longer and then made his way to the door, saying over his shoulder, 'And don't ask me what I mean by that because I don't know. But I'll see you in court tomorrow.'

Geoffrey didn't catch up with him until he had reached the street. 'So you've made up your mind at last,' he said, falling into step beside his friend. 'I thought it was only a matter of time once Norma Martin went back on her evidence.'

'It wasn't that,' said Antony, almost absently. 'But while we're on the subject, do we still need to call Amanda Herschell? After all it turned out that all she could say for certain was that she'd seen no evidence that Osmond had been entertaining another woman while he knew her.'

'I think,' said Geoffrey deliberately, 'there's every reason to call her.'

'What . . . oh I see,' said Antony, enlightened.

Nothing more was said until they reached the place where Geoffrey had left his car. 'I'm not going back to the office,' he said then. 'Can I give you a lift?'

'Thank you, Geoffrey, but no. I think I'll just look in at chambers on the off chance that Uncle Nick may still be there.' Something in his tone made Horton stand staring after him until his tall figure had disappeared round the next corner. Then he sighed and started to walk towards his car, fumbling for his keys as he went.

III

He hadn't really expected to find his uncle still in chambers. It was growing late and the clerks' office was dark, but there was a rim of light under Sir Nicholas's door. Antony tapped and went in without waiting for a summons, and only when he was half way across the room realised that he was lucky not to have interrupted a late-running conference. Sir

203

Nicholas took off his spectacles, sat back in his chair and looked his nephew over rather closely. He had obviously been working, and the papers on his desk were in their usual state of confusion . . . usual, that is, if he had had five minutes alone with them. Antony went across and began mechanically to straighten them.

'So one of the prosecution's witnesses didn't come up to proof,' Sir Nicholas observed, watching him. 'Or so Halloran tells me, and he's generally well informed. I hope you realise it won't do your case a hap'orth of good in the long run.'

'Of course I do, Uncle Nick. I've been over it all exhaustively with Geoffrey and Derek, and also had the pleasure of explaining the situation to our client after we left court. But that wasn't what I wanted to see you about.'

Sir Nicholas, who had been about to invite Antony to accompany him home, assumed the air of one who had all the time in the world at his disposal. 'Something is worrying you, Antony,' he said. A statement, not a question. Maitland ceased his task of creating order out of chaos and raised his eyes quickly to meet his uncle's.

'Is it so obvious?' he asked.

'To me, yes. But if you've realised all along that even if this girl is telling the truth—'

'I'm sure she is.'

'—your client's motive is no less strong, and it could even be argued that with resentment added to the fear of losing his daughter—'

'It isn't that, Uncle Nick.' Maitland interrupted for the second time, and for once in his life Sir Nicholas allowed the solecism to pass unrebuked. Antony went to the window and back before he spoke again, and then returned to his former place at the corner of the desk, looking down at the older man in a troubled way. 'I think I've been wrong all the time,' he said, 'and let Robert Osmond down very badly.'

'You're telling me, if I understand you, that you've come to believe that he didn't murder his wife,' said Sir Nicholas eyeing his nephew with something of the apprehension that a man might afford a ticking bomb.

'Yes, I have, Uncle Nick. When I talked to him tonight . . . well, never mind my reasons, they'll wait. But I ought to have been concerning myself all this time with finding out what other possibilities there were. If I'd insisted, Geoffrey would have gone along with me, he's done so any number of times and never counted the consequences. Only I wasn't sure.'

'And now you are? What has Geoffrey to say to that?'

'Come to think of it, I didn't ask him. Does it matter?'

'Not particularly, but I think you'd better tell me, Antony, what has happened that has changed your mind.'

'It isn't easy to explain. In fact I don't think there's any concrete reason I can give you. It's just that when we were talking to him after old Conroy had adjourned this afternoon it came over me . . . he isn't that kind of man.'

'That kind of thinking, Antony, as you very well know, is a cardinal sin for a lawyer.'

'I know. I also know that I've complained of it myself in other people any number of times. But that doesn't alter how I feel.'

'You still may be wrong,' Sir Nicholas pointed out.

'Of course I may. Do you think I don't know that? But I'd no right to pre-judge him, and now I don't know what to do.' He was fiddling with a letter-opener he had picked up from the desk but now he looked up and his eyes met his uncle's in naked appeal. 'I need your help, sir, your advice as to how I should go on. If there's anything I can do; but it's too late now . . . don't you think?'

'You've kept me reasonably up-to-date about the progress of the case so far,' said Sir Nicholas slowly. 'Perhaps it would help if you tell me in a little more detail than Halloran could exactly what happened today.'

'Yes, of course.' But he resumed his pacing as he did so and the tale came out jerkily. Sir Nicholas was silent for a moment after he had finished.

'Being unsure of your client's innocence until this talk you had with him just now, that went at least three-quarters of the way towards convincing you, you were nevertheless determined to do your best for him,' he said at last. 'Stand still a moment, Antony, I can't think with you whirling around the room like a dervish.'

'I'm sorry, sir,' said Maitland, coming to a halt and picking up the paper knife again. He half expected a request to stop fidgeting but none came.

'What line were you proposing to follow? From your questions to this man Brodie it would seem that you had something definite in mind.'

'Only to try to prevent the jury from considering the Osmonds' affairs in a vacuum as it were. Phillipa had a life outside the one she shared years ago with Robert and Jennifer, but the prosecution's case gives no inkling of that. Other people knew her and may possibly have had reason to wish her dead. If I'd taken the trouble to find out in more detail—'

'You can't accuse Brodie of killing her even if he was at one time her lover, or because he may have been jealous when he knew she was going to marry again.'

'Of course, I can't, though I'm pretty sure he was. I think now that she'd no intention at all of paying for his services in cash, and most likely he preferred it that way but she wasn't willing to pay quite the price he had in mind. There's this chap Ringfield too. Conroy wouldn't let me go far into his acquaintanceship with Phillipa, but Geoffrey tells me his sister didn't like her, and he thinks – Geoffrey, I mean – that that was because Ringfield took a fancy to her. Then there's Phillipa's brother, who inherits what she had to leave. Not a fortune, but from what I hear of him he's pretty hard up. And her partner has the option of buying her shares in the firm very cheaply. But it's all so vague, nothing to build on, while there's Robert Osmond with a damned good motive and all the opportunity in the world. He doesn't deny that, though I think I might possibly have shaken Ringfield about the identification if I'd tried. When he appeared in the Magistrate's Court he said he recognised Osmond from a newspaper photograph *after* the murder, but today – and in the statement Geoffrey had from the prosecution – he said he'd known him when he saw him because Phillipa had once shown him his picture. But I think he probably genuinely remembered that, and came to believe it was how it had actually been, and there didn't seem any point in bringing it up, as our client admitted being in St John's Wood. So why should the jury look any further for the guilty party?'

Sir Nicholas was frowning. 'I'm afraid at this stage you

206

must reconcile yourself, Antony, to doing the best you can with the material at your disposal. In the absence of any concrete evidence your plan of endeavouring to widen the jury's horizons seems to me the best you can follow.'

'But, Uncle Nick—' Maitland protested.

'I know, in your present state of mind you don't think it's enough. But consider for a moment, my dear boy, what other course is there to follow? Continue on the lines you've laid out for yourself—'

'And I shall be able to tell myself afterwards that I did my best!' said Antony savagely.

Again his uncle ignored the interruption. 'I was about to say, like Mr Micawber, that something may turn up,' he corrected mildly. 'If you've made up your mind as to Osmond's innocence – and I think you have, even though you claim to have moments of doubting it – there's nothing I can do or say to stop you from blaming yourself, but that doesn't alter the fact that you're extremely foolish to do so.'

Maitland's attention was obviously wandering. 'I shall be opening the defence tomorrow,' he said, 'but I doubt if we'll get further than Osmond's evidence, or perhaps Amanda Herschell's as well if Garfield isn't in too captious a mood. I thought we might dispense with Miss Herschell's evidence as Norma Martin had changed her story, but Geoffrey says very definitely not.'

'Geoffrey is wise,' said Sir Nicholas, but again his nephew took no notice of the remark.

'If you and Vera would excuse me tomorrow night there'd be time to have a word with Wheeldon and Spencer.'

'I suppose you're referring to Mrs Osmond's brother and her partner. What good would it do for you to see them at this stage? You must have read their statements.'

'Yes, of course I have,' said Maitland a little impatiently. 'But it might help to get some personal impression of them before I have to examine them in court.'

It was Sir Nicholas's private opinion that the proposed interviews would do no good at all, but if there was a chance of the exercise doing something to soothe his nephew's over-active conscience he wasn't going to say so. 'We should certainly excuse you,' he said, 'but I doubt if what you propose will make you very late. Will these two men be at the court, waiting to give their evidence?'

'No, Geoffrey told me he'd asked them to attend on Wednesday. Our client's evidence will take some time, and with Garfield cross-examining . . . you know how he goes on and on.'

'I do indeed,' said Sir Nicholas, who had suffered himself from his learned friend's loquacity from time to time. 'But even so, if you visit them immediately after the adjournment I doubt if it will delay you very long.'

'No, I don't think so either. Geoffrey can get in touch with them at lunchtime and we'll just have to hope that they'll both be available. I quite realise Uncle Nick,' he added, 'that you're itching to tell me I shall be wasting my time. But anyway I'm grateful to you for listening.'

IV

They shared a taxi back to Kempenfeldt Square and parted in the hall, where Gibbs succeeded in conveying without a word said that the blame for their late arrival must obviously be Maitland's. When he let himself into his own quarters, Jenny had obviously heard the creak of the door and was already pouring sherry by the time he reached the living-room.

'Unless you'd prefer something stronger,' she asked, turning with a glass in her hand and getting a good look at him for the first time.

'No, love, that'll be perfect. I'm sorry I'm so late.'

'It doesn't matter.' She placed the glass invitingly next to the chair at the left side of the hearth, and went back to her own favourite corner of the sofa where she curled up in a relaxed way that she was very far from feeling. One look at her husband had made it obvious that he was tired and in some pain, and she wasn't going to worry him further with questions. When he was ready to talk he would do so. 'Dinner won't spoil,' she said, 'so there's no hurry unless you're hungry.'

'As a matter of fact, love, I'm ravenous, and I expect you are too.'

Antony gulped down his sherry in a way quite unlike him, and Jenny rose without comment to refill his glass. 'Conroy didn't sit particularly late,' he said, 'but I wanted to talk to Robert Osmond afterwards, and then I had a word with Uncle Nick before we left chambers.'

'Well, if Uncle Nick came home with you he'll probably be in trouble with Mrs Stokes for being so late,' said Jenny, smiling. 'But I don't suppose Vera will mind taking care of that.'

'I suppose not. What a lot of trouble we do cause you, love.' He was sipping his sherry with more appreciation now. 'And in case you're wondering how we got on today I'd rather give you the whole story later, but that's what I was talking to Uncle Nick about. You see I'm ninety-nine per cent sure now that our client is innocent.'

'And you think you ought to have realised that before and tried to do something about it,' said Jenny, who – at least where Antony was concerned – never needed to have things spelled out for her.

'Yes, of course. Uncle Nick told me not to be a fool.'

'That doesn't sound very helpful.'

'No, but he also went so far as to approve the line I'm taking in court as being as likely as any other to produce some result. And that's not saying very much, love, it's definitely a forlorn hope, but talking to him did give me an idea. If Geoffrey will go along with me—'

'Geoffrey always goes along with you,' Jenny observed.

'Yes, I know he does and I'm grateful. But what I was going to say was that if he can arrange matters there are two witnesses I think now I ought to have seen before, who won't be called until Wednesday, so we could talk to them tomorrow evening. It will mean my being a bit late home, but Uncle Nick has absolved me in advance, and I know you and Vera will.'

'Yes, of course.' His glass was empty and she got up in a purposeful way. 'If you're hungry we may as well eat right away,' she said. 'And it might be a good idea to open a bottle of wine.'

They ate their meal in a companionable silence and had just finished clearing the table when the house phone rang. It was almost a quarter to ten – a very little longer and Gibbs would have retired firmly from his own interpretation of his daily duties – and the sound surprised them both. If Roger Farrell had decided for some reason to visit them at this late hour he would have been let into the house and left to make his own way upstairs, being so frequent a visitor that even Gibbs approved this informality. 'I can't imagine who it could be at this time of night,' Antony grumbled as he made his way to the phone, but he was soon to be enlightened.

'A gentleman to see you,' said Gibbs's voice almost approvingly in his ear. 'Sir Alfred Godalming.'

For just a moment Maitland was silent through sheer surprise. But then he recovered himself. 'You're slipping, Gibbs,' he said. 'Sir Alfred is a policeman.' The butler's attitude towards members of the force, however exalted, was well known; he generally referred to them in a disparaging way as 'persons', and it was a pretty safe bet that the information would cause him to change his attitude towards the visitor even if only in a subtle way.

'Indeed?' he said. 'Do you wish to see him, Mr Maitland?'

The true answer to that would have been a resounding, No. Antony considered the matter for a moment. The wisest course would certainly be to enlist Sir Nicholas and Vera on his side, but for some reason this evening that course didn't appeal to him. 'I suppose I must see him,' he said reluctantly. 'If you'll start him on his way upstairs, I'll meet him half way.' He turned from the phone to find Jenny staring at him.

'Who—?' she began.

'Godalming,' he said briefly. 'So that's what Geoffrey meant when he insisted on calling Amanda Herschell.'

That last remark naturally meant nothing to Jenny. 'That awful man!' she said indignantly. 'At this time of night I think you'd every right to refuse to see him.'

'Put it down to curiosity, love,' said Antony, though he was pretty sure in his own mind of the reason for the Assistant Commissioner's call. 'But I'd better go and meet him, I don't want him to get lost half way up.'

'Shall I make myself scarce?' she asked, following him into

the hall, and he paused with the front door half open.

'Not on your life!' he said. Jenny, he knew, had a weakness for knowing the worst, and she might as well hear what Sir Alfred had to say at first hand without his having to repeat it to her later.

He found the visitor on the first-floor landing looking around him as though in some bewilderment. 'One more flight, I'm afraid,' he said. And then, deliberately over-formal, 'I don't know what the purpose of your visit may be, Sir Alfred, but I must tell you I appreciate your coming yourself instead of sending one of your minions.'

'Do you expect me to reply, It's good of you to see me, Mr Maitland?'

They were already on their way up the stairs. 'Certainly not, Sir Alfred, I wouldn't expect so much courtesy,' said Maitland over his shoulder.

'I was about to add,' said Godalming coldly, 'that you will be well advised to listen to what I have to say.'

Antony ignored that, closed the door carefully once the visitor had followed him into the hall, and then led the way to the living-room where Jenny, contrary to her usual habit, had decided to seat herself in what was usually regarded as Sir Nicholas's chair. This was so unusual that Antony checked momentarily at the sight of her, but seeing the prim way she was sitting he decided that she had felt the wing chair would lend her a little dignity. This was enough to bring a note of amusement to his voice as he turned to perform the introductions. 'I believe you haven't met Sir Alfred Godalming, love,' he said. 'He's the new – well, comparatively new – Assistant Commissioner (Crime) at New Scotland Yard. My wife, Jenny, Sir Alfred.'

'I'm naturally delighted to make Mrs Maitland's acquaint-ance,' said Godalming, in a cold tone which gave the lie to what he was saying, 'but I'm sure she will forgive me if I tell you that what I have to say will be better kept between the two of us.'

'I have no idea what that is, of course,' said Antony; and that too was a lie – he was pretty sure he knew now what this was all about and was only surprised that it hadn't occurred to him before.

211

'I must insist—' Sir Alfred started.

'I'm afraid you're not in a position to insist on anything,' Antony informed him. 'It is, if you'll forgive me for mentioning the matter, rather a late hour for a social call. I'm sure you wouldn't wish to add to your inconsideration by turning my wife out of her own living-room.'

'In your own interests, Mr Maitland—'

'In my own interests, Sir Alfred,' Antony interrupted him again, 'I should very much prefer to have a witness to our talk.' And suddenly he was angry, too angry not to allow it to show. 'We w-will have our meeting on my t-terms or n-not at all,' he said. 'Otherwise p-perhaps you'll remember my adv-vice to you on our previous m-meeting. You can g-go to the d-devil.'

'Sit down, Sir Alfred,' said Jenny in her quiet way. 'Then we can all be comfortable while you tell my husband what you want of him.'

'Thank you.' Godalming almost threw himself into the chair opposite her. 'It is about the Osmond case, Mr Maitland,' he said.

Antony went past him, propped one shoulder against the high mantel, and looked down at him negligently. 'In that c-case, I should have th-thought you'd have d-delegated the m-matter to Eversley,' he said.

'In the circumstances, that would have been highly improper,' said Sir Alfred stiffly. 'As a witness for the prosecution in a case in which you are appearing for the defence—'

'You're his s-superior officer. Doesn't that m-make you equally involved?'

Perhaps Godalming could think of no reply to this question, uttered in a tone of rather overdone politeness, even if the effect Antony was trying for was rather marred by the slight, angry stammer. In any case, the visitor ignored it and asked bluntly, 'How much did you pay that girl to go back on her evidence?'

Antony heard Jenny catch her breath sharply, and his temper, which in any case was held on a not-too-tight a rein, was lost irretrievably. 'I'd n-never s-seen her b-before today,' he snapped.

212

'I presume you were briefed on what her evidence would be.'

'C-certainly I w-was.'

'And only when you saw her in court did you come to the conclusion that of the three witnesses to your client's – I can only call it immoral behaviour – she was the one who could be the most easily broken down?'

'You have no r-right at all to ask these q-questions, and no r-reason either, unless you're b-becoming as obsessed as Chief Superintendent B-Briggs was. If you want the whole s-story I'll spell it out f-for you. Before Mrs Osmond's d-death there was the question of the c-custody suit she proposed to b-bring against her husband, and at that t-time Mr Geoffrey Horton, my instructing s-solicitor, had enquiries made about the three w-witnesses, and the man who was said to have unearthed them, Stewart B-Brodie. This, m-may I remind you, was before Phillipa Osmond's d-death, and that is the only contact – except through their s-statements which were sent to Mr Horton by the prosecution – that either of us has had with them. And if you w-want to know what I think, they were all lying until that poor g-girl told us the truth in court today, because it was a different m-matter telling lies in a murder case than in one where it was just a question of w-which parent a child should live with.'

'You can't prove that!'

'No, I c-can't, it's up to the jury to make up their own minds. And if you're insinuating that I b-bribed a witness your story would be m-more reasonable if you accused me of t-tampering with evidence in a way that would be of assistance to my c-client.'

'I am quite well aware—'

'Yes, and so am I. If I'd been going to b-bribe anyone I'd have looked for s-somebody whose evidence was more damaging to the defence. Wilfred Begg for instance, or that r-rather pathetic chap, Ringfield. Though c-come to think of it that might not have been s-such a good idea, Phillipa Osmond obviously had him exactly where she w-wanted him.'

'Mr Begg is a man of integrity.'

That was too much for Maitland's sense of humour, which

213

was never very far below the surface. He laughed and said, 'Meaning I'm not?' For the moment his anger had left him and the slight stammer with it. 'Don't be so pompous, Sir Alfred. You've almost got me believing you believe in this nonsense yourself.'

'In that case you would be wise to follow your instincts, Mr Maitland.' Godalming came to his feet as he spoke. 'I don't know what other ideas you have up your sleeve, but in view of this very obvious attempt to subvert justice I should warn you that any further action of the kind will be only too painfully obvious.'

'Oh, what's the use!' Antony came erect to face the other man, their eyes level. Godalming was slimly built and his hair, which was now an indeterminate colour, was growing well back from his temples. He had a thin face and at the moment a rather predatory look, so that Antony was suddenly visited with a vision of a fox terrier, its teeth clamped into the scruff of a rat's neck. The image amused him again, because though he had called himself some pretty bad names in his time no kind of rodent had figured among them. All the same, it was painfully obvious that the idea Briggs had harboured for so long – that he himself was capable of any skulduggery for the sake of winning a case, had found a new home and was now fixed just as powerfully in the Assistant Commissioner's mind. 'Are we to have this argument every time I accept a brief for the defence in a criminal case?' he wondered.

'That is up to you, Mr Maitland. I will leave you now but I would advise you to be very, very careful.'

'Heaven and earth! Can't you be m-more original than that?' Antony asked. And then with a return to his former manner, which he hoped Godalming would find as annoying as he found the insinuations that had been made, 'Must you go, Sir Alfred? It seems to me we've hardly touched the edge of the subject.'

'Enough has been said, Mr Maitland, for me to realise that my errand was useless. I will say good night to you, Mrs Maitland, and apologise for the intrusion.'

For the moment Jenny stared back at him blankly, so that Antony wondered just how upset she was and whether she had for the moment lost the power of speech. Then, 'Good night, Sir Alfred,' she responded in a haughty tone her husband had never heard before. 'I won't say you'll be welcome any time you care to visit us, for that would be untrue. But if, when you have thought matters out, you feel that an apology to my husband would be in order—'

'I have expressed my regrets to you for disturbing you in your home, Mrs Maitland.' He turned and made for the door, and his final remark was made over his shoulder. 'As for the rest, Mr Maitland and I understand each other I think, and he will agree with me that no apology is called for.'

'Don't be a b-blithering idiot,' said Antony, following the unwelcome visitor out of the room. Godalming didn't speak again as they went down the stairs, and they parted on the doorstep without even the curtest of good nights. Maitland paused a moment, wondering whether to speak to his uncle immediately. But it was getting late and Jenny might be more upset than she seemed. He crossed the hall and mounted the stairs again.

Jenny was still sitting where he had left her and she looked up and gave him a rather wavering smile as he went in. 'It's so late I don't think I'll make coffee,' she said. 'It would only keep us awake. But I should like a drink of some sort, and I daresay you could do with one too.'

'I certainly could! What is your pleasure, *Madame la Duchesse*?'

She relaxed suddenly and laughed. 'Is that what I sounded like?' she asked. 'I know now why you can't stand the sight of that horrible man. I'd have liked to have scratched his eyes out!'

This remark made her husband pause for a moment or two. 'Have I shocked you?' she asked anxiously.

'Far from it, love. My sentiments exactly.' He did not add that he had never expected to hear them echoed, least of all by Jenny, who hated to think ill of anybody. 'The real trouble is that he's doing his best to infect his department with his ideas,' he said. 'Eversley's one of them, they knew each other before either of them came to London. But as I've said a hundred times—'

'I know, Antony. As long as you stick to the straight and

narrow,' she said. 'But what did you mean when you turned away from the telephone and said you knew now why Geoffrey wanted to call Amanda Herschell?'

'Because he foresaw what Godalming's attitude would be when he knew that Norma Martin went back on her evidence this morning,' Antony told her. 'In a very small way Amanda can confirm what she said . . . not that it'll make much difference to our friend's attitude.' He crossed the room and started rummaging in the cupboard where the drinks were kept. 'You didn't tell me what you'd like, love, but I think I shall give you cognac, and some of Uncle Nick's special brand at that. And while we drink it I'll tell you what happened today in court, and perhaps you'll have some ideas as to what I should do. I admit I'm stumped, and Uncle Nick just advised me to follow the path I'd already mapped out for myself.'

'Do you think these two men you mean to see tomorrow will be able to help at all?' asked Jenny when he had finished.

'I very much doubt it. By stretching the imagination a little, either of them could be said to have a motive, I suppose, but even if I decide there's reason to suspect one of them, I've no way of finding anything to back up the idea.'

'That man Brodie provided you with an alibi without being asked,' said Jenny. 'Won't the jury find that suspicious?'

'They're more likely, by the time Garfield has finished addressing them, to think the unfortunate witness was intimidated by the wicked counsel for the defence,' said Antony, and produced a smile for her edification which didn't convince her in the least that he was regarding the matter lightly.

'Antony,' she said, 'what about the little girl?'

'That's one of the worst things about it, Jenny. What's going to happen to her?'

'I know, but I meant how is she . . . now?'

'Amanda says she's behaving fairly normally but I think she's convinced herself that nothing can possibly happen to keep her father away much longer. And she still won't talk about what happened the day her mother was killed, or the day before that either.'

'Do you think she might be more willing to confide in a stranger?'

'She might, of course, but if she did we don't know what she'd say.'

'I know you said that before, but it was when you were wondering if she might know something that would make matters worse for her father. Now you've made up your mind about him—'

'Yes, that does make a difference, though it's difficult to see how she could know anything that would help.'

'I think you ought to try everything,' said Jenny firmly. 'After all, she might have been to see her mother as you wondered at first, and even seen someone else there whom Mr Osmond didn't recognise when he saw them leaving. But if she was with Phillipa she must have been still there when Mr Osmond left for home, which surely means her mother was still alive at that time.'

'Logic from you, love?' asked Antony, smiling.

'It's just that I can't see any little girl finding her mother's body and not rushing out screaming.'

'She might not have recognised her. Osmond thinks she doesn't remember Phillipa at all.'

'*Any* body,' Jenny insisted. 'In any case, I'm sure he's wrong about that.'

'It's a very long shot, love.'

'Yes, I know, but if all else fails we could at least try.'

'We?'

'I thought perhaps,' said Jenny hesitantly, 'that she might find it easier to talk to a woman.'

'My dearest love, you don't need to rub in the fact that she probably regards me as an ogre,' said Antony, but now his amusement was quite genuine. 'If I don't get any inspiration from the two witnesses I'm seeing out of court tomorrow, I think we should give it a try. Only it's a bit difficult to see how we could fit it in.'

'Nothing easier,' said Jenny, suddenly unusually decisive. 'You could go to Mrs Osmond's partner's office first thing, and talk to him before you go to court. And when you adjourn in the afternoon . . . does this Mr Spencer live very far away?'

217

'No. Not a very good address, but pretty central.'

'Then you can see him, pick me up here in a taxi – that'll save time rather than my getting the car out – and we'll go out and see Jennifer together. If it's still necessary, of course.'

'You're in a very decided mood this evening, love. What are Uncle Nick and Vera going to do while we're gallivanting about?'

'I won't ask Uncle Nick to put up with one of Mrs Stokes's cold collations,' Jenny assured him. 'If I leave things ready Vera will be only too happy to do everything that's necessary – sometimes I think she envies me my own kitchen – and we can eat when we come back and tell them what's happened. If anything,' she added. 'I know it's not very likely but—'

Suddenly Antony was on his knees beside her, their eyes now more or less on a level. 'My dear and only love,' he said, 'do you remember what you told me once, years and years ago before we were even married?'

'As we've known each other all our lives I must have said a good deal,' said Jenny practically.

'Yes, but this was serious, and I've never forgotten it even though I may sometimes have seemed to. You said – I can remember your exact words – you said, "It isn't failing that matters, it's trying and trying and never giving up."'

'If it was before we were married I must have been quite young at the time,' said Jenny apologetically. 'It does sound a little . . . childish.'

'Well, perhaps. But it contains an undeniable truth and a good deal of wisdom. Out of the mouths of babes—' said Antony, and didn't attempt to finish the quotation. Instead he put his hands over hers, holding them firmly. 'I'll make you a solemn promise, Jenny, that if Robert Osmond is convicted I'll go on doing everything I can to clear his name.'

'That's good,' said Jenny, but it had to be admitted that her thoughts were more for her husband than for his client. If the pact they had just made comforted Antony that was quite enough for her.

TUESDAY,
the fourth day of the trial

I

Late as it had been when they finished talking the night before
Antony had phoned Geoffrey to tell him of the change in
plans that would take him to Calvin Wheeldon's office before
the court convened. 'I'll call for you at a quarter to nine,' said
Geoffrey without hesitation. 'If we're waiting for him when
he arrives at his office there's a good chance he won't already
have got caught up with appointments. Yes, I'm coming with
you,' he added, when Maitland started to assure him that he
could perform the errand alone. 'I've got a very strong feeling
we should do everything by the book. But I don't know what
good you think it's going to do us.'

'None at all, I daresay, but I'll explain tomorrow,' Antony
promised. And did so during the short drive to their
destination. Geoffrey said, 'I knew it!' when told of Sir Alfred
Godalming's visit, but made no attempt to dissuade his
companion from a course of action which he himself thought
so useless as to be foolish. 'I'll come with you to Spencer's, of
course, but if you decide to see Jennifer I doubt if there's any
need for me to come along as well. It would probably put her
off; the fewer people who are present the better, and anyway
it's completely unofficial. Whatever she has to tell us I doubt
if it would do any good asking Osmond's permission to call
her as a witness.'

'All I'm hoping for is a starting point,' Antony assured
him. 'But I'm not particularly hopeful about finding one.'

Against their expectations they found Calvin Wheeldon

219

already at his office, a very modern, clean and shining place, which – together with all the paraphernalia of the architect's profession – made it look very strange to both of them. They were led past a door with Phillipa Osmond's name on it and into Wheeldon's presence. Not as tall a man as Robert Osmond, he was squarely built and with a pleasantly ugly face. It must be admitted that Maitland's eyes went immediately to his hands, which were also square and strong-looking. The medical evidence which they had heard the previous week had made him perhaps a little over-interested in the point.

'You told me I wouldn't be needed in court before tomorrow, Mr Horton,' said Wheeldon before Geoffrey could introduce his companion. 'Are you here to tell me you were wrong about that?'

'No, it was just that Mr Maitland felt he would like to have a word with you before seeing you in court,' Geoffrey explained. 'This is Mr Maitland, Robert Osmond's leading counsel.'

'Well, I didn't see how I could help in court, and still less how a preliminary conversation can be of any use,' said Wheeldon. 'A thankless task, isn't it?' he added, glancing at Maitland. 'Defending Robert under the circumstances, I mean.'

'What makes you say that, Mr Wheeldon?' Antony asked him.

'I've seen nothing of him since Phillipa left him, but I know well enough he's devoted to that brat of theirs. What Phillipa wanted, Phillipa usually got, one way or the other. And she was very sure that she was going to get custody of Jennifer.'

'Can you tell us a little more about that? What she said to you about it, for instance.' As Geoffrey had expected, Maitland had taken over the questioning. Which was fair enough, seeing that the solicitor was merely there to lend a little orthodoxy to the proceedings.

'Nothing much. Just that she could prove that Robert wasn't a suitable person to have charge of a sensitive child. Which may or may not be a good description of Jennifer, I just don't know. Phillipa's attitude left me in no doubt that she was quite sure of herself.'

'When was this?'

'Oh, two or three weeks before she died, I suppose. I wasn't particularly interested . . . I have troubles of my own.'

'I'm sorry to hear that.'

It was only too obvious that Wheeldon was in a mood to make use of any willing and sympathetic ear, which made Maitland congratulate himself on his decision, because certainly in court the other man would not be so forthcoming. 'I'd known for about four months,' Wheeldon said, 'that she was going to marry again. They even threw an engagement party to which they invited me. That, if you want my opinion, is why she wanted Jennifer, though she talked a lot about the natural affection of a mother for her child. Leighton struck me as a sentimental sort of man. I did try to persuade her she'd be bored stiff without a job of work to do, she couldn't spend all her time looking after the kid. But there was no doing anything with her, she was sick of work and that was all there was to it.'

'You didn't want to lose her as a partner?'

'Not on your life! Her face was her fortune,' Calvin said, smiling rather wryly. 'Our fortune, I should say. Not that she wasn't a damned good architect, she was. If you want the whole truth, Mr Maitland, a damned sight better than I am.'

Being in no position to contradict this statement, Antony ignored it. 'What we really wanted, Mr Wheeldon, before we get into court, is anything you can tell us about Mrs Osmond's friends and acquaintances outside the office. We met her only once, and Mr Osmond, of course, knows nothing of her life recently.'

'I suppose you can say I don't know too much about it either,' said Wheeldon. 'She came to me when she qualified. We weren't in these offices then, but I soon saw the difference she made to our workload and I offered her a partnership as one way of keeping her. It was a bit difficult from the time Jennifer was born until Phillipa left Robert, but somehow we managed, and there was nobody like her for the personal touch. And then she let me down like that, though I suppose you could say it doesn't make any difference now.'

'So during all that time your relationship was a purely professional one?'

'Certainly it was. Not that I'd have been averse to having a fling with her,' said Wheeldon, who seemed to be in an extremely confidential mood, 'and from what I know of Phillipa I daresay she wouldn't have minded it either. But I know better than to mess around with business associates.'

'You said, "from what I know of Phillipa". Could you tell me what you mean by that?'

'I may be wronging her,' said Calvin hastily. 'Only I know she put out every bit of sex appeal she had when there was a contract in the air, and sometimes, of course, I wasn't really sure how far it went.'

'I see. Was there anybody recently in her life who might have been jealous when he knew of her proposed marriage?'

'Not to my knowledge, unless it was that chap Brodie. Come to think of it, it's odd he wasn't at that engagement party I mentioned. They were always in conference together just when I wanted to talk to her about something important. And I daresay you're thinking I was jealous too. Well I was, but not in that way. I could have wrung her neck when I knew she was leaving me, only I didn't.'

'I suppose the police came to see you after the murder?'

'Yes.' Calvin's grin made his ugly face almost attractive. 'Only I wasn't quite so open with them as I've been with you, Mr Maitland, and I hope you won't expect me to be quite as frank when we get into court. Even so, they did ask for an alibi.'

'Did they indeed?' said Antony, trying to sound as uninterested as he could.

Wheeldon rose to the bait, in the same way as people so often will to the lure of silence. 'With any luck I should have had a perfect one,' he said rather ruefully. 'I went out to see a client, the representative of a company we're building a huge block of offices for at Maida Vale. The chap didn't turn up, he said afterwards his secretary must have forgotten to make a note of the appointment.'

'But surely you saw somebody you knew at the site?'

'No. I'd had a long talk with the construction people early that morning – by telephone, that is – but everything seemed to be proceeding on schedule, there was no need to trouble them again. However, my car was parked nearby for a full hour before I decided I'd better go and find a telephone. I should think somebody must have seen it.'

'Yes, I should think so too,' Antony agreed cordially, though a miniature map of that part of London was forming itself in his mind. 'There's just one more thing I should like to ask you then, Mr Wheeldon. Do you know Phillipa Osmond's brother?'

'Rudolph? Oh yes, I know him quite well.'

'What do you think of him?'

'He's a playwright, very much in the minor league. Not that he isn't a clever chap in his own way. What's lacking in him is Phillipa's business flair; that and a sense of application, I suppose. But a nice chap, quite harmless.'

As a recommendation Antony didn't think that was exactly what he would have liked to hear about himself. Still, in the circumstances it might be a useful one. 'Did he get on with his sister?' he asked.

'Well, if she'd been my sister I'd have been ready to strangle her,' said Calvin frankly. Then he pulled himself up. 'It's awfully easy to use phrases like that, isn't it? I'd better be careful when I get into court. I say' – a sudden thought struck him – 'you aren't intending to set me up as an alternative suspect, are you?'

'As a matter of fact, no,' said Maitland, thinking as he spoke that ten minutes ago the answer would have been a lie. But he didn't think that a man with anything to hide would have been quite so free with his opinions.

Wheeldon was explaining himself. 'All I meant was, she was always nagging at him to make something of himself, I think that's how she put it. But he's too good-natured, or at least too lazy, ever to do that.'

'Then I think that's all we need to ask you, Mr Wheeldon,' said Antony, getting up, 'and I'm sorry to have taken up so much of your time.'

'That's all right.' Calvin Wheeldon also rose to his feet. 'But still,' he added, looking from one of them to the other, 'you want me to appear in court tomorrow, or whenever.'

Geoffrey interposed at that point. 'Yes, Mr Wheeldon, we do,' he said firmly. 'In particular, I think Mr Maitland will want to know your assessment of Mrs Osmond's character as

223

you have just given it to us, and to make that convincing, of course, he would have to ask you how long you knew her.'

'Would it make it any better for Robert for the court to know she was a bit of a bitch, if an extremely attractive one?' asked Wheeldon curiously.

'I think it's an important point,' said Horton, sidestepping that one neatly.

'Well you can rely on me in that case.'

They made their farewells, and nothing more was said between them until they were in the street outside and had turned in the direction of the car park. 'Thank you, Nanny,' said Maitland grinning.

Geoffrey didn't pretend to misunderstand him. 'We need all the confirmation we can get for Norma Martin's story,' he said firmly. 'And don't go forgetting that when it comes to the point.'

II

It seemed to Maitland at the time that that day was one of the most unpleasant he had ever spent in court. His own opening address – carefully prepared, and of necessity considerably altered in the early hours of that morning – gave him no great trouble. It was his habit to say as little as was reasonable at that stage, and in the present instance he had to admit there wasn't much that he could say. But he was still suffering from pangs of conscience, and the talk with Calvin Wheeldon that morning had made him realise more clearly even than before how little was to be expected from a similar interview with Phillipa Osmond's brother. And behind it all was the small lingering doubt . . . in spite of what he felt, in spite of his own conviction to the contrary, was it possible that his client would have killed to retain custody of his daughter?

Robert Osmond, when he took the stand, made a good witness, but even to counsel's prejudiced ears his story could not sound other than unconvincing. Maitland managed to restrain him from going into more detail than was necessary

224

about his feelings concerning the custody suit, but the fact of his being in St John's Wood on the afternoon of his wife's death had to be brought out in order that he could explain his presence and deny having actually seen her. Mr Justice Conroy adjourned for luncheon as soon as he had finished his examination-in-chief, and Geoffrey took advantage of the recess to have one last interview with their client to try to prepare him for what was to come; but if Antony had entertained a secret hope that Norma Martin's retraction of her evidence would have given counsel for the prosecution any kindlier view of the prisoner he was soon to find out his mistake.

It was only too obvious that Garfield's most puritanical mood was on him when he rose to cross-examine when the court re-convened after lunch. 'You would have us believe, Mr Osmond, that your marriage to the deceased was a happy one until she suddenly and inexplicably left both you and her young daughter?'

'I didn't say that exactly. I said I wasn't conscious of anything wrong until Phillipa became pregnant. I don't think she wanted a child, and I don't think she liked all the things that had to be done after Jennifer was born.'

'You didn't try to arrange for a legal separation?'

'No.'

'Why was that, Mr Osmond?'

'Because I thought it might bring the matter of custody to the forefront.'

'If your view of Mrs Osmond's character is the right one there could surely be no question that she would want to take the child from you?'

'I'd come to realise she could be spiteful. That was why I didn't agree immediately to a divorce when she suggested it, not until she assured me that there was no question of her wanting to take charge of Jennifer.'

'Was that really the reason, Mr Osmond? Was it not rather that you feared what might come to light if the case was brought to court?'

'She said she had evidence of infidelity. It wasn't true, and I think I'd have taken my chance in court if it hadn't been for the assurance she gave me. But later, when she decided she did want custody of Jennifer after all, I realised more vividly

225

than ever that she was capable of doing anything to get what she wanted.'

'You told us she had no interest in the child. How then do you explain the desire she then expressed?'

'My lord! It is not up to my client to explain Mrs Osmond's wishes,' Maitland objected.

Conroy agreed, but the impression had been made. 'Let us turn then to the proposed custody suit,' said Garfield, quite as well aware as his opponent was that he had made his point. 'We have heard the evidence of three witnesses as to your habit of entertaining your mistresses in your own home . . . a small flat where privacy would have been difficult, even if you desired it, which it seems you did not.'

That brought an outburst from Osmond. 'There wasn't a word of truth in any of it, and if there were I couldn't think of a word bad enough to describe it. A sort of perversion. I'd never have done anything to harm Jennifer like that. What would be the point anyway? I could have found plenty of opportunity if I'd wanted that kind of life.'

'You deny that you were acquainted with any of the three women who gave evidence. That you ever saw them until they appeared in court.'

'Of course I deny it, and I'm telling the truth. Besides that last one . . . yesterday morning . . . *she* told the court what had really happened.'

'Contradicting a statement she had already made under oath. Let me suggest to you, Mr Osmond, that she changed her story out of pity. After all, she was the last of the three to have known you, perhaps she had some lingering feeling for you, in which case she may well have felt that telling her story at a murder trial was rather more serious than at a hearing concerning the custody of your child.'

'I suppose that's what she did feel but not because her first story was true. The whole thing was a pack of lies from start to finish.'

'Then we will consider the alternative. How would you have felt, Mr Osmond, at the prospect of losing your daughter because of evidence that had been faked.'

'I'd have been as mad as fire . . . as I was. I'm trying to tell you it was all an invention.'

: 'I think, my lord' – Garfield turned towards the bench – 'the prisoner means that he was extremely angry.'

'Thank you, Mr Garfield,' said Conroy solemnly. 'You may proceed.'

'I'm obliged to your lordship. So, Mr Osmond, we have two possibilities. Mrs Osmond had proof, very adequate proof, that you were an unfit person to have charge of Jennifer; or the witnesses to your depravity are lying. If the latter is the case, could you have proved it?'

'I should have tried to.'

'Very likely, but had you any real hope of being able to do so?'

'No.'

'Then I put it to you, Mr Osmond, that in either of the two situations I have outlined your motive for disposing of your wife must be regarded as overwhelming. You say you are devoted to your daughter—'

'I'd do anything for her . . . but not murder,' he added quickly.

'But you will agree, will you not, that if you had been genuinely conscious of your innocence of Mrs Osmond's accusations, that would have merely been an added incentive?'

'I've already told you I was angry, and I'll admit – because it wouldn't do much good if I didn't – that knowing she was lying made it worse. If I'd had murder in mind . . . but I didn't!'

'So you say. Why did you go to St John's Wood on the afternoon of Mrs Osmond's death?'

'I've tried to explain that as clearly as I could. I thought perhaps I could talk some sense into her.'

'But you say you did not see her.'

'No, I suppose you could say I lost my nerve. Her attitude . . . we'd only have quarrelled.'

'Is that not what really happened? You went to see her, after some hesitation, and either in anger, or because you knew your case to be hopeless, you killed her.'

'No, it wasn't like that.'

'Perhaps you will tell us exactly how it was then, Mr Osmond.'

'I've told you again and again. I waited . . . oh, perhaps an hour. Only I knew – I suppose I'd known all the time – that it was hopeless to talk and what was the use of adding even more bitterness to the feeling between us?'

'So you went in with the one purpose in mind . . . to kill her?'

'How many times must I tell you that I did nothing of the sort? I didn't go near her, at least no nearer than the street outside.'

'It was a cold day,' said Garfield thoughtfully.

Osmond's temper had been showing signs for some time of growing ragged. 'Yes,' he said, 'and I was wearing gloves, and I remembered not to take them off until I got my hands round her throat and to put them on again as soon as I knew she was dead! And don't take that as an admission of anything,' he added savagely, turning quite improperly to address the jury directly. 'I've been listening to the evidence too . . . remember?'

'Really, Mr Maitland,' said Conroy in a complaining tone. 'You must keep your witness in better order. Are we to take that as a confession of guilt?'

'Certainly not, my lord,' said Maitland coming to his feet in a hurry. 'I didn't interfere before because I felt sure that the court would understand, as I do, the intolerable tension my client is under. Which of us in similar circumstances might not be tempted to indulge in a little sarcasm?'

'That's all very well, Mr Maitland,' said the judge, eyeing him suspiciously. 'All very well and very specious. But he distinctly said—'

'In the heat of the moment, my lord, and under what I'm sure your lordship will agree was intolerable pressure. To be telling the truth, and constantly to be accused of lying . . . I will take it on myself to apologise on my client's behalf, and I'm sure I can promise you that there will be no further outbursts of any kind.'

'Very well, Mr Maitland, very well.'

'The court has already heard my client say that his words were not intended as an admission,' said Antony insinuatingly.

228

'Then we will leave the matter there. You may proceed, Mr Garfield.'

And proceed Garfield did, back and forth over the same ground until the afternoon was growing late. Maitland did what he could to break the impact of the questions hurled at the prisoner, but beyond a certain point he knew it would be useless, and even as it was Conroy's patience with him was growing very thin indeed by the time Garfield sat down.

'Have you any further questions, Mr Maitland?' The judge asked him in a resigned tone.

'One only, my lord.'

'Very well.'

'You have found my learned friend's questions very trying, Mr Osmond, but this of mine requires only the shortest of responses. You are on oath. Remembering that, please tell me quite simply: did you or did you not kill Mrs Phillipa Osmond?'

'I did not,' said Osmond.

'Thank you. In that case' – he glanced enquiringly at Garfield – 'I think you may step down.'

It was already so late that Mr Justice Conroy adjourned immediately, and Amanda Herschell went home without having been called upon to give her evidence. Antony was so sure after his talk with Calvin Wheeldon that he and Jenny would be making the proposed visit that evening that he had taken the opportunity during the luncheon recess to warn her of it. She looked a little puzzled, but said very willingly, 'Of course you must do what you think best.'

'I don't want to get your hopes up, Amanda. It's – I suppose you could call it a counsel of despair.'

'And, of course, even if she will talk to Mrs Maitland we don't know what she has to say,' said Amanda. 'But—' She broke off, looking at him with sudden excitement so that he realised that in spite of what he had said she found his request encouraging. 'It means – doesn't it, Mr Maitland? – that you've decided you believe that Robert wasn't mixed up with those women, and that he'd never have dreamed of laying a finger on Phillipa, if only because she was Jennifer's mother.'

'Something like that,' said Maitland, and smiled at her. But the fear that he might have raised false hopes only added to his depression.

As soon as he had unrobed he joined Geoffrey. Derek Stringer had already left for home. After many years of friendship he was still something of an enigma to his leader . . . ready to follow even the most unlikely theory, but never expressing an opinion of his own on a client's guilt or innocence, only – when he felt it advisable – on the expediency or otherwise of some proposed course of action.

So Geoffrey and Antony together made their way to Rudolph Spencer's lodgings. As Maitland had said, they were not too far from Kempenfeldt Square, but the old, rather shabby house might have been in another world as far as appearances went. Even with the fairly late adjournment they were prepared for a fairly long wait before Phillipa Osmond's brother got back from his office, but to their surprise the woman who opened the door admitted that Mr Spencer was in his room and gave them specific directions for finding it.

A tap on the door she had indicated brought a rather absent-minded call for them to come in. They obeyed and found themselves in an attic room, cool enough, even on that pleasant May evening, to make it necessary for its occupant to wear a heavy sweater. He was huddled over a desk under the dormer window, scribbling industriously and surrounding himself with untidy sheets of completed script. 'Yes, what do you want?' he asked without looking round, and Horton was forced to begin his explanations without any real assurance that his audience was attending. But he needn't have worried, the word 'solicitor' seemed to act as though there was some magic in it. The man at the desk swung round.

'You're not Wilfred Begg,' he said accusingly. 'Oh no, of course I know who you are. Your name's Horton, or something like that.'

'Yes, I—' said Geoffrey, uncharacteristically taken aback by this greeting. 'It's about your evidence tomorrow. This is Mr Maitland, who is Robert Osmond's counsel.'

'I . . . I was going to say, I see, but I don't see at all. There's nothing I can tell you that will help you.'

'Let us be the judge of that,' said Antony. 'Why did you think it must be Mr Begg?' he added curiously.

230

'Because he's taking the deuce of a time to settle matters.'
Antony made no reply and after a while the other man went
on. 'I'm talking about money. I'm Phillipa's heir, after all,
and I have my rent to pay. I don't think Begg understands
that.'

'Probate takes time,' Geoffrey explained, perhaps with
some feeling of sympathy for the absent Mr Begg.

'Yes, but in the meantime . . . it's not as if there's anyone
to dispute my claim.'

'Osmond's daughter, perhaps?'

'Jennifer?' Rudolph smiled. 'She's a nice kid, and we were
great friends until Phillipa decided to strike out on her own.
But what Phillipa had to leave wasn't a fortune, though it
seems like that to me. I don't suppose Robert would think it
was worth bothering about.'

'Perhaps not.' Geoffrey had dumped a pile of newspapers
on the floor and seated himself in the room's only armchair,
leaving Antony to take a rather hard, wooden one. 'I'm sorry
we disappointed you,' said Horton, 'but if you're willing to
help us there are a few questions Mr Maitland would like to
ask you. We came here rather than to your office as soon as
we left court this afternoon, but I expected we should have to
wait for you.'

'Oh well,' said Spencer casually, 'they can't expect me to
go in when I may be called to go to court at any moment.
Besides,' he smiled suddenly, obviously the visitors had been
forgiven for any misunderstanding as to the reason for their
visit, 'I'd just thought of a good ending for the first act and I
wanted to get it down on paper.'

He was, Maitland thought, almost as tall as himself, but it
was difficult to judge while the other man remained seated.
Spencer's hair was dark and sleek and he was decidedly
good-looking . . . rather like his sister, in fact, except in his
colouring, though in a thoroughly masculine way. Antony
could visualise him as an actor rather than as a writer of plays,
but perhaps his talents didn't lie in that direction. 'I hope
we're not disturbing you,' he said, taking over as he knew
Geoffrey expected.

'Don't worry, that bit's done. Not that I expect it to ever
see the light of day,' he added, 'except perhaps in some

231

horrible little garret in the suburbs. You don't write yourself?'

'No. As Mr Horton told you, we're both lawyers.'

'Then you won't understand. There are times when you just have to get it out of your system,' Rudolph confided. 'But I still don't quite see why you thought it was worth your while to come here.'

'To ask you questions, as Mr Horton told you.'

'I've nothing against Robert, but Phillipa could be damned annoying at times.'

'He's pleading Not Guilty,' Antony pointed out, 'but you know that of course. We're trying to find out something about Mrs Osmond's circle of friends since she left her husband, and it occurred to me that you might be the best person to help us, and perhaps more likely to do so if we spoke to you in private rather than in court.'

'You're not thinking of me, I hope.'

'If you mean as an alternative suspect, I imagine you were at work.'

'Not that day, I was nursing a cold.' He grinned again, confidingly. 'That first act,' he admitted. 'I had a great deal of trouble with it. And as far as I know Mrs Matthews was out, so there'd be nobody to confirm I was here.'

'Well, leaving that aside for the moment,' said Maitland, trying to match his light tone, 'what can you tell me about your sister's friends?'

'She must have known a lot of people I've never heard of, through her business connections, you know. Have you tried Calvin Wheeldon?'

'Yes, we saw him at his office first thing this morning.'

'Well, if he couldn't help I don't think I can. You know she was engaged to be married?'

'Yes, I know that.'

'Nice enough chap . . . a bit of a stick-in-the-mud, but a nice enough chap. I'm sorry for him now, though he might not,' he added reflectively, 'have got quite such a bargain as he expected when he married Phillipa.'

'What on earth do you mean by that, Mr Spencer?'

'Sibling rivalry,' said Rudolph, waving a hand vaguely. 'I

232

suppose that covers it well enough. To put it bluntly, Mr Maitland, if you didn't do things just her way my dear little sister could be a pain in the neck. I'm quite sure Mr Leighton – somehow I find it difficult to call him Matthew – had no idea of this when he proposed, as far as he's concerned she was all sweetness and light. But once they were married it would have been different.'

'You're very frank, Mr Spencer,' said Antony, taken aback.

'That's what you wanted, isn't it? Then there's Calvin. He was absolutely furious, if you want to know, because she was leaving him to get married. And not without reason.'

'He conveyed as much to me, but I admit I couldn't quite see why. After all he was in business before Mrs Osmond qualified and joined him.'

'In a small way of business,' said Rudolph. 'It was Phillipa who made the firm what it is, and with her gone ten to one it will go downhill again. Why am I telling you all this? That's going to be the next question, isn't it? I think it's because I like Robert and I love Jennifer and I don't want to see both their lives ruined.'

'Are you telling us you think Mr Wheeldon might have been upset enough at what he may have thought of as your sister's desertion to have killed her?'

'Oh no, that's nonsense. I'm sure Robert must have done it, and in the circumstances I don't blame him. But you want to confuse the court, isn't that the idea? I'm quite willing to help you do that.'

'That wasn't exactly our idea,' said Maitland slowly, but he couldn't help smiling a little as he spoke. 'I happen to believe in Robert Osmond's innocence, and if I could have found out who was really guilty – I suppose I should say, if I could find some legal proof that someone else was guilty – I'd have been glad enough to produce it in court. Vague accusations would be no use at all, even if I felt it would be fair to make them. And as you know Mr Wheeldon I ought to assure you that I've no such idea about him.'

'If you're going to give me a lecture in ethics—'

'Nothing of the sort,' said Antony hastily. 'I want background material, and that's what you're giving me. I just need a pointer, that's all, something that might perhaps lead to that proof I spoke of.'

'Isn't it rather late in the day for that?'

'There's always the Court of Appeal, and if new evidence turns up—'

Rudolph Spencer didn't seem to have been listening. 'I suppose I'm a little vague about legal matters,' he admitted, 'but I have heard of reasonable doubt. I thought perhaps if you could stir that up in the minds of the jury Robert would get off, Jennifer would be happy, and nobody would be very much harmed.'

'Don't you care who killed your sister?'

'I didn't want her dead, if that's what you mean. But I suppose . . . oh well, you do feel a bit queer when somebody you've known all your life gets killed this way. But we hadn't one single thing in common, unless you can say that my urge to write good plays is somehow comparable to her urge to build magnificent structures. I shan't really miss her, and I can't pretend I shall.'

It was one thing to come prepared to ask impertinent questions, and quite another to find yourself in receipt of the answers without the trouble of putting them. 'Tell us what you know about Robert Osmond,' Maitland invited.

'Robert? I told you he's a good sort of chap. Too good for Phillipa, or so I always thought.'

'Why do you think Mrs Osmond left him?'

'There was some story she told me at the time. I didn't believe it, quite frankly, and I can't even remember it now. I think it was just because she found Jennifer a tie, a burden she wanted to be rid of.'

'And yet after all these years she suddenly decided she wanted custody of the child?'

'Yes, and that had me flummoxed,' said Rudolph. 'Frankly, when she first told me I didn't believe her. I've been racking my brains about it ever since.'

'What reason did she give you?'

'Oh, some bromide about motherly love. Suppressed all these years out of consideration for Jennifer's welfare. Now that she wasn't going to work any more she'd have time to be a real mother, which was what a girl of that age needed. And if you ask me – it's just occurred to me – that must be the clue to the whole puzzle. She was marrying a rich man; devoting herself to Jennifer would only have meant putting the child in charge of a nurse or governess or something of the kind. She'd be hurting Robert, and she'd have enjoyed that, without putting herself to any particular trouble.'

'You're not painting a very pretty picture of your sister, Mr Spencer.'

'I'm trying to tell you the truth as it appears to me.'

'Yes, and I'm grateful. Do you know the grounds on which she intended to base her claim for custody?'

'Yes, she told me, and I found that hard to believe too. Not that Robert should not have had an affair or two – he's human, after all – but to do anything that might harm Jennifer . . . I don't see that, I'm afraid.'

'Now, that I do find interesting, Mr Spencer. You may not know that one of the women went back on her evidence.'

'No, I didn't as a matter of fact. Doesn't that help?'

'No, because it can be taken two ways . . . either she was still fond of your brother-in-law and changed her story to try to help him, or the fact that he was being wrongly accused made him angrier than ever. But you think the witnesses were lying?'

'If you want my frank opinion,' said Spencer, obviously determined to give it, 'I wouldn't trust Stew Brodie an inch.'

'Perhaps not, but if he was engaged in an elaborate deception he must have had some motive.'

'He thought that Phillipa was the sun and the moon and the stars,' said Rudolph in a rather bored tone. 'Would you say that was sufficient motive?'

'How did she feel about him?'

'To tell you the truth I haven't the faintest idea. You never did have with Phillipa. As far as I could make out she could make any man believe black was white without too much difficulty. Stew might have thought she returned his feelings.'

'That wouldn't explain the three witnesses he unearthed.'

'Everybody has his price,' said Rudolph negligently. 'And I don't know about you two, but I know all about being hard up.'

235

'That was what the third of the witnesses said, that they were being paid for their evidence.'

'Then I should think she was telling the truth. And from what Wilfred Begg tells me about Phillipa's finances she could have afforded that well enough, within reason.'

'That's very interesting,' said Antony sincerely. 'Well, I'm more grateful than I can say for the frank way you've talked to us, Mr Spencer.'

'Even though you did find it a bit off-putting at times,' said Rudolph, grinning. 'Have you any sisters?'

'No.'

'Well, if you had you might understand better. On the other hand, I suppose you might not. I daresay there are sisters *and* sisters. Anyway, now that you're here you might tell me what's going to happen to Jennifer if Robert is convicted. I understand Robert was going to re-marry too and that the girl is with Jennifer now, but I don't suppose the authorities would allow that arrangement to go on.'

'I'm afraid not.'

'I suppose that means some ghastly social service . . . but what can I do? No one would consider me a proper person to look after a child that age.'

'Perhaps not.' Antony couldn't help smiling. 'I believe you have some unorthodox opinions, Mr Spencer, from most people's point of view. But I'm not so sure they'd be altogether right about that.'

III

'Well?' asked Geoffrey as soon as they were outside again. 'I admit I'd still like to call him because of some of the things he said, but are you sure you can keep him in order?'

'I can try,' said Antony rather doubtfully. 'But I wouldn't count on his discretion when Garfield gets hold of him.'

'Well, we've all night to think about it.'

'You think about it,' Antony suggested. 'If we can find a taxi I'll take you back to the car.'

236

'No, that would be just wasting your time. I'm not particularly late, and the sooner you and Jenny get this job done the better. If it *can* be done,' he added doubtfully.

'Yes, precisely. If it *can* be done,' Antony echoed. 'Thank you for your help anyway, Geoffrey, and I'll give you a call later in the evening to let you know what's transpired.'

So he went straight back to Kempenfeldt Square and Jenny must have had her coat ready because she came down to join him in a moment. They talked very little on the journey. Jenny looked composed but he sensed a nervousness in her which he didn't find altogether surprising.

Amanda was glad to see them and said so, and it was obvious that she and Jenny took an immediate liking to each other. 'And I've had no luck with Jennifer,' she added in a low voice, glancing over her shoulder at the living-room door. 'I don't know whether she'll be any more willing to talk to a stranger, but it's certainly worth a try. Do you know much about children, Jenny?'

'I'm afraid not. Only friends' children.'

'Well, I ought to – I did a stint in the children's ward for a while – but I've had absolutely no success at all.'

'I just thought . . . I know Antony's as worried as you must be about this business, so trying to get Jennifer to talk seems to be the last hope. And I did wonder if perhaps she might prefer to talk to someone she doesn't know than someone as close to her as you are. And then again I thought perhaps she'd prefer to talk to a woman than to a man.'

'I'd be very glad if you could get her to tell us what's troubling her, because I don't think it's any good for her to be bottling things up,' said Amanda. 'But when I think about it I'm not quite sure what good it will do Robert even if we do find out what happened to her.'

'The main question is where she went the afternoon she disappeared,' said Antony, thinking of Jenny's theory as he spoke, and wondering how likely it was to be right. 'And I suppose whatever was said to her the day before is connected to that in some way.'

'The afternoon Phillipa was killed,' said Amanda thoughtfully. 'Well, we can but try,' she said again, trying to sound more hopeful. 'If we sit at the far end of the room, Mr

237

Maitland, I think it will be the best thing. Too many people would only confuse Jennifer, and that way Mrs Maitland can have a free hand.'

When they trooped into the living-room the child greeted the two newcomers with her usual careful politeness. 'Mr Maitland and I have some business to talk over,' said Amanda cheerfully, 'so you must keep Mrs Maitland company while we talk.' She led the way firmly to the other end of the room, settled herself at the dining-table, and motioned to Antony to sit down near her.

As he did so he heard Jennifer saying, 'Won't you sit here, Mrs Maitland? It's the most comfortable chair, daddy says. It was nice of you to come to keep me company.'

'I thought I'd like to get to know you,' said Jenny. 'You see, my name's Jennifer too, though nobody ever uses it in full, so it seemed only right that I should meet my namesake.'

For a while Antony concentrated on giving Amanda as clear a picture as he could of what had happened in court the day before, and trying to explain exactly how much and how little could be expected from it. But after a while there was no more to say. Amanda had just one comment, 'I always knew', and then she too was silent, obviously thinking over what she had heard in more detail. All the time he had been talking Antony had been aware of the quiet murmur of Jenny's voice in the background and of Jennifer's polite but rather stilted replies. Now he gave them his full attention, and realised that they were completely absorbed in each other, and that the child at least wouldn't notice that the conversation at the other end of the room had ceased and they were being overheard.

'You see,' Jenny was saying, 'it's a question of helping other people, especially people you love.' This time the child didn't reply and after a moment Jenny went on. 'You'll find when you grow older that if you don't try your best to do that you'll always regret it afterwards. Do you understand what I'm telling you?' Antony took a moment to wonder how she had brought the conversation to this particular point.

'I don't know.' Jennifer's voice was strained. 'You were telling me stories about the farm you stay at sometimes; it sounded an awful lot of fun, and now all of a sudden

238

everything seems to have become more serious.'

'You're old enough to understand, Jennifer, that things are serious, very serious indeed. You love your father, don't you?'

'Of course I do. Do you mean I hurt him terribly when I said he'd lied to me about mummy being dead?'

'Do you still think that?'

'That he deliberately lied to me? No, I don't think that any longer. You're quite right, I should have known that straight away, and now I can't tell him I'm sorry.'

'Why did it upset you so, Jennifer?' Jenny's voice was very quiet, almost casual, but Antony didn't need telling that the conversation was almost as much a strain on her as it was on the little girl. 'Was it what the man said who spoke to you in the school playground?'

'Not only that. I can't tell you . . . it was too awful.'

'He told you awful things?' Jenny was frowning in her concentration. 'He said your mother was alive and that she wanted you to live with her. Was there anything else?'

'Yes, but—'

'What else, Jennifer?'

'He said bad things about daddy. They don't matter . . . I didn't believe him . . . only I couldn't tell him, or Amanda.'

'Would you have liked that? To live with your mother?'

'No . . . oh no!'

'Then what was so terrible?'

'He said – the man – that she'd force daddy to let me go to her.'

'And that frightened you?'

'I can't tell you.'

'Things we keep to ourselves have a way of getting bigger and bigger in our minds,' said Jenny. She was hammering away at the first day the child had become upset, not getting to the real point at all, but Antony had the sudden conviction that in this her instinct was sound. 'You say that wasn't what frightened you.'

'I wasn't frightened exactly, I knew daddy would look after me. Oh, I can't tell you!'

'If I had a daughter,' said Jenny steadily (and only her

husband knew how much the words cost her), 'I'd hope she'd always be ready to confide in me when something was troubling her.' And suddenly Jennifer's hands went up to hide her face and after a moment there were tears trickling through her fingers.

'I can't tell you, I can't,' she said. 'It was too wicked!'

Jenny left her chair then and joined the child on the sofa, putting an arm around her shoulders and pulling her close. 'Who was wicked?' she asked gently. 'The man who spoke to you?'

'I was, I was!'

'You know, I find that very difficult to believe,' said Jenny in a rallying tone. 'And I'll tell you something else, I think if we examined this wickedness of yours, we'd find perhaps that it wasn't so very dreadful after all.'

'You don't know.' Jennifer sounded heartbroken, and very forlorn.

'No, but you're going to tell me,' said Jenny confidently, and suddenly the little girl raised her head. Her words had been muffled, but now she spoke very clearly.

'Don't you see, Mrs Maitland, I was glad when I thought my mother was dead? That's wicked, isn't it? That's a dreadful sin.'

'It's . . . not very usual,' said Jenny. Antony, watching her, was again very conscious of the strain she was under. 'But now you've told me so much I think you'd better tell me the rest, Jennifer. You had some reason for feeling like that, and if we look at it together you may find you weren't so very wicked after all. Besides, you were only three when she went away—'

'Nearly four,' said Jennifer quickly, contradicting her just as Antony had heard her contradict her father that first day.

'Even four isn't a very great age,' Jenny pointed out. 'I don't suppose you can remember her, can you, or hardly at all?'

'Of course I can remember. I can remember all sorts of things when I was that age and even younger. I remember one day I was in this very room alone; mummy had gone out and I knew she would be back before daddy came home because she told me never, never, never to tell him that she sometimes left me alone.'

'You were going to tell me something that happened when you were alone here,' Jenny prompted her.

'Only that I suddenly realised I was a person, Jennifer Osmond, not just "my little girl", and rather a nuisance to everybody.'

'I'm sure your father never thought that.'

'No, daddy was different but he wasn't always here. I'm only telling you this to show you I wasn't a baby, Mrs Maitland, and I knew perfectly well what was going on though I didn't understand it then. It's only this past year I realised – the girls get together at playtime, you know, and all kinds of talk goes on – that married ladies don't spend a lot of time with other men or make you call them "uncle" when they're no relation at all. Then I just knew that she'd take me with her to different places the days she was supposed to stay at home with me. Sometimes it might be to a hotel, or sometimes to somebody's home, but always there was a man there. And she'd say very casually, "This is Jennifer. It's a damned nuisance but I had to drag her along with me. I can't imagine why I ever let myself be saddled with an – an incubus like her." I remember the word very well, though I didn't know what it meant . . . just that it was something she didn't like. And then they'd go away together somewhere alone and I'd be left with a picture book to wait and wait. She'd say it was a business meeting and I didn't know any better then. I only knew I hated it.'

Maitland was thinking, so Osmond was wrong when he said he thought marriage to him had satisfied Phillipa sexually. And another thought crossed his mind; Norma Martin saying that children always knew more about what was going on around them than you gave them credit for. 'Have you anything else to tell me about that?' Jenny was prompting gently.

'Not much. Only that she always told me, you must never tell daddy, he doesn't understand that I can't be with you all the time. And when he'd ask us in the evening what we'd been doing that day she'd say, "Oh, we went to the park," very quickly before I had time to say anything else. And I didn't know what to do because grown-ups always tell you

you have to be obedient, but they also tell you you mustn't tell lies.'

'I don't think your feelings were so very dreadful,' Jenny assured her. 'You were very young, and very confused.' She turned her head slightly so that her eyes met Antony's for a moment. 'Now you're going to tell me what happened the day you ran away,' she said, turning back to Jennifer.

'I didn't exactly—'

'The day you disappeared then. It might be very important.'

'Is that what you meant, Mrs Maitland, by helping people you love?'

'That's exactly what I meant. My husband wants to do what he can for your father, and to do that he needs help very badly. Do you understand about that?'

'Of course I do. I shall be nine next week,' said Jennifer, as though that settled the matter. Obviously the business of being treated as a grown-up was very important to her. 'And you're truly not shocked about what I told you?' she insisted.

'I'm truly not shocked,' Jenny echoed. 'And I don't think anybody else would be either.'

For a moment Jennifer looked at her, obviously weighing up the truth of what she was saying. Antony could tell by his wife's very stillness how intent she was on the child; she seemed to be holding her breath. He glanced at Amanda and put a finger to his lips, in reply to which she nodded emphatically. 'I think I will tell you,' said Jennifer at last. 'I'd been thinking and thinking about what the man said and he seemed so sure that she'd get her own way and that I might have to go and live with her. So I thought I'd try to find out if he was telling the truth, because before she always thought I was a nuisance and I couldn't understand why she'd want to take me away from daddy now.'

For an instant Jenny again risked an agonised look at Antony, as though by doing so she might somehow be inspired to know the kind of questions she should ask now. All he could do was nod to her encouragingly, and after a moment her eyes went back to the child by her side again. 'All I know is that Mrs Arbuthnot took you back to school

242

that afternoon and saw you go into the playground. What happened after that?'

'I waited until I was sure she had gone and then I came out again. There's a telephone box on the corner and I looked in the directory and found my mother's name. I've never made a call from a box before but the instructions were quite clear and I'd brought some change with me. The phone rang for rather a long time and I thought mummy must be out, then suddenly she answered. She sounded a little out of breath.'

'You wanted to find out whether what the man told you was true?'

'Oh, I didn't believe the bits about daddy. He isn't that kind of man at all. Miss Bell at school once told us that people are inclined to see their own faults in others,' said Jennifer, obviously quoting, 'so after a while I worked it out that that's what must have happened. Mummy thought things about daddy that were true about her. But what I did want to know was whether I was really going to have to live with her again.'

'So that's what you asked her?'

'I didn't get the chance to just at first. She said "Oh, it's you," and sounded terribly disappointed. And then she said "I might have known if you wanted to call you'd choose a time like this. I only just got in and heard the bell ringing and haven't even had time to take my coat off."'

'Did that upset you?'

'No, it – it encouraged me,' said Jennifer. 'I thought it meant she felt about me just as she'd always done, and it couldn't possibly be true that she wanted me to live with her. So as soon as I could get a word in I asked her right out and her manner changed immediately. She said, "Of course I want you, baby," which is a thing I never liked being called, even when I was little. She started to tell me she wouldn't be out all day as daddy is and we'd have wonderful times together. And she said I should tell the lawyers I wanted to live with her because a girl needed a mother. And I told her I'd have one anyway as daddy was getting married again and that made her cross for a moment but then she went back to – to cooing at me. She said, "I'm going to get married too, darling, to a wonderful man. He's a little older than daddy but very kind and he's longing to have a little girl of his own. And we won't be living very far from where you are now so you can go to the same school and everything. He has a big house in Tilney Square." And that isn't very far away, and suddenly I had an idea that perhaps if I could talk to him he could persuade mummy not to try to take me away from daddy. So I asked her exactly where he lived, rather as if I was coming round to the idea, and she told me his name – Matthew Leighton – and the number of the house where he lived.'

'So it was Mr Leighton you went to see.'

'Yes, of course. If I was going to have to live with him and mummy I wanted to know what he was like. But I did think too that if he was in love with her and I could persuade him that I would rather live with daddy he might be able to make her change her mind. So I walked straight round to his house and it was only when I rang the bell I thought most likely he'd be at his office. But he wasn't, he was at home. Just getting ready to go down to the country for the weekend, he told me. But first there was a man who came to the door and asked my name. I told him, Jennifer Osmond, and he went away and then came back to say Mr Leighton would like to see me.' She was talking very quickly now, as though, once started, she couldn't get the story over fast enough. 'And I didn't really like it when he greeted me by saying "My little daughter!" and trying to kiss me, but he was very kind, a really nice man. I came to realise that after I'd been with him for a while.'

'What did you talk about?'

'Well, first he had to tell me how much he loved my mother and how very happy we'd all be together as a family. How much he'd always wanted a daughter. So I told him, please I don't want to leave daddy, and couldn't he persuade mummy to give up this idea she had and just forget all about me.'

'What did he say to that?'

'He said he could understand that I was fond of my father but I must also understand – I was quite old enough now – that he wasn't a fit person to have the care of me. That really made me cross, though he meant to be kind, I know, but I

244

could see I wasn't getting anywhere and when he started to tell me how much my mother loved me and how she'd only left me where I was for my own good I burst into tears. He came and sat by me then, just as you're doing, Mrs Maitland, only on the arm of my chair, and said I must understand that when a marriage ended the two people concerned sometimes felt very bitter about each other and I mustn't take any notice now of things that my father had said about my mother because they just weren't true. And I said he hadn't told me anything, I had thought she was dead. And he asked me, wasn't I pleased she wasn't, and I blurted out, "No, because I hate her," and then I was crying more than ever. And when I thought about it afterwards I knew that was wicked too – what I'd said – and perhaps not quite true. He didn't seem shocked, just tried to comfort me and persuade me that I was all wrong in what I thought. So I told him – I was crying so hard I wonder that he could hear me – just how she really felt about me and about being an incubus and about the uncles. And he took me by the shoulders and shook me a little and said very seriously, "Little girl, do you know what you're saying?" And I told him I didn't know then but I did now and it would be all right when I was at school but when I had to be at home all day I just couldn't bear to have it start all over again. So he gave me a clean handkerchief and made me wipe my eyes and said "Stop crying, Jennifer, and don't worry. I won't let anything hurt you." '

'How long were you there?'

'I wasn't noticing the time, but I think perhaps about half an hour.'

'Then you didn't go home straight away.'

'No, I'd been crying so much I knew it would show and I felt . . . very odd, Mrs Maitland, as if I didn't know who I was any more. I'd told him things I'd never told anybody else, and I felt so guilty I just couldn't talk about it, until now I've told you. So I just went into the park and found a seat there and meant to think about things only I couldn't think clearly. And I got colder and colder and at last a policeman came and I went home with him.'

'Well, don't worry about it any more, Jennifer,' said Jenny gently. 'You needn't be frightened about your future any

245

more,' (Heaven send she's right about that, thought Antony) 'and you needn't worry about what you think of as wicked. It was very natural to feel as you did.'

'Do you really think so?' For the first time something like hope had crept into her voice.

'I'm absolutely sure of it,' said Jenny firmly.

'It's Mr Maitland who wants to know all this, isn't it? Shall I have to tell it to him?'

'You forgot, he's at the other end of the room with Amanda. He's been there all the time.'

Jennifer sat up a little straighter and shook herself, rather as if she were coming out of a dream. Then she looked around the room. 'I'm glad you heard,' she said, dividing a rather watery smile between Antony and Amanda. 'Now I shan't have to talk about it ever again. But I don't understand what Mrs Maitland says about helping.'

'Don't worry about that either,' said Antony.

'But daddy—'

Jenny glanced at her husband and saw in his face a look of blazing excitement not altogether unfamiliar to her. 'Your daddy will be all right,' she said, 'Mr Maitland will see to that.' And perhaps some of her new-found confidence conveyed itself to the child. Jennifer got up and went across the room in something of a rush.

'Did you hear that, Amanda?' she demanded. 'I know daddy trusts Mr Maitland, so I think we should too.'

IV

Nothing at all was said until they got home, though Jenny held on to Antony's hand really hard all the time they were in the taxi. Vera and Sir Nicholas had finished dinner and everything was cleared away except the two covers that had been left for them. 'But I don't think I could eat anything just yet,' said Jenny. 'I don't know whether I may have done something awful. Was I right when I thought what Jennifer said had really given you an idea, Antony?'

246

'Perfectly right, love, I'll tell you all about it in a moment. First sit down and I'd better get you a drink because you deserve one.'

'I'll do the honours,' said Sir Nicholas. 'For once in his life, as it seems to be Jenny's story, perhaps Antony won't object to enlightening us.'

'I didn't really do anything,' said Jenny sitting down beside Vera on the sofa.

'Except be yourself, love.' Antony sat down too and leaned his head against the high back of the winged chair. The momentary excitement which had buoyed him since he heard Jennifer's story was draining away now and he was aware of being very tired. There were difficulties ahead, and for the moment he could see no way round them. But Uncle Nick and Vera deserved to have their curiosity satisfied, and with a clearer tale than any Jenny would give them. As soon as Sir Nicholas had finished his self-imposed task he began to tell them what Jennifer had said, and for once Sir Nicholas was content to sip his cognac and listen without any interruption.

It was Vera who spoke first when the tale was finished. 'What an iniquitous thing!' she exclaimed. 'And that poor child. What on earth were you doing to give her – and the girl too, who must be equally worried – the idea that this somehow cleared her father?'

'I'm afraid that was my doing, Vera,' said Jenny, before her husband could speak. 'You see Antony looked suddenly so excited I knew he had an idea, and I'm afraid I spoke without thinking about whether he could prove he was right or not.'

They were all of them looking at Antony now, knowing him well enough to realise that the child's trust, if he was unable to justify it, would be very hard for him to bear. But there was no point in giving him time to dwell on that. 'What was this inspiration of yours?' Sir Nicholas asked.

'I'd better begin by assuring you that I realise we aren't out of the woods yet,' said Antony. 'You know I've been looking for an alternative suspect, and I haven't had time to tell you about the two men I saw today, but in my own mind I ruled them both out. Stewart Brodie isn't a man I admire exactly, and I thought up various rather complicated motives he might have had and dismissed the lot of them. Derek noticed

Matthew Leighton among the spectators in court on Monday, so he certainly must have heard what Norma Martin had to say and been very much hurt by it. I've noticed him myself once or twice since then, but until now I'd no idea he knew anything about Phillipa Osmond's goings-on before the murder. Jennifer's story gives him a motive where before I thought he hadn't one.'

'That is not the same thing as saying – let alone proving – that he's guilty,' Sir Nicholas pointed out.

'I know that only too well.'

'And in spite of that you think he killed Mrs Osmond?'

'Yes, I do. I keep thinking of my talk with him, which at the time seemed perfectly commonplace, but what we've just heard changes that. For one thing he gave me no hint at all that his feelings towards Phillipa had changed, as they must have done if you believe Jennifer, as it seems he did. My own feeling is that he might have condoned her extra-marital affairs – though perhaps not if she'd been married to him at the time – but not unkindness to a child. And that idea doesn't rest only on what Jennifer said; Leighton practically told me himself that it was Phillipa's desire to regain custody of her daughter that finally prompted him to propose to her.'

'As a theory that is . . . not unreasonable,' Sir Nicholas conceded. 'But what do you propose to do about it? These two men you saw today, have you decided against calling them as witnesses?'

'No, Geoffrey insists we must because their view of Phillipa Osmond in some ways may be held to confirm what Norma Martin told the court.'

'A very proper attitude,' his uncle approved.

'Yes, I thought you'd see it that way, but as far as Osmond's defence is concerned there's not much point in it. The only thing I can think of is for Geoffrey to get Cobbold's on to finding out whether Leighton was in St John's Wood that afternoon, though of course he may have been there without being seen. That might give us some new evidence to take to the Court of Appeal, but once Osmond has been convicted, I don't think they'd consider it enough to reverse the verdict.'

'Quite sure you're right,' said Vera. 'And if you slap a *sub poena* on him to appear for the defence tomorrow, always supposing it could be done in time, you couldn't attack him in court on what you've got.'

'I could ask him, I suppose, about Jennifer's visit to him,' said Antony slowly. 'That was the first thing that occurred to me, naturally. But if he denies that the child went there at all . . . no, he can't do that because his manservant saw her. Still, he could make up some story about their conversation, and unless Osmond changes his mind and allows us to call Jennifer that would be the end of the matter.'

'Unlikely to change his mind,' said Vera. 'However careful Garfield was, if she was contradicting what Leighton had said he'd be bound to question her pretty closely.'

'Yes, I know. I don't like the idea, but the only thing I can think of is to let things take their course, and then see what Cobbold's can dig up.' He paused there and looked around the circle of anxious faces, then said in a lighter tone, 'I could, of course, telephone Leighton. Something on the lines of "Fly at once, all is known." But I can't help feeling that would be suspiciously like blackmail.'

'You're right about that.' Sir Nicholas's tone was faintly regretful. 'And if we understood Jenny's rather tangled story about your visitor yesterday evening correctly, I imagine it would be no use appealing to the police. A request from the prosecution for an adjournment might be listened to, where one from you wouldn't.'

'Yes, I haven't a hope of getting Eversley to listen to me, let alone do anything about it.'

'In that case you must just let things take their course, as you said. And that was a rather interesting remark of her teacher's that Jennifer repeated to you,' Sir Nicholas went on, probably in the interests of turning his nephew's thoughts, even if it was only to a different aspect of the same subject. 'That people see their own faults in others.'

'Yes, but do you think Phillipa really believed her husband was doing the things she said of him? It doesn't seem like that to me, because it would mean that Stewart Brodie was deliberately deceiving her.'

'No,' said his uncle thoughtfully, 'but I do think that what she'd been doing herself gave her the idea for the plot against

249

her husband, imputing her own faults to him. But that's enough of Robert Osmond's affairs for tonight,' he added bracingly. 'We're agreed that nothing more can be done immediately, so you and Jenny may as well have your meal in peace, and we'll regard the subject as closed for tonight at least.'

V

But Sir Nicholas was over-optimistic if he hoped that Robert Osmond's affairs would not obtrude on their attention again that evening. Antony and Jenny had barely finished eating when the house phone rang; Jenny continued to pile their plates together, and Antony went across the room to answer it. 'A Mr Matthew Leighton has called to see you, Mr Maitland,' said Gibbs's voice in his ear, still conveying well enough his displeasure at being disturbed so late on two evenings in succession. 'Do you wish to see him?'

'Just a minute, Gibbs.' Antony placed one hand over the mouthpiece, and naturally enough, after an association of so many years, it was to his uncle that his appeal was addressed. 'It's Matthew Leighton, Uncle Nick. Here. What should I do?'

'See him, of course. There's nothing to prevent you from doing so,' he added rather impatiently, when Maitland seemed to hesitate. 'He is not a prosecution witness, and I imagine from what you've told me this evening that there are things you might with advantage discuss.'

'But Geoffrey—'

'As Geoffrey lives in the suburbs it would take some time for him to get here. If you want a witness to your conversation, Antony, I shall be very willing to join you. Tell Gibbs to show Mr Leighton into the study.'

Antony obeyed, but it was not without misgivings. As was perhaps inevitable he was assailed by doubts of his own theory, and perhaps the more so because Sir Nicholas seemed suddenly to be taking it for granted that he was right. He

250

made some sort of an apology to Vera and followed his uncle out of the room and down the stairs.

When they reached Sir Nicholas's study it was obvious that Matthew Leighton was nervous. He had seated himself, but he jumped to his feet as the door opened, so that they both got the impression that he had been seated only on the edge of his chair. 'I wanted to talk to you, Mr Maitland,' he said, and then broke off, eyeing Sir Nicholas doubtfully.

Antony performed the introductions. 'If it's about the Osmond case—' he added, but wasn't allowed to finish the sentence.

'What else could it be that would make me intrude on you so late in the evening?' said Leighton. 'I should apologise for that, but I have a particular reason for wanting to consult you.'

'I was about to add that any approach should have been made to Robert Osmond's solicitor, Mr Geoffrey Horton,' Antony told him. 'But if you feel the matter is urgent, I'll do my best to help you. However, I do feel it would be as well if my uncle sat in on our talk . . . to see fair play, if you like to put it like that,' he added on a lighter note.

Matthew Leighton looked at him for a long moment, obviously weighing up the implications of what he had said. 'It seems my visit isn't a surprise to you, Mr Maitland,' he said then.

'Well yes, it is a surprise,' Antony admitted. 'But you have been very much on my mind, so you could say it's a coincidence your turning up like this. Have you any objection to my uncle's presence?'

'None at all.'

'Then perhaps you'll tell us why you wanted to see me.'

'I can put it very simply,' said Leighton. 'I want you to tell me what you think of Robert Osmond's chances of being acquitted.'

Before Antony had a chance to speak Sir Nicholas had broken in. 'But, my dear sir, you can't expect my nephew to tell you that. It is, after all, up to the jury.'

'Besides,' said Antony, 'you must know almost as much about that as I do myself. My junior, Mr Stringer, noticed that you were one of the spectators in court, on Monday at

251

least, though I've no idea if you've been there since the trial began.'

'Yes, I have. I doubt if you'll deny that I have a – a certain interest in what is going on.'

Maitland ignored this. 'My uncle is quite right,' he said. 'I can't answer your question exactly as you put it. I don't need to tell you that one of the witnesses Mrs Osmond intended to call in the custody suit has denied her former evidence, though I must be honest and admit that I can't say how this will be regarded by the jury. It may even be said that the knowledge of his own innocence of the charges would add fuel to the fire of my client's indignation. There is, however, one other thing that I think I can tell you without impropriety.'

'What is that?' asked Leighton in a rather harsh tone.

Maitland glanced for a moment at his uncle and was encouraged by an almost imperceptible nod. 'That Jennifer Osmond has told me exactly where she went and what she did on the afternoon of her mother's murder,' said Antony. 'I'll further admit to you that I drew certain conclusions from what she told me,' he added and then wondered if he had gone too far.

'Well, I'm glad on the whole that the child talked to you.' To Antony's surprise Matthew Leighton sounded sincere. 'She was obviously very upset and I've been reproaching myself ever since for letting her leave the house alone. As for your conclusions—'

'That's all they are, they can't be proved.'

'No, I understand that, but I don't think it makes any difference really. I think I made up my mind before I came to you, there's no way I can justify to myself letting another man suffer for something I did. Besides, I promised Jennifer—' He broke off there, obviously deeply moved, and Antony could hear the child's voice completing the sentence, *he said I won't let anything hurt you.*

'Just a moment, Mr Leighton.' That was Sir Nicholas speaking into the brief silence rather more hastily than was his custom. 'I'm not quite sure what this is all about but if you have something to tell us about Phillipa Osmond's murder, I ought to point out to you that as officers of the court we

252

can't keep silent about it. Neither my nephew nor I represent you, and the usual lawyer–client relationship doesn't apply.'

For the first time Leighton smiled. 'Thank you for saying that, but I understand the position very well,' he said. 'You know already what little Jennifer told you, and I think you can understand my shock and horror at what she had to say. I loved Phillipa so very deeply.' He paused there, and for a moment it seemed as if he was about to go off into a reverie. 'If you'll forgive me for being sentimental,' he went on, 'she seemed to embody all that is best in women and to have a genuine love for family life which is something of a rarity nowadays. And to be told by a child . . . her child . . . that my image of her was a false one was almost more than my reason could stand. But there was no doubt that Jennifer was telling the truth, the things she didn't understand were as revealing as the ones she did, or perhaps more so. And the fact that Phillipa was at home when she had said she had a business engagement was just one more small weight in the scale. So when Jennifer had gone, I took my suitcases and set out for the country just as I had intended, only I went to St John's Wood on the way. The little girl did get home safely, didn't she?'

'Yes, Mr Leighton. Rather later than her father expected, but she got home safely.'

'I couldn't tell you exactly when I got to Phillipa's flat. I finished packing before I went, but I was more or less in a dream. All I could think of was getting to Phillipa and confronting her with what I had learned, and I suppose there was still some faint hope in the back of my mind that perhaps she would be able to convince me that there had been some dreadful mistake; though in my heart I knew that if I allowed that to happen our future relationship would be a sham on both our parts.'

'But she didn't try?'

'She didn't even try. First she said, "Oh, that child!" when I told her that Jennifer had been to see me. "She always was a nuisance," she said, "and now she's still trying to spoil things for me." So I repeated what I'd been told and she didn't even try to deny it, just laughed at me. She said, "You may as well understand, darling, I've always taken my pleasure where I found it and I don't intend to change." I went over to stand by her chair and she looked up at me, still laughing. I'm a powerful man, I strangled her with my bare hands.'

Antony for the moment could think of no comment on that. It was Sir Nicholas who spoke, after what seemed like an endless moment. 'I think we're both glad you came to us with this information,' he said, 'but I should like to know what you had in mind in doing so. Your own solicitor—'

'We've already been into that.'

'You said you came because you wanted to know whether Robert Osmond was going to be convicted or not,' said Antony, coming to life suddenly.

'Yes, but I think I knew all the time that whatever you said I'd tell you the truth anyway. I think I wanted to commit myself, to make it impossible to turn back. And now I've told you . . . it's a relief really. I couldn't have lived, knowing Osmond was in prison and the little girl was homeless.' He looked from one of them to the other. 'What should I do now?'

'I'll give you the credit for meaning what you say' – again it was Sir Nicholas who answered – 'and that being so I think there's only one piece of advice I can give you. I think you should rouse that solicitor of yours, out of bed if necessary, tell him the whole story, and go with him to the police. You know, I suppose, that it is Detective Chief Inspector Eversley who is in charge of the case. That is—' he added, suddenly doubtful.

Matthew Leighton was coming to his feet. For a moment he sounded genuinely amused. 'I shan't change my mind, and I shan't let my solicitor change it for me,' he said. 'But to tell you the truth' – he looked from one of them to the other, asking their understanding if not their sympathy – 'ever since . . . nothing seems to matter any more.'

EPILOGUE

The start of the trial was delayed the following morning at the prosecution's request, and when the court eventually convened it was to hear the announcement from Paul Garfield that certain facts had come to his notice that made it necessary to withdraw the case against Robert Osmond. Antony, Geoffrey and Derek joined Sir Nicholas at Astroff's for lunch, but Maitland was inclined to be more silent than usual and after a while Geoffrey said in a rallying tone, 'What's worrying you now? Osmond doesn't believe what's happened, but he's in seventh heaven now that it's all over.'

'I think it would be nice,' said Antony, 'just once, if you could help one person or set of people without hurting someone else.'

'My dear boy,' said Sir Nicholas, his tone disguising whatever sympathy he may have felt with this point of view, 'Matthew Leighton was hurt by Phillipa Osmond long before you came on the scene, and hurt just about as badly as it is possible for a man to be.'

'I suppose that's true. What will happen to him, Uncle Nick?'

'His solicitor, being mainly engaged in commercial law, has already been in touch with Paul Collingwood, and Collingwood has talked to Mallory,' said Sir Nicholas in rather a smug tone. 'The idea seems to be that I should accept a brief to defend him.'

For a moment his audience seemed to be struck dumb by this announcement. 'Well, that's a good thing, I suppose,' said Antony at last.

'It is hardly polite to sound quite so doubtful, Antony,' his uncle informed him. 'I am very much inclined to think that the judge and jury will feel as sympathetic towards him as we do.'

'The prosecution will go all out for manslaughter, I imagine,' said Geoffrey, 'and I suppose you can say that's bad enough, but since he isn't denying anything he may get out of prison quite quickly.'

'With his whole life in ruins,' said Maitland, declining to be comforted.

'Yes, I'm afraid he took Phillipa Osmond's defection very hard,' Sir Nicholas agreed. 'And if you're going to try to blame yourself for that as well as everything else, Antony, I can only say I wash my hands of you.'

'There's one thing to be said for it,' said Derek, entering the conversation suddenly. 'Money may not bring happiness, but it can help you to be miserable in comfort.'

'Good heavens, Derek, I didn't know you had it in you to be so cynical,' said Antony, surprised.

'A point in his favour,' said Sir Nicholas approvingly. 'I've told you time and time again, my dear boy, all lawyers should have a certain amount of cynicism in their make-up.'

Some four weeks later Robert Osmond and Amanda Herschell were married quietly and Antony and Jenny attended the ceremony. Jennifer was there – a different child, quite radiant – and made a point of telling them after the ceremony was over that she would be going with daddy and Amanda on their honeymoon. 'I didn't want to interfere,' she said in her serious grown-up way, 'but they were adamant.' She produced the word proudly, probably quoting her father. 'Amanda says families should always stick together, and as a matter of fact' – she slipped her hand into Jenny's as she spoke – 'I shouldn't really care to have been left alone just now.'

'So there's your happy ending, for you,' said Jenny when they were back home again. 'The only thing is,' she added with a sidelong glance at her husband, 'I do think Mr Osmond should have invited Chief Inspector Eversley to the wedding.'

'Heaven forbid!' said Maitland piously. 'Talk about skeletons at the feast.'

'I didn't really mean it,' Jenny assured him in a serious tone, and went off to the kitchen to make a cup of tea, leaving her husband helpless for the moment with laughter.